Fly Me to the Moon

Bipolar Journey Through Mania and Depression

H. E. Logue, M. D.

Outskirts Press, Inc.
Denver, Colorado

Fly Me To The Moon
Bipolar Journey through Mania and Depression

v2.0

Outskirts Press
http://www.outskirtspress.com

ISBN-10: 1-59800-696-7
ISBN-13: 978-1-59800-696-4

Library of Congress Control Number: 2006930285

Printed in the United States of America

CONTENTS

Foreword

by Marc D. Feldman, M.D.

Fly Me to the Moon: Bipolar Journey through Mania and Depression fills a niche in the mental health industry throughout the U.S. and elsewhere. The storyline captivated me to read it in two sittings, however it is thoughtfully segmented to meet any reader's pace. This book is deeply engaging while never sacrificing medical/psychiatric authenticity in the service of character development. Instead, it constitutes a most compelling and immersive way for anyone to learn about Bipolar Disorder. You will enter into the private world of Eileen Robbins. Her story is enjoyable and don't be surprised to identify with her as she lives through mood swings, altered behavior, and treatment. You will feel her struggles as she reluctantly accepts a diagnosis that will change her life forever. Although *Fly Me to the Moon* serves as an excellent resource book, it is primarily an appealing novel with a rich message that is a welcomed innovation.

Regardless of the impetus behind your interest, you will learn what you need to know about Bipolar Disorder. Healthcare professionals will gain a deeper understanding of the disorder enhancing their level of patient care. For members of the public who have not had personal contact with Bipolar Disorder, its stigma will be erased and its myths will be debunked.

And for individuals with Bipolar Disorder and their loved ones, this book will not just be enlightening, but its insights will also give you realistic hope.

Fly Me to the Moon: Bipolar Journey through Mania and Depression is a powerful mechanism for education about Bipolar Disorder. I am confident that readers will enjoy, learn, and benefit from Eileen's story.

Dr. Feldman is the author of four psychiatric-related books and approximately 80 peer-reviewed articles and book chapters. He has served as Vice-Chair for Clinical Services and Professor at University of Alabama in Birmingham's (UAB's) Department of Psychiatry, Assistant Professor of Psychiatry at Duke University and Medical Director of Hill Crest Hospital.

Acknowledgements

Having been so richly blessed with the encouragement, assistance, and unfailing help of so many, I genuinely and lovingly thank and acknowledge the following who helped to make this book possible.

My wife, Kathy, in guiding me to choose this topic for my oeuvre and subsequent counsel regarding content, and to my daughters, Virginia (Ginger) M. Logue Menendez and Janine R. Wooten, for their critical analysis and early editorial input. To my daughter, Ann I. Bondi, for guidance and helpful CME strategies.

Special thanks to Marc D. Feldman, M.D., author of Munchausen by Proxy, Playing Sick, and others, for his close reading and valuable counsel and encouragement.

Special thanks to Tamara V. Shadinger, Ph.D., for her exhaustive efforts to gather information, provide editorial counsel, and coordinate continuing education opportunities.

To Josh Menendez for early stylistic suggestions.

To Kay McLean, R.N., M.S.N. and Jeana Russell, R.N., L.P.C. for their reading and insightful feedback.

To colleagues, patients, health professionals, and community citizens who voluntarily lend their names for authenticity: Samuel Saxon, Ph.D., Richard Ince, Ph.D., Gerald K. Anderson, Ph.D., Don Spargo, R.N., Dianne Moore, MHT, Linda Pilato, Sanquetta Copeland, Lola Beasley, R.N., and Jody Dean, R.N.

To Peggy Holly and Dianne Moore, MHT, for their unfailing support in innumerable ways.

Special thanks to Bradley Y. Dennis, M.D., Medical Director at Brookwood Medical Center, Birmingham, Alabama: Laura Ann Walley, Credentials Chairman, and Ms. Diane Oetting, Director of Education for the State of Alabama, for invaluable assistance and guidance in helping to produce this book in a continuing medical education acceptable format, and to Brookwood Medical Center for sponsoring the CME Program.

And finally, with gratitude in general, to my patients, colleagues, and to my profession.

Introduction

As a psychiatrist with thirty-three years in private practice and clinical research, I have treated in excess of one thousand patients with Bipolar Disorder (formerly Manic Depressive Illness). My patients and their families have frequently asked for a book to help them understand Bipolar Disorder. In assessing their response to the several notable good published books, I have, unfortunately, not been able to obtain a patient consensus on a favorite book to recommend. *Fly Me to the Moon: Bipolar Journey through Mania and Depression* is my offering to fill that need. There are three million persons in the U.S. alone who have the Bipolar gene. Millions more including their family members, friends, close associates or co-workers also need to understand the illness.

Treating patients with Bipolar Disorder has been a passion of mine throughout my thirty-three years in psychiatry. It is tremendously gratifying to be part of a patient's conquest of a raging destructive beast within. It is rewards such as this that keep doctors in the practice of medicine despite expanding hardships and difficulties.

Imagine being untrained and placed on a wild stallion and forced to ride it until it is tamed. The beast of Bipolar Disorder has stallion-like power, stubbornness and endurance. Without appropriate help, one could be exhausted, maimed or dead before the beast is subdued. The same dangers are present in a person with Bipolar Disorder.

Fortunately, treatment options have dramatically improved, and many lives are now saved and afforded the opportunity to live and enjoy reasonably normal lives.

Eileen is a remarkable character who carries the Bipolar story phenomenally well. She interacts with the powerful and influential effortlessly. With the less fortunate she displays equal warmth and grace.

Eileen's co-characters are a host of authentic people interacting with fictional characters weaving a novel of interest, intrigue, suspense, and romance in which she faces life and death struggles, deceit, corporate greed, and bias. Eileen's Bipolar symptomatology characteristically promotes vicissitudes which a professional woman with mental illness might expect.

Eileen's story provides the reader with an enjoyable novel while providing substantial understanding of Bipolar Disorder and the day-to-day struggles of patients with Bipolar Disorder and their families.

Fly Me to the Moon: Bipolar Journey through Mania and Depression is written in a manner to bridge the gap between the patient, public and the professional. Continuing education credits are available to professionals who satisfactorily complete a post test.

Writing this book has been a joy. I trust it will help demystify and destigmatize the organic mental illnesses.

To your health,
H.E. Logue, M.D.

Fly Me to the Moon

Chapter 1
Eileen Flies

Eileen Robbins' flight touched down at Washington National Airport five minutes past ten on Thursday morning. Her appointment with Senator Samuel Johnson was scheduled for two p.m. 'Plenty of time' she reasoned. While deplaning, she flashed her characteristic beautiful, infectious smile to the Eastern pilot. "Thank you for the nice flight."

"Thank you for flying Eastern," the handsome pilot quickly replied. 'Gorgeous,' he observed, wishing that he could be her escort. Eileen defined beauty. She stood five feet eight inches tall; a svelte brunette with professionally coiffured hair, cut sharp and close. Her large hazel eyes sparkled with energy and enticing excitement. Her full cherry lips showcased her perfect teeth. An eye-catching, camera worthy outfit tastefully accentuated her cover girl figure.

Eileen's energy level was high and her mood great. She nimbly negotiated her way through the crowded terminal, retrieved her checked luggage, hailed a cab, and proceeded directly to the Willard Hotel.

"Your hotel is quite charming. I was told it would be." Eileen commented to the registration clerk.

"Yes, thank you," the receptionist rotely bounced back her reply while proceeding to efficiently assign Eileen to a luxury room.

A bellman escorted Eileen to her room. While arranging her luggage, he offered standard introductory remarks about the Willard. He departed promptly after receiving his tip, but no conversation from his guest, obviously preoccupied with the room layout.

Eileen converted a corner of the room into a study. She opened her attaché case and removed a copy of her proposal. 'I'll just go through it one more time;' she determined. The title page excited her with each reading. “Project Moon City, A Proposal for Senator Samuel Johnson by Eileen Robbins.” Eileen smiled with satisfaction. She needed the powerful fifth term Alabama Senator's help. He chaired the Ways and Means Committee. 'Finally within reach,' she was confident.

Eileen slowly turned the pages scanning every word, each graph and all projections. The proposal was polished to perfection, a recognized Eileen Robbins trademark. Nevertheless, she used her remaining time to rehearse her presentation. 'I can't wait to place a copy in the Senator's hands.'

Eileen closed the proposal, kissed it, and placed it back inside the attaché case. Only then did she realize that she had worked through lunch.

Eileen checked her appearance, freshening her make-up and rechecking her smart blue suit with white blouse and light blue silk scarf. Approving the woman in the mirror, she took a deep breath, picked up the attaché case and departed for her ambitious appointment with Senator Johnson.

The short taxi ride to the Sam Rayburn Senate Office Building rekindled her admiration and awe of the massive marble and granite monuments and buildings. Eileen first engendered these feelings on her initial and only other trip to D.C., her senior high school class trip. She remembered her impressions of strength and power. 'Perhaps,' she fantasized, 'Now I am a participant rather than an observer.'

Inside the Rayburn Building Eileen entered the empty elevator and pressed the third-floor button. She marveled at the polished mahogany surrounding her. Confirming its authenticity she touched it approvingly as she ascended. Eileen lifted her eyes upward and offered a quick prayer, 'Oh, God, please let Senator Johnson like my proposal.'

Eileen entered the Senator's office ten minutes early. A masculine, rich wood and leather decorum confronted her. Eileen intuitively sensed, 'A strong and honest feeling, traditional and conventional, yet I'm confident he has a grasp of the future. After all, it is 1975.' She approached the receptionist, who reeked of longevity 'not unlike Senator Johnson' Eileen mused.

“Hello, I'm Eileen Robbins. I have an appointment with Senator

Johnson at two o'clock. I realize I am a few minutes early."

"Miss Robbins, I'm Ms. Sanders. I spoke with you on the phone. Welcome to Washington. Senator Johnson is looking forward to seeing you. He always enjoys visits by his Alabama constituents. Unfortunately, the Senator is running a little behind schedule today. I hope you won't mind a short delay. Please have a seat and make yourself at home. Could I get you anything to drink?"

Ms. Sanders looked and sounded efficient and business-savvy, but her practiced pleasantness left Eileen questioning her sincerity.

"No thank you. I'll be fine."

"The Senator knows your grandfather. He says he hasn't seen you since you were a small child. He is looking forward to hearing about you and your grandfather."

"Thank you for the heads-up Ms. Sanders." 'That was nice, perhaps she's OK.' Eileen looked around the spacious waiting area, and chose a chair suitable for proper sitting by a lady in a skirt.

Eileen smiled at the mention of Senator Johnson remembering her as a child. She held the thought as she sat down and studied his portrait, which hung prominently on the opposite wall. 'When could Senator Johnson have seen me? How old was I? Did I behave? Did he like me?' Her eyes lifted toward the ceiling, 'I wish I could remember. That was so long ago.'

'Perhaps he came to my elementary school, or maybe I was with papa on a trip to the Senator's office. Oh, well, hopefully I made a good impression.' Eileen's eyes closed in a flood of memories.

Eileen worshipped Papa Allen Robbins. 'Papa always gave me treats and invariably invited me on short trips, business and pleasure. Papa was an entrepreneur, perhaps some of my adventurous spirit stems from my early days with Papa Robbins.' He had been one of the first major contractors in the over-the-mountain bedroom communities of Birmingham, Alabama. It was he who had established their Robbins pedigree name. Her own father, Herschel, was much less aggressive and even less entrepreneurial, though he cultivated keen management skills and business acumen. Herschel joined his father in the family construction business, and became an invaluable asset in the continued growth of the Robbins construction empire. The two of them were uniquely complementary.

'Dad and Papa never argued. They talked out their differences. Papa was a dreamer and a doer, but a good listener. Dad was a thinker and a manager, but he rarely challenged papa. Yet if Papa's dreams couldn't withstand Dad's pencil and paper analysis, they mutually called it a gamble and wouldn't attempt it. I'm lucky to have learned from two of the best. I couldn't have had better role models to prepare me for my position as CEO of Space Travel, Incorporated.'

'I am lucky to have been blessed with so many advantages; living '*over-the-mountain*,' south of Birmingham. Dad and Papa helped to build much of it. My brother and I always ranked high on the national achievement tests. Mama made me feel that excelling was the Robbins' credo.'

Eileen's lifelong best friend, Missy, had once described her as: "friendly, likable, popular, intelligent, attractive, industrious, trustworthy, loyal, conscientious, athletic, and healthy; the everything girl." Eileen cherished her admiration and frequently sought it during her "funky" lows.

Eileen had flown bodily to Washington, now with welcomed unusual energy, she was mentally flying around through her past. She skimmed through the years, assessing herself, and with piqued curiosity that Senator Johnson remembers her.

Chapter 2
Graduation

Months before Eileen's graduation from the University of Alabama she applied for a position with the accounting firm of Levine, Randall and Smith. An invitation for an interview was promptly returned. Accepting the invitation, Eileen prepared for it as she might for a major course exam.

The meat of Eileen's interviews with the firm's principals covered the nuts and bolts of a general interview, "Hello, Mr. Levine. Thank you for the opportunity to interview. I have heard so many good things about you and your firm. It's a pleasure to meet you; it would be an honor to work with you. I worked hard at the university preparing myself to be an asset to a prestigious firm such as yours. I have a strong work ethic. I am loyal, conscientious, and industrious. I can start anytime after July tenth. I'm happy to answer any questions that you might have of me." Eileen learned that his sporting interest was horse racing. She decided not to learn who the current favorites were but simply commented, "I understand that you enjoy horse racing. I tried to make some sense of it but it must take a great deal of patience and unique ability to follow horse racing. I'm impressed that you have chosen such a difficult sport, especially being so isolated from it here in Birmingham."

"Well." said Levine. "As a matter of fact there are a number of enthusiasts here, and sooner than you think, we may bring horse racing to Birmingham."

"Oh, I hadn't heard. How fascinating. I assume you might be a part of that enterprise?"

"I best change the subject for now."

"Oh, I see," said Eileen, "I think you have done a super job of incorporating your hobby into your office decorum. I like it."

"Thank you very much."

Eileen would use the same technique in each of her interviews. It was part of her preparation, be genuine, be friendly, be yourself, enjoy people, and let them like you.

LRS, short for Levine, Randall and Smith approved the office interviews and invited Eileen to dinner for a final interview. Eileen joined the three principals at the Relay Club on the top floor of the Bank for Savings Building. She was seated with the window to her left, 'It feels too open but the city view is pretty.'

Eileen observed, 'No spouses. I'm the only female present. I can expect more business questions. Fine, I'll just enjoy the evening.'

When the appetizers were served, Levine gestured to Eileen.

'How clever of him' Eileen perceived. 'He's handed off the hosting to me, their guest.' Eileen picked up the appropriate utensil and effortlessly led them through all six courses.

"In my research of accounting firms in Birmingham I continuously heard high praise and comments about LRS. I learned that you decided to remain independent. I understand you rejected an opportunity to join one of the big eight firms. I like that. It shows confidence and strength. Besides, you don't have to go to New York or LA and then wait for a decision."

Levine responded, "Your research paid off. You're correct. In fact that was one of our questions for you this evening. We wondered if you would be, shall we say, put off by the fact that we are strictly local with no national aspiration? We prefer local control and ownership."

"Not at all. I am relieved. Birmingham is home. I'm looking for a professional home. I would not want to build up a clientele who trusted me only to be told to transfer to another city."

"That's our attitude," Randall offered. "Levine, Smith and I put this company together fifteen years ago. We are quite pleased with our accomplishments."

Smith said, "So you can see that we are interested in bringing on new people with like minded philosophies."

"Yes, of course. Isn't it nice that I fit perfectly? I am happy to have my impressions and thoughts of LRS confirmed. I do hope you will seriously consider offering a position to me. I am a good worker and I'm sure that I will be a positive addition for you."

The following morning Eileen received a phone call, "Hello."

"Miss Robbins?"

"Yes."

"This is Jack Levine. Of course, we will put this in writing but on behalf of LRS I would like to extend an offer for employment to you."

"Oh, that's great Mr. Levine!"

"I'll send over a sample contract. Just give me a call when you've had a chance to study it."

"I'm sure it will be just fine. I will get back to you just as soon as possible." Eileen was elated. It was Friday. On Sunday she would return to the University of Alabama in Tuscaloosa to begin her final semester.

'I wonder if I'm the first to land a job. I haven't heard of anyone else with an offer. I can't wait to tell Mom and Dad. I'll not say anything at school until others start mentioning their jobs. Some,' she remembered, 'were concerned about their potential for finding a job.'

Eileen read through the LRS contract with minimal retracing, 'Alright. This is super. They are being straightforward. They are not selling me short. They are offering me the going rate for men. I earned it and I got it.' Inwardly she speculated that the original interview came easier and quicker because of her name and family status.

Eileen held no delusion that her progression would be as rapid as her male counterparts. 'I wonder how long it will take me to break the glass ceiling.' She was undaunted. 'I'm likeable and more ambitious than most. I'll work hard and become one of their top producers. They will want me to become a partner.'

Eileen sent a graduation invitation to LRS and tucked inside a small note; she telegraphed youthful eagerness by writing, "see you soon," then drawing a smiley face, and signed, Eileen. After the ceremony, while visiting with her parents and grandparents, she heard a vaguely familiar voice. "Miss Robbins. Hi, Bill Randall. Congratulations on your graduation and especially Summa Cum Laude. We couldn't resist your invitation. I'm privileged to be representing LRS and I have a little something for you." Randall handed her an envelope and a small wrapped present.

Eileen introduced Randall to all of her family members.

Instinctively, Eileen knew, 'This is the executed contract. It was contingent on my graduation. How neat of them to take this opportunity to bring it, but what is this present?' She opened the envelope first, "Oh, I am so happy you've taken this occasion to bring this. I will get it back to you shortly." Eileen opened the present. "Oh, this is great. How clever. Thank you so much Mr. Randall and it's practical as well." Eileen held up a gold-plated Cross pen and pencil set. It had been inscribed "Eileen Robbins 1972." The occasion afforded a bonding for Eileen and Randall.

'Graduation and contract on the same day. Wow, my career is launched.'

After graduation Eileen took a well-earned respite before beginning work August first. She relaxed, visited friends, and spent a week at their beach house on the Gulf. Eileen's next four weeks in Europe rekindled her space fantasies. While in London she had déjà vu experiences. 'I feel at home. It was here that I witnessed the unfolding of the greatest technological event in history. President "Jack" Kennedy's promise was achieved. Apollo XI of the United States flew three men to the moon. (Two, Neal Armstrong and Edwin "Buzz" Aldrin), landed on its surface July the Twentieth, Nineteen Sixty-Nine. Then they flew safely home. People everywhere were transfixed, always near and watching a television.' Eileen was no exception. In fact, she was more enthralled than most.

Studying abroad that summer semester, every facet of her life resounded with wonder and promise. Her fascination with space travel became entrenched and a recurrent unyielding obsession. 'I'm traveling to Europe. These guys are traveling to the moon. One day I'll go to the moon. How long will it be before the rest of us can travel in space? With boats, cars and airplanes it only took a few years between invention and public application. Space travel will surely follow the pattern.' Eileen resolved to be involved in its development.

Mrs. Sanders answered a phone call, interrupting Eileen's train of thought. 'One fifty-five, I'll be waiting longer. I wonder if the Senator knows my credentials.'

Chapter 3
Beginning Work

On the first Monday of August Eileen arrived at LRS five minutes before nine. She wore a navy blue skirt, white blouse with long sleeves and buttoned down collar with a small bow, tied at the collar. Her navy blue pumps matched her navy purse. Her black attaché case clinched a professional appearance.

Preparing for the day, the receptionist was seated behind her desk arranging items as Eileen approached. "Good morning. May I help you?"

"Hi. I'm Eileen Robbins. This is my first day to work here. I'm to meet Mr. Randall.

"Oh, hi, Miss Robbins. I'm Betty. I'm the receptionist. I'm new in this position. Let me get Cynthia for you. She's our office manager." She pressed the intercom button, "Miss Robbins is here to meet with Mr. Randall and start work." "She'll be right out, Miss Robbins."

"Hi Miss Robbins. I'm Cynthia the office manager. It's a real pleasure."

"Hi Cynthia, I'm Eileen. It's my pleasure. Thanks for meeting me. Mr. Randall mentioned that he would be meeting with me this morning."

"Yes indeed. I'm going to give you a quick tour of the office. I'll introduce you to our staff and show you to your office. I'll explain our phone and intercom system. Mr. Randall will join us there. He will meet with you for a few minutes before the nine thirty planning session. I will rejoin you there. We have these each Monday. They usually last thirty-five to forty-five minutes. The first one of the month frequently lasts longer. This morning you will be introduced to all of the firm's members. You should be quite a hit. You're our first lady you know. You'll do just fine. You look quite professional and smart. That's what it takes."

"Thanks for the heads-up and the compliment. I'm sure I will need plenty of guidance in transitioning from the university to the real world."

"No you won't. It'll be as easy as one-two-three but if I do say so, we have a good staff and we are always here to help."

"That's comforting Cynthia."

Eileen repeated every staff member's name as she was introduced to them. If she said the person's name while looking at them it somehow clicked in her memory. She had always had that knack.

"This will be your office, Miss Robbins."

"Thank you, Cynthia. It seems adequate."

"Well, we don't have an office that's been decorated for a lady. Everyone expects you to make some changes and add some feminine warmth. They told me to tell you that would be fine."

Laughing, Eileen said, "Maybe I will make a few changes. Let's see if we can make it feel a little more inviting. I'll think about it."

"Mr. Randall will be here shortly. He will take you to the meeting. Is there anything further I can do for you? Oh, I almost forgot. Let me show you the basics of the intercom system. I'm here all the time, so drop in anytime you have any questions or just buzz me and I'll come around. It's very nice to have you here."

"Thank you. It's very nice to be here."

Randall walked into Eileen's office just as she withdrew her pen and pencil set from her attaché case.

"Oh, hi Mr. Randall. My first act of settling in" gesturing to her pen set. "That was so nice of LRS, again, thanks."

"We're glad you like it and glad to have you here at LRS. Coming through the office, on the way here half the staff told me how nice you are and how glad they are that you are here."

"Only half?" Laughing, "I'll just have to try harder."

"No. No. I didn't see the other half. It was a hundred percent of the ones I encountered."

"Whew, that's a relief. Thanks for the clarification."

"That's nothing. All of the accounting team already likes you even though some of them haven't met you. I'm here to give you a little tip.

Levine enjoys putting new people on the spot. If he treats you the same as he treats everyone else he will have each person introduce themselves to you. Then he will ask you to introduce yourself and to tell everyone about yourself."

Eileen's lips parted with surprise, she had not anticipated giving a speech about herself. 'Not a problem,' she reassured herself. She had memorized all the members' names from the letterhead. It should be easy to place names with faces. 'I just need to find a way to connect with them.'

Fortunately for Eileen, Levine's format was to introduce her personally to each of their eight members.

Levine said, "This morning we will be discussing any unique problems and collectively work on solutions."

'Maybe I have dodged the bullet. He's going to treat me differently.'

"But first," Levine continued, "As is our tradition here, we like for our new members to tell us about themselves, so Miss Robbins would you, for the benefit of those who haven't had the opportunity to get to know you, tell us about yourself?"

'Well, at least so far I am treated equal,' she thought. "Why Mr. Levine that's all the direction you're going to give me? Where should I start?"

"Anywhere you like."

"Fellow accountants, thank you for inviting me to join you at LRS, and thank you for the warm welcome and solid handshakes. You have made me feel comfortable and for that I am grateful. I knew early on in life that accounting was what I wanted to do. In my junior year at The University of Alabama I began asking around about accounting firms. By the beginning of my senior year I knew that LRS was where I wanted to make my professional home. I applied here first. When my interviews felt positive I decided not to apply anywhere else. Thank you for choosing me because you were my only choice. So, Mr. Levine, Mr. Randall, Mr. Smith, Mr. Skinner," Eileen looked at each member and successively called them by name. "I consider you my professional family, my mentors, and my friends."

"I study hard, and I work hard. I exercise regularly, and I don't smoke. I don't use or believe in illegal or recreational drugs. I love life and enjoy people. I restrain from religion and politics at work. I am an adventurer. I love excitement and I'm simply enthralled with space travel. I hope, one day, to travel in space. Will that be sufficient Mr. Levine or was it too much?"

"Perfect Miss Robbins, perfect." Levine himself began the applause.

Eileen listened intently through the forty-five minute meeting. Levine and Randall made sure that she was included but she was not otherwise challenged throughout the meeting. At the meeting's conclusion, Eileen proceeded to her office.

'That went well. Everyone seemed nice. I am going to work with a passion. I will be as good as anyone, better than most, I hope.' She knew her first assignments would be subordinated to partners, taking care of details for those with heavy schedules. She knew that everything she did would be reviewed by senior members. 'I'll double-check everything myself before submitting anything. I'll pay my dues and bide my time. I'll watch for opportunities and be ready when they present themselves.'

Several months into Eileen's employment, Randall informed Levine, "Eileen's knowledge is solid. She even makes appropriate and significant suggestions. She's conscientious. Her work is impeccable. Everyone likes her, the staff, the other members, the clients; no doubt we've got a winner. I believe we should back off on the overview and save ourselves the effort. She's solid."

"Glad to hear it. That's record time for a new employee right?"

"You're absolutely correct."

After the first year, LRS began assigning new clients to Eileen. She easily won their confidence and loyalty. Her credo was "Be timely and accurate." Typical was a comment from Mr. Eddings. "Miss Robbins, it's a real pleasure to work with you. You hear what I say. You do what I need and you get it back to me when you say you will. Thank you."

"Thank you, Mr. Eddings. I enjoy working with you. In fact, I enjoy people and I enjoy my work. A great combination."

"It sure is. I'm glad I found you."

It became office SOP for anyone, especially the staff, to let Eileen know when there was anything on the radio or TV relating to the Apollo project or for that matter, anything that related to space and space travel. She watched everything, take offs, splash downs, and anything in between. She read all that she could find in the newspaper and in the popular magazines. At night she drew sketches of fantasy spaceships, interconnected rooms for space stations, and buildings for barren, airless, interplanetary destinations. Primarily though, she was focused on Earth's moon.

"Do you still want to be the first woman in space Miss Robbins?"

"That would be nice Betty but I'm sure some hotshot pilot will beat me to that. I'll just have to settle on being the first tourist to the moon."

"That's cool. Take me with you?"

"We'll take lots of people."

"You're a dreamer aren't you?"

"I guess so Betty but who else were dreamers? The Wright Brothers, Henry Ford, Werner von Braun. Hey, I'll take that company any day."

"Well, dreams are one thing but work is reality, speaking of which I better get back to mine. Have a nice day."

'Betty was right, work is reality. I've got dual dreams, success at LRS, and getting to the moon. I better get to work on both.'

At two minutes past two Mrs. Sanders approached Eileen. Miss Robbins, "It's going to be several more minutes before the Senator can see you, may I get something for you, coffee, soft drink, or water?"

"Perhaps some water, thank you Mrs. Sanders."

Eileen returned to reconstructing her professional growth, as if somehow this would make the Senator aware of her accomplishments.

Chapter 4
Opportunity

Early in nineteen seventy-four, only eighteen months into her career at LRS, Eileen's opportunity was literally handed to her.

Eileen watched Mr. Skinner come through her open door with a client folder in hand. He gestured that she needed to take the folder. His voice was crisp and his face firm, "Eileen, I'm really in a bind. I need your help. This has to be ready by Monday morning and there is no way I can get it done with my heavy schedule. Mr. MacInough has been a client of mine for several years. He's asked that I refigure his estate planning along with the tax treatment of his business dealings. Would you have time to take a look at it for me? I would be very grateful."

'MacInough. I've heard that name. He's important. I wonder if Skinner has other clients more important or more pressing.' "Of course, Mr. Skinner, I'll be happy to take a look at it. Show me what you have." Eileen skimmed through the folder. "Let's get together Friday morning?"

"Sounds good."

Eileen knew that of all the people at LRS, Skinner was the least conscientious in keeping up with new trends, regulations, and tax codes. 'I'm going to look at every conceivable possibility.' She felt a surge of energy. Her mind was sharp, clever and cunning. She had anticipated this type opportunity. 'As the first female at LRS it's my moral responsibility to demonstrate our capabilities even if I have to connive a bit here and there.'

Eileen was certain that Mr. Skinner's Monday morning meeting with Mr. MacInough would be to deliver the proposal to him. These meetings always inserted a buffer of time to accommodate changes. She methodically calculated her plan.

On Friday morning Eileen approached Mr. Skinner, "Here's a draft proposal for Mr. MacInough's business arrangements, estate planning and tax treatment. They are fairly standard for business dealings here in Birmingham. You might want to suggest to him that he could be a little more aggressive in his expense deductions."

Pleased, Skinner semi thanked her, "That's a great idea. I'll be sure to mention it to him."

"I have some other ideas I'm researching, but it's too premature to discuss any numbers. I will continue working on them."

"Fine."

Eileen thought, 'You wouldn't think it fine if you knew how badly these new numbers will show you up. How could anyone be so incompetent or miss such great opportunities with one of your prime clients?'

Late Friday afternoon, Eileen provided the finished product to Skinner. "This is the finished product of the proposal we spoke about this morning. I wanted you to have an opportunity to see it before you meet with Mr. MacInough on Monday." "I'll do a proforma on the other thoughts this weekend."

"Thank you Eileen. I'll study this over the weekend."

Late Saturday morning Eileen called Mr. MacInough at home, "Mr. MacInough, I'm Eileen Robbins. I'm one of the CPA's at LRS. I'm helping Mr. Skinner with your tax planning. I wanted to make sure that you won't mind if we at least look at a few alternative opportunities."

"Of course not. Please look at all opportunities. Thank you for calling."

"Thank you very much. I'll see you on Monday."

Skinner had not invited Eileen to the Monday meeting. However, she vowed, 'This is one party I'm going to crash.'

On Monday, Eileen waited until Skinner initiated the meeting with Mr. MacInough. She surprised them by entering the conference room unannounced. She closed the door behind her and approached them with her file folder in hand. "Hi Mr. MacInough. I'm Eileen Robbins; I spoke with you about working with Mr. Skinner on your business plan and tax treatments. I brought my notes in case you have any questions after Mr. Skinner explains it to you, but I can leave if you would rather discuss this privately?"

"No. Please stay Miss Robbins. The more the merrier," MacInough answered preempting Skinner.

Eileen sensed MacInough's satisfaction. She exercised the patience of a master chess player and the precision of an atomic physicist to calculate the appropriate moment to interject herself further. Mr. Skinner discussed the ramifications of his proposal just as Eileen had given it to him. When it was apparent to Eileen and MacInough that the session was about to conclude, Eileen struck. She rescued MacInough from financial disaster and Skinner from his inadequacies.

"Mr. Skinner, when you and I reviewed Mr. MacInough's needs we discussed the idea that perhaps we could be more aggressive in structuring his business and estate planning, and perhaps utilize some of the new tax maneuvers available to businessmen such as Mr. MacInough. I assumed you wanted me to follow-up these thoughts, so over the weekend I prepared an alternate proposal. Thank you for letting me develop this. It appears to me that Mr. MacInough can save in the neighborhood of a quarter of a million dollars over the next couple of years through using new techniques available to us. Of course, continuing to use these will provide annual savings beyond that. Mr. MacInough should be very grateful to you, Mr. Skinner."

With fixed gaze, Mr. MacInough sat in shocked awe. After a short, uncomfortable silence, MacInough cleared his throat and turned towards Skinner. "Wow. You guys are geniuses. I hoped you could help, but this is phenomenal. How soon could you draw up the papers for the alternate proposal?"

"I assumed you would like the alternate proposal so I took the liberty of preparing the necessary paperwork. Naturally, you will want to have your tax attorney bless it. Would that be Mr. Levine? He is our expert."

MacInough was hooked, "I'll use whoever ya'll recommend. I'm very appreciative."

Skinner was upstaged. But, how could he complain? 'Eileen made me look good to MacInough. Not only that, she saved MacInough a bundle of money and now LRS can refigure our research, development and preparation time.' Suddenly his fee looked much more lucrative.

As the meeting was ending Mr. MacInough inquired, "Miss Robbins, are you any relation to Samuel Robbins?"

"Why yes sir, I am, he's my uncle. Do you know Samuel?"

"Yes I do, Samuel and I are big buddies. In fact, we were in college together. We joined different fraternities but we were always best of friends. After college we maintained our friendship and have been involved in several mutual business ventures. He's a fine man. Looks like you were cut from the same cloth."

"That's a real compliment. I appreciate it. I can't wait to tell Uncle Samuel." Skinner separated himself from them and the conversation which obviously did not include him. He walked to Levine's office contemplating, 'How do I relate this to Levine? I have to think of something.'

Levine's door was open. Skinner walked in. "Jack, you're going to be interested to hear this. You know old MacInough. We've been doing his accounting for about ten years, but we never could get him to break away from Sam Jones, his tax attorney. Well, Miss Eileen just did the job for us. She assisted me on a project of his business set-ups and tax planning. I thought maybe we could save him some money. By golly when she ran the numbers sure enough we'll be saving him about a quarter of a million dollars during the first year or so. Of course, then there will be annual savings after that. He told us we were geniuses. Then she told him he should have a tax attorney check it out and suggested you were the expert so Sam said, 'That's fine with me,' so you just wound up with a new client."

Levine looked straight at Skinner taking a moment to digest the remarkable news. "Well Bob, you've done a helluva job here. You realize there was lots of research on that don't you?"

"Oh yeah, I've already thought of all that. It's just a matter of reconstructing just exactly how many extra hours of work went into that research and preparation."

Levine and Skinner laughed heartily.

Internally, Eileen laughed hardest, 'That was smooth as silk. That should get me some attention.' Actually, she could hardly wait to share the encounter, and her excitement, with Missy.

At five past two, Mrs. Sanders approached Eileen with a glass of water. Eileen accepted the water and thanked her, but returned to her own absorbing line of thought.

Chapter 5
The Payoff

Not a full week had passed before Eileen received a fortuitous phone call. "Hello, this is Eileen Robbins."

A strong pleasant, but authoritative voice announced, "Miss Robbins I'm a friend of Bob MacInough. He told me about the marvelous job you did for him. I find myself in a similar situation and was wondering if we could meet. Currently all my business is at one of the big eight firms. I would appreciate meeting you prior to saying anything to them. My preference would be to meet somewhere other than your office, at least initially. Perhaps we could have lunch and explore potential possibilities? If you are agreeable we will meet at Brittlings Cafeteria. Would that be all right with you?"

Eileen's thoughts were racing faster than the fingers of an abacus expert. 'The door is open. The MacInough deal has paid off.'

"My name is Broadman. John Broadman, but I will ask you to keep it confidential in case it doesn't work out. Do you mind?"

'So much to answer. I don't even know him. A total stranger. What do I say? I can't refuse this type of opportunity.' "Well sir, if you are a friend of the gentleman Mr. MacInough to the point that you discussed private matters such as he and I have reviewed, you must be trustworthy enough for a public meeting. I will be happy to meet with you sir."

"Fine, what about tomorrow at eleven thirty for lunch?"

"That will be fine. I will describe myself to you."

"That won't be necessary 'ma'am, Mr. MacInough has done a decent job of that."

"How shall I recognize you?"

"Don't worry I'll see to it that we get to the same table."

Eileen pushed back from her desk stood up, walked around and looked out the window. She stretched forth both arms mentally embracing all of the outdoors. 'Fantastic! I have to make sure the meeting goes well. This could be my big opportunity.' Eileen had no idea how big.

Her energy soared through the afternoon and into the evening. 'Why am I so revved up? I need to slow down. I've got to use this energy. I have to collect my thoughts for my meeting with Mr. Broadman. What will I put in my attaché case? I want to make sure I'm dressed to kill. He needs to see me as professional. He needs to like me. I hope I can save him some money. He is with the big eight; they do really good work. I have to win his account. He will send me others just as MacInough sent him. I'll have my own clientele. I'll break that glass ceiling. I'll become a partner. I've got to get some rest.' Nothing seemed to slow her down. Eileen showered and prepared for bed. 'I'm not sleepy. It's eleven thirty.' She went to the closet and selected an appealing ensemble for the following day. She checked for soils or wrinkles. She vacuumed the apartment, dusted the lamps, sorted her laundry. It was twelve thirty a.m.

'It's sinful to feel this good.' But her mind rebelled at this line of thought. She told herself, 'No. I've earned it. I've worked for it. I will enjoy it.' Her thought pattern switched rapidly. 'I'm so lucky, so fortunate, so smart.' She felt guilt and chastised herself for the egotistical thoughts.

Eileen's eyes and mind searched the room for something, anything to corral her thoughts, relax her body and bring her sleep. The clock taunted her, two a.m. She hadn't noticed that book before, even when she dusted everything in the room, but there it was, the Holy Bible. 'I haven't been reading the Bible lately. Perhaps if I read a little, God will know how grateful I am.' Opening the Bible she skimmed the pages and spotted the passage, "Ask and it shall be given. Seek and ye shall find." Eileen closed her eyes and thought, 'How lucky to have a God so generous and the Bible pointing the pathway directly to Him. God grant me the right words for Mr. Broadman and give me peace and sleep.' She shortly dropped into a sound sleep with the Bible lying beside her, unclosed.

Eileen awoke late the next morning. She realized she would not get to work by eight o'clock if she followed her usual routine. She popped in two pieces of bread for toast and poured a glass of milk. 'This will get me through the morning. It's a crucial day. She took time to double check her make-up, and scrutinize her outfit in the full-length mirror.

At the office Eileen paced more than usual. She scribbled thoughts and doodled drawings, then crumpled them, half-filling the wastebasket. She nervously made several trips to the break room.

'What's happening to me? Am I just excited? I was out of control last night. I'm nervous. I'm too excited. I must calm down. Broadman can't see me as anxious.'

Eleven thirty seemed interminably far away. Her mind raced forward to meeting Broadman. 'Who is he? What kind of person is he? Does he have a big account? Can I win his account? Be calm. Be yourself. You can win this account on your own.'

Eileen stepped through the door at Brittlings Cafeteria at exactly eleven thirty. She felt out of place despite previous visits. Brittlings was so public, so utilitarian, but she knew that was precisely the reason Broadman had chosen Brittlings.

John Broadman was seated alone in the private dining room. Through the open door, he could see Eileen enter. 'What a fine looking woman. MacInough was right on the first count. I hope he's right on the second count. Maybe I should have taken her to the country club. Maybe next time.'

A dark complexioned waiter who wore a patch over one eye picked up the signal from Mr. Broadman and immediately stepped up to Eileen, "Miss Robbins, I believe? My name is Horace. You will be the guest of the gentleman over in the private dining room. Nobody else in the room today. It will just be the two of you. You just go through the line 'ma'am, get anything you like. I'll be at the end to pick it up for you. Will that be all right ma'am?"

"That will be quite fine, Horace." Eileen had seen him there several times previously. Though she had not known his name, she had admired him. He was a pleasant man, a good worker, and he never mentioned or complained that he was blind in one eye. He never worked without a black patch over that eye. Presumably, it hid a deformity.

Eileen went through the line and selected a light lunch consisting of cottage cheese, fruit, chicken salad, and sweet iced tea.

"Won't there be anything else, 'ma'am?" Horace was asking.

"No, that will be fine, Horace."

"You just let yourself on in 'ma'am and I'll be right along."

Eileen entered the medium-sized meeting room. Mr. Broadman stood as she entered.

'He's rather pleasant-looking, handsome, tall, salt and pepper hair.' The vibes were good. She was already relaxing. 'There's that southern gentlemanness already showing. I love it.'

Mr. Broadman walked toward her with an extended hand. "Miss Robbins, I'm John Broadman, it's a pleasure to meet you 'ma'am. Please have a seat. Bob told me how pretty you were and also how smart. We'll see if you check out as well on the second part as the first part. He told me that in a couple of years you'd be saving him a quarter of a million dollars."

Horace entered with Eileen's tray. She noticed that he had added a glass of ice water and two nice slices of lemon.

'What a nice touch,' Eileen noted, 'A real thoughtful waiter.'

Horace sat everything on the table and inquired, "What else can I get for you 'ma'am?"

"Nothing Horace, but thank you very much."

Turning back to Mr. Broadman Eileen commented, "Well Mr. Broadman, that's very kind of you. I try to do a good job, and when Mr. Skinner asked me to work out that proposal for Mr. MacInough I just did the best I could."

Mr. Broadman quickly framed a tone of straightforwardness for their relationship, "Now 'ma'am, let's start this meeting shooting straight. Skinner hasn't read a book or journal since he left college and you know that as well as I do. Bob said you did a good job of letting him save face and he went along with it, but he knew exactly what had happened, and he damned sure appreciated it."

Eileen was blushing. Her assumption had been confirmed. 'I love his frankness. He must already like me. This is great. His eyes are warm and his words are engaging. He's an honest man, I can tell.' She answered him simply with her warmest smile.

They sat down to eat. While she nibbled at her food, Broadman ate heartily. “Well, you're like all the pretty girls, you eat like a bird and keep that pretty figure and I eat like a horse and look like one.”

“Why Mr. Broadman, you look just fine sir. You actually remind me a bit of John Wayne.”

“My goodness 'ma’am, I've not had flattery like that in years. That'll get you anywhere you want to go, you know.”

With a quick wink, “Well, why don't we start with your account, Mr. Broadman?”

“Hold on there. All in due time. Tell me first how you figured out what you could do with Bob's business dealings and tax structuring. How did you come up with the idea anyway? Are you quite sure it is legal?”

“Well sir, Mr. Levine wanted to make sure, so he's checked it out thoroughly. He's very comfortable with it. He's gone ahead with all the preparations for Mr. MacInough. I believe we can consider it perfectly legal. Everyone's needs will be individual, and require personalized creativity. I would very much appreciate an opportunity to see what we can do with yours.”

“Not we, Miss Robbins. You. I don't want Skinner or the rest of them working on it. I just want you to take a look at my situation and tell me if in your opinion we can do better.”

“I understand. Frankly that's exactly what I would prefer.”

“Well Miss Robbins, I have a unique situation. My wife, bless her heart, has been a mighty good woman to me, bore me three fine boys and raised them right. The doctor found a big lump in her breast last year so they operated and took it out in December. They are trying to give us as much hope as possible, but I've seen and heard and read too much in my lifetime to not see the writing on the wall. I'm not going to have my sweet bride much longer. Bob tells me you said the best time to do any estate planning is before you need it. That's why this meeting is so urgent. I talked to my accountant about it in early February. He said he would look into it. I suppose he is still looking because he hasn't called me back. I hadn't figured there would be a whole lot he could do; so, I haven't been pushing him. When I heard what you had done for Bob I decided to give you a call. Do you think you can help me, Miss Robbins?” “I don't mind paying a fair share of taxes but I've worked hard for my money and I've paid Uncle Sam his due. I'd rather he not get most of it just because I won't have my wife to pass it along to."

"Mr. Broadman, I'm so sorry to hear this sad news. I do hope you are wrong about your wife. I can tell you that Uncle Sam is still going to want a slice of your estate. With proper planning however, and with due thought and consideration to your wife's final desires, your desires, and family planning, we probably could get Uncle Sam to take less than you might have expected. It's definitely worth exploring."

"I would be mighty obliged to you, 'ma'am. This is what I propose we do. We'll set up a formal appointment at your office. I will come over for a proper appointment. I'll bring my papers outlining my current situation. I will leave them with you for your analysis. After you have studied them and prepared a response, you let me know and we'll set another meeting and I'll come back. I would appreciate it if you would keep this confidential for the time being."

"Of course. All we do is confidential."

"I understand, just wanted to say it."

As they stood to leave they were face-to-face. The lingering eye contact was unmistakable. Both recognized it but neither acknowledged it. A mini-bear hug was brewing, but he refrained and she didn't invite.

She walked out into the sunshine. 'It's a beautiful day. It's a wonderful world.' She drew a deep breath. Her thoughts were so strong that she felt they were audible. 'Broadman is going to be my first big client.'

It was fifteen past two. Mrs. Sanders noticed Eileen glancing at her watch. "I am so sorry. The Senator will be embarrassed. I'm sure he will be out shortly."

"I understand," Eileen obligingly replied.

Chapter 6
Expectations

In the short drive back to her office Eileen's lips formed a knowing smile. 'Mom and Dad are going to be proud.' But the smile vanished without a trace, as she began thinking instead, 'They will be surprised. It's always a surprise when it's me. They expected this of Brad but not me.' Brad was her older brother by four years.

She recognized a familiar feeling, anger at herself. Why did she continue to compete with her brother? After all, he betrayed the family dreams and expectations. It had hurt so badly that his name is never mentioned.

Eileen had spent hours with Dr. Saxon, a psychologist. He counseled her to understand her individual worth, her need to develop a personal path and goal. He enlightened her that being the second of only two children, and especially behind an unusually talented, bright and personable brother, she was trying to compete on an unequal playing field. He focused for her that she must appreciate her gifts: intelligence, personableness, beauty, and an uncanny sense about other people's expectations." She used this knowledge to cope with her parents 'I measured up, even usually exceeding their expectations. These same talents and techniques would help me to forge ahead in the world of unmerciful competition.' Saxon had observed that she "needed a contentedness about this." She remembered those words. 'Why can't I be content? Nothing is ever good enough, or fulfilling enough. It has always been that way. Would it be so forever?'

At first it had been fun being 'Brad's little sister.' Everyone would say, "Oh, you're Brad's little sister. He's so cute." And then an invitation would ensue, "Come on in." Brad was her ticket to everything. It didn't hurt either that mama made sure that she wore the finest clothes. From the earliest years she was socialized with the elite of the "over the mountain folk."

Grade school was formative for her individuality. Brad was not in the room with her. The separation of their paths was subtle but distinct. As a bright and cheerful child she was a teacher favorite.

Eileen continued replaying her past. 'Ms. Swindall was so nice.' "Eileen, honey, you have such a brilliant mind for numbers and logic. Study your math dear; it's your forte." Eileen looked up "forte" and beamed with pride. Swindall became a favorite teacher and a major influence on her love of math.

Perfection in the Robbins' household was an expectation. Brad had perfect teeth. Eileen's were almost perfect. Not good enough. She would be required to endure braces for two years. An A on a report card was never good enough. An A+ was acceptable. Handwritten accolades were expected. At least in this, she excelled over Brad. He had always produced straight A's, but it was Eileen who consistently had the A+'s and the teacher accolades.

Brad was tall, reaching the height of six feet three inches. He was muscular and good looking. Brad enjoyed basketball and had been Captain of the team in his senior year. Their team made it to the finals before losing that year to a rival across town. Yet, his athletic prowess was good enough to earn an invited interest from several colleges and universities.

Brad had been a difficult person to understand. He would be the life of the party, fun loving and joyful. He would be everyone's friend. He was able to make anyone feel better, but on the darker side his moods were black as soot. No one could pull him out. He withdrew from friends, and insisted on being left alone. His moods would last for days, but then he would snap out of them. Mr. and Mrs. Robbins tolerated his moods having learned that they didn't last long. When left alone and nurtured, he would come around. They convinced themselves that he was not on drugs as many of the young people were. Brad had a steady girlfriend during his junior and senior year though the relationship was rocky. They broke up three times only to repeatedly reconcile. At the end of the senior year they were dating, but continuing to struggle. She would be going to Princeton and he was going to the University of Alabama. He would do the family proud by accepting a basketball scholarship. He looked forward to studying engineering; however, mom was still pushing him toward pre-med. No one thought any of this was a big deal. They assumed it would sort itself out during the first couple of years at the University.

One week after graduation Brad took his father's pistol out into the backyard. He placed the barrel in his mouth and ended his life. He was eighteen years old. He left no note. There had been no good-byes. There were no hints that anything was wrong. His girlfriend, Jennifer, was devastated. Mom and Dad were in shock. They looked outside for blame. Surely his girlfriend must be pregnant or she must have hurt him very deeply some way. These thoughts evaporated as Jennifer and her parents mourned as grievously as they did.

Eileen's shock and horror was unfathomable. She was fourteen years old. It can't be true. Is he really dead? How long will he be dead? Is he mad at us? What can we do to make it all right? He shouldn't hurt me like this. I'll get him for this. Now I won't have to compete with him.' Later at the funeral she watched his casket slowly descend into the earth, she finally realized Brad was not coming back. Outwardly her body folded around her weeping face and broken heart. Inwardly she was screaming, 'No! That's my brother; you can't do that to him!' She needed him to stay. 'I'll be alone. He will be alone. Should I go with him? How could he do that to himself?' Her thoughts were flying in every direction, making little sense. 'Some of that is as vivid as yesterday, some of it like a distant vague dream.'

Mr. and Mrs. Robbins called friends to get suggestions for a child psychologist. They got several names but Dr. Sam Saxon was mentioned most often. It was consistently mentioned that he believed in spiritual guidance as well as psychological counseling. They forced her to see him.

'I liked him well enough. He was very understanding, easy to talk with. He was witty and made me laugh a few times after the first couple of sessions. He was quite helpful. I had guilt feelings thinking perhaps I caused Brad's suicide. Dr. Saxon helped me understand that I had nothing to do with his suicide. I thought I might wind up with the same need to escape. He assured me that was a personal choice. There are many ways to solve dilemmas and relieve stress. My willingness to look at alternatives was a plus. My ability to work in therapy, learn about myself, and develop coping strategies gave me a head start should I ever feel those kinds of urges or impulses. It is reassuring that someone like him would always be available. He also assured me that Mom and Dad would be there for me, whatever my needs.'

Dr. Saxon helped her to understand that even in our enlightened twentieth century, some families, unfortunately, allow their second born and their daughters to feel they are second class. We instill in people to believe the Bible, but use it to reinforce the rights and heritage of the firstborn, specifically the firstborn son. He pointed out the many accomplishments of modern day women, Eleanor Roosevelt, Claire Booth-Luce, and Amelia Earhart. Eileen remembered thinking, 'Yeah, Earhart died trying to prove herself.' Eileen thought, 'At least we should have equality between the sexes. After all, we live in the United States of America, where everything is supposed to be equal and fair.' Dr. Saxon said, "Supposed to be is fantasy. You must live in the real world. There is pervasive injustice and too little fairness. Luck is not usually something you find but rather something you create. You are a bright young lady. I hope you will keep your eyes open. I'm not trying to teach you to be paranoid, just cautious."

Eileen surmised that, 'my parent's big question for Dr. Saxon had been, were they at risk of losing me the way they lost Brad.' They insisted there had been no warning signs. Sure, they told Dr. Saxon, "once in a while in one of his blue moods he would say, 'Life sucks' or 'why did I have to be born?', but he never said he would kill himself. Once he said 'If anything happens to me, make sure that Jennifer gets my varsity sweater,' but he seemed perfectly upbeat when he said it."

Brads' moodiness distressed Eileen. She did not consider herself to be moody. There were times when she was a little testy as she was labeled, usually when challenging Brad or feeling ignored in the presence of Brad being praised for something.

Mr. Robbins seemed to withdraw somewhat after Brad's death but Mrs. Robbins seemed to have redoubled her energy and effort. She made sure that no desire went unfulfilled. Eileen wore the best clothes, drove the best car; she had at least as much spending money as any other over the mountain child. It was a foregone conclusion that she would be a debutante in the Ball of Roses. She dated Jay Coker, the popular President of the sophomore class. Mrs. Robbins discouraged the relationship with various disparaging remarks about Jay and his family. In Eileen's junior year she dated Roy Putman, Captain of the football team. Mrs. Robbins thought he was too old for Eileen and likely to take advantage of her. Whomever she dated Mrs. Robbins would find or invent fault. Eileen was also a solid member of the high school track team. During her senior year she was captain and they won the State Championship. Mom was very supportive and ever present. Dad was supportive but never present. She remembers him saying, "Great job, kid." But she thought 'If it were Brad, he would be there with his chest poked out.' In reality, she knew he also missed most of Brad's basketball games.

At the University of Alabama, Eileen enjoyed the independence and freedom that comes with college and distance from home. She partied, dated, and studied, excelling in each.

Naturally gregarious and fun loving, Eileen accepted most of the early party invitations. During the first party she drank little alcohol and observed others. Emboldened by the experience, she increased her participation during the second party. She consumed more alcohol and discovered: 'I feel good. This is fun. I want to dance.' Her inhibitions were dissolved. 'I have to dance.'

"Hi there, my name is Eileen; what's your name?"

"Bruce."

"Bruce, nice to meet you. Let's dance." Eileen pulled him to the center of the floor where they danced and danced. She ignored his protest that he was not a dancer. Bruce, reluctantly, evolved into a great dance partner. He and Eileen became friends, and quickly were steady dates. Bruce was the second son of a banker in Mobile. Eileen's bubbly gregariousness was the perfect complementary match for Bruce's reticent manner. He depended heavily on her. Eventually, the need to prop Bruce's courage became a chore. She took a break and asked for time to think. Bruce pleaded that he loved Eileen.

"I'll do anything you ask of me. I don't want to lose you."

For whatever reason, Eileen's energy had sunk too low to cope.

'I can't do this. I am barely able to get to class. Why can't he see I'm exhausted? He needs me and he's such a good person. I'm cruel to dump him. Where does my black cloud come from? Maybe he could accept it better if I took an overdose. What's the use anyway? I'll never feel good again. I'll never be happy.' Eileen's black mood lasted nearly three weeks.

There was no discernible reason that the Friday morning should be different. On awakening however, Eileen was different. 'Wow! I feel good. Maybe I had a bug. I've got to go over my notes for this afternoon's exam. It's not too late to make plans for tonight's party, should I call Bruce? No, he's been pulling me down. I can't risk it!'

Eileen's guilt over Bruce gave way to her infatuation with her next love, Stewart. His father was a wealthy oil man from Louisiana. Stewart was astute and flamboyant. He was a welcome relief from Bruce. Stewart needed no support. He inundated her with presents, flowers, romantic cards, dinners, and drinks. 'This is wonderful,' boasted Eileen. Her girlfriends, however, asked, “How do you put up with that creep?” Eileen's answer, “I know he's got an ego but he treats me like a princess.”

Eileen abruptly ended the relationship with Stewart when she woke up one morning with him in her bed. 'What have I done? The bastard got me drunk and took advantage of me. I should never have gotten drunk. I know the kind of person he is. I was stupid to ever date him.' Eileen was embarrassed. She never told anyone. She was plunged into another black spell.

Eileen became sensitive and cautious regarding men. She knew that she was good at her studies. She would focus her energy academically. She went to the University of Alabama with the intention of becoming a certified public accountant. It had not been intellectually challenging. She was at the top of her class from the beginning to the end. She expected she might do the same with employment. If she was unable to reach the top at LRS she would take her learning and earnings and move to a better opportunity. She could have had a job with one of the big eight firms, but in Birmingham LRS was prestigious, and, by sheer numbers she should be able to move up more timely.

Eileen wondered if the Senator would cancel her appointment and thought of asking Mrs. Sanders if she should reschedule; but she decided against it.

The time was nineteen past two.

Chapter 7
Partnership

Broadman sat at the conference table listening intently to every word of Eileen's presentation. He studied each overhead with a poker face and steel eyes. Eileen had worked tirelessly through every available morsel of information referable to Broadman's business affairs. She had tediously crafted a fascinating intricate tax structure, including trust funds and imaginative business machinations. She presented her proposal with confidence, exuding joy in her work, and pride in her product. To the best of her ability she had researched everything, making sure not to wander into disallowable traps. All calculations were based on the assumption that Mrs. Broadman would survive a minimum of twelve months after executing the proposed plan. Broadman and his heirs could expect to legally avoid approximately twenty-two and a half million dollars in federal tax alone. One by one she presented the overheads, each one projecting intriguing ideas or suggestions, and most with estimated savings. She knew Mr. Broadman was keeping a mental tally. The next to the last overhead read, "Projected Grand Savings." The one line on the last overhead simply showed in bold numbers, "$22,500,000.00." When she projected it onto the screen Broadman's poker face blinked. She read surprise and delight from his expression. Eileen stated her obligatory disclaimer, "If all works out as we have calculated, this number fairly represents your expected savings."

Broadman had digested every word. He had known Eileen was talking of millions but had not anticipated a total of twenty-two and a half million dollars. He didn't even give Eileen the pleasure of instant "at-a-girl" applause or exclaiming; "Fantastic!" he sat there as if he might be channeling his adrenaline and searching his mind for the right thing to say.

Eileen patiently outwaited him.

Mr. Broadman finally spoke, "Miss Robbins, that's one helluva job."

"Thank you, sir. It's special, just for you."

"No need to flatter me, you're just damned smart, which I appreciate. Is Levine still the head of the firm?"

"Yes sir, have I done anything wrong?"

"Where's the old codger? Is he here now?

"I think he might be."

"Go find him. Tell him I want to see him. Tell him who I am. He'll come."

Eileen, stunned, obediently replied, "Yes sir, just a moment please," and exited the room. She went directly to Mr. Levine's office who fortunately was just finishing with a client. She whispered, "I need to see you sir, it is rather urgent." Mr. Levine said, "I believe you know your way out Bill, I will have this ready for you by next week."

"Thank you, Mr. Levine; I'll see you next week."

Eileen continued, "I've just outlined a proposal for Mr. John Broadman. He hasn't told me what he thinks of it but he insisted he talk to the head of our firm. I hope he is pleased. I don't think I've done anything wrong or offended him. I would really appreciate it if you could come in. I need your help."

"Sure, I'll smooth this out. Don't worry."

Together they walked to the conference room. Eileen closed the door behind them.

Mr. Broadman stood and extended his hand, "Mr. Levine sir, I'm John Broadman, President of Alabama Syndicated Mines, Inc."

Mr. Levine replied, "Yes sir. I recognize you from the many pictures in the paper. It is a pleasure to have you in our office, sir. What may I do for you?

"I was impressed with what Miss Robbins did for one of my friends so I asked her to look over my financial situation. Are you aware of this proposal she has just outlined for me?"

"Well, no sir. She told me she was working on a proposal for an anonymous client but that it would be later before the name could be revealed."

"Damn, you really kept my name confidential?"

Eileen said, "Well, yes sir, that's what you asked."

Broadman admitted, "Well, I'll be; that's great. I guess I don't expect this kind of truth and trust this day and age. I am obliged to you, ma'am." He then turned again to Levine, "Now see here, Levine. This lady has shown me probably fifty overheads. She has figured out ways that I can make some legal business moves that could potentially save me twenty-two and a half million dollars, but time is of the essence you see. I got only a short period of time to do it and she can't guarantee the legality of it though she believes it to be proper and legit. Now, you are the legal guru here and you are the head of this place. You need to hear me clear on this; I don't deal with anything less than the best. So far, no one has shown me anything half this good. Now, if she's right, she is the best. It's your job to tell me if she is right. I want to know that by tomorrow, and like I said, time's of the essence. If she is right, I've got to do this now. Can you do that for me?"

"I'll sure give it my best shot."

"Half promises, Dammit, Levine, that's not what I asked. I asked you if I could have the answer tomorrow."

Levine, beginning to perspire said, "Yes sir, Mr. Broadman, we will have the answer tomorrow."

"Now, one other thing. If she is right, I want her as my accountant. Is that all right?"

"Of course, sir."

"Well, before you answer so quickly hear me out. I don't deal with junior partners. If she is my accountant she is a full partner in your organization, do you agree to that?"

Levine sputtered, "You know the Board will have to look at this question, uh, uh, it's quite different from our past pattern. We never looked at potential memberships this way before, we just, just, never..."

"Untie your tongue, Levine. You are trying to say, you've never had a woman partner before. Well, I never had a woman accountant before either. I want her and I can see no reason why you shouldn't also."

Eileen, fearing a backlash, immediately interjected, “Mr. Broadman, sir, with due respect, that is an internal decision by our Board and I would never presume...”

Mr. Broadman interrupted saying, “Hold your thoughts Miss Robbins, I'm talking with Mr. Levine. My account at this firm will likely be their largest and you're the one that's earned it. Now, if that hasn't earned you partnership status, then I believe I can set you up in your own business, ma’am.”

Mr. Levine interjected, “Mr. Broadman, uh, sir, give us, give us some time to think this over and talk about it.”

“I thought you understood. I did. I gave you twenty-four hours. That's all the time I have. I'll expect to come back here tomorrow at one o'clock and get the answers: number one, is all of this proposal legal? Number two, is Miss Robbins here a full partner in your organization? If so, you have my business. If not, I'm going to try to buy her way out of your organization. Good day, sir.” With that, Broadman retrieved his attaché case and exited; closing the conference room door behind him.

Eileen was relieved that the door had been closed. She immediately retreated, at least ostensibly. “Mr. Levine sir, I had no idea. Please understand, I didn't expect anything like this.”

Levine growled, “That old coot. Everybody in town knows how difficult he is, always demanding this and ordering that. Maybe that is how he got to be so powerful. Everybody is afraid to turn him down. If he comes into the firm, his one account would increase our revenue by at least twenty percent. So, it is hard to just discount what he says.”

Levine looked at Eileen. “You have been very good for the firm. We've never made anyone a partner here in the second year. We've never even had a woman partner. I don't know if I can sell this.”

“I understand sir. I would like you to consider it. It would be an honor. I would work hard to make you proud.”

Levine looked her straight in the eye and asked, “Would you leave if I can't sell this idea?”

Eileen sheepishly replied, “Mr. Levine sir, you know I wouldn't want to. This firm is my dream, but it’s not like I'll get many opportunities as lucrative as this one sir. Wouldn't it be better for all of us if the Board could see some wisdom in this?”

Levine grumbled, “Just as I thought. I'll go round up the boys. You organize all that stuff to make our job easier to check behind you. You've put us in a damned twenty-four hour bind."

"Yes, sir. I didn't mean to, sir. Honest, I didn't. I'll get on it right away, sir."

In the called Board meeting that evening, Levine grumbled his way through presenting what has happened.

Skinner snorted, "That little bitch. She's been nothing but trouble since she got here. Somebody ought to take her down to size."

Randall offered a different appraisal, "Looks like we're the ones taken down to size. You gotta give her credit. She has done nothing illegal. She has been pleasant. She has worked her ass off. She's come up with plans and opportunities that none of us thought of, and if she lands this account she has put us on the map in Birmingham, maybe in Alabama."

Smith spoke up, "Dammit, we're already on the map in Alabama. We are a respected firm."

Randall rejoined, "Yes, we are, but we don't have Broadman's account and there are quite a few more out there like his. Think of the positives. Suppose we make her a partner. We will all get a bigger year end bonus because of his one account. She's going to get a raise and be incentivised to do more of these things. Broadman is going to tell his friends. Hell, I bet that writer down at the Birmingham News, Menendez, would do a feature article on her. Of course, our firm would be mentioned prominently. There's no telling how much this one account can do for this firm. We'd be damned fools to ignore this request. Why, she would be the youngest professional woman in Birmingham, to make partnership in a major firm, maybe even in Alabama. Yes sir, I make a motion we make her a partner today."

Skinner said, "Let's discuss that."

Randall spoke again, "I tell you what, you can discuss it all you want, but if you don't make her a partner, I'm going to ask her to take me as a partner in her new firm, how's that?"

Levine decided to do the chair's job and bring closure, "Hold on, lets not get divided and fight with each other. This is going to happen one day. It might as well be today. Our male chauvinism should die a peaceful death right here, right now. All in favor of the motion, say aye."

Aye's were heard from all except one.

"All opposed, ney."

No neys were heard. One had abstained.

Chapter 8
Meeting the Senator

At twenty-minutes past two, Eileen reasoned, 'If a maitre d' tells me its going to be a few minutes, but time lingers, how much more should I expect to wait for a Senator?' Almost reflexively, she began rehearsing her presentation. How should she abbreviate it? She had prepared a thirty-minute presentation. 'Some of my time may be eroded. Will the Senator extend my time as he has with his current guest or will I be the one cut short? Obviously, that depends on who the two-thirty appointment is and how my proposal is being received. I'll have to be at my top performance.'

'I must be confident, but not cocky. I need to show respect and honor, but I can't appear intimidated. I'll be articulate and knowledgeable, but careful and not condescending. I'll be humble and thankful for his audience, but I'll be professional and worthy of his time. I'll ask for his consideration and support of the project. At a later meeting, I'll seal his support.'

Eileen's eyes closed again. 'So much has happened since the nineteen sixty-nine Apollo XI moon landing that captivated me and set this process in motion. Neal Armstrong's statement was so poignant. "That's one small step for man, one giant leap for mankind." I felt my adrenaline rush as if I were there. I yearned to be there. I thought everyone deserves to experience such an adventure. Why not?! 'Anything the government can do, private industry can do better and more efficiently. All it really takes is an idea, an entrepreneur and a financier. Now, only six years later, we have come this far.' Eileen outlined her idea into developmental stages even before Apollo returned to Earth. 'If I could find a financier I could be the entrepreneur. If feasibility studies pan out for a private space vehicle why not have regular trips to the moon? Technical know-how had just been proven and witnessed by millions on worldwide television. No one would doubt the possibility; surely the plausibility could be successfully marketed for its feasibility and probability. The public loves adventure and is willing to take risks. For such a spectacular adventure people would undoubtedly accept a degree of uncertainty.'

Eileen planned to enlist the services of a marketing firm but decided to wait until the project was nearer completion. She reasoned, 'Most successful people are risk-takers; consequently they will be the target clientele.' As for market segments, anyone with financial means would be welcomed due to the anticipated high maintenance for the program. She would screen out only the over-demanding.

Birmingham, although not a large city, was blessed with a significant number of wealthy businessmen. 'I have been fortunate to gain significant in-roads through my family and John Broadman. Perhaps Senator Johnson will help expand my roster of investors statewide or even nationally.'

'We are exceeding our goals. Already, ten million dollars have been committed. Broadman took the lead with one million and deposited a check for one hundred thousand dollars as seed money. Four of his friends in Birmingham pledged a million dollars each and five of their friends in Birmingham, Montgomery, and Mobile have also committed a million each.'

The firm of Jacob, Black & Hall assigned securities experts to incorporate them as Space Travel, Inc. Eileen was designated President and CEO. Mr. Broadman became Chairman of the Board. Eileen received and appreciated a generous expense allowance.

Eileen hired Ralph Smith, an engineering consultant from the Huntsville Space Center who had extensive experience with the Apollo Program. At first he consulted at night and on weekends. Later she expanded his duties to full-time. He made plausible preliminary projections regarding the overall cost of the project and the time schedules. He enlightened Eileen on the technological requirements which were outside her field of knowledge.

Smith insisted that once a shuttle bus was developed, "The original tourists should function dually as tourists and construction workers. On each trip they will transport building materials. While there, they will assemble a series of airtight rooms, halls and buildings, each connected by automatic airlocks. Eventually, a giant complex will emerge at the edge of the light and dark sides of the moon avoiding the extremes of temperature. The dwelling complex will be equivalent to a hotel. Adjacent sections will be for dining, for entertainment, a service area and an infirmary."

Eileen exclaimed, "My word. You are talking about a small city."

"Yes, that's exactly what I am talking about."

"Then that's it, our project will be *Moon City*. Eventually we will promote other exciting adventures such as traveling to Mars or circling Venus, but for now our business will be traveling to and from Moon City."

Eileen heard Mrs. Sanders' voice. "Miss Robbins. The Senator will see you now."

Mrs. Sanders led Eileen into the Senator's office and closed the door behind them. Eileen's approval of the spacious and sumptuous office comforted her. The Senator rose from behind his desk and came forward, "My, My! Eileen Robbins. Granddaughter of Allen Robbins. He would bring you with him to our lake to fish. I declare you Alabama ladies get prettier every year. I sure hope you are representing us this year in the Miss America Pageant. If so, you sure have my support."

"Well, thank you Senator." Thinking to herself, 'Time is ticking away. I need to present my project.'

"This is my assistant, Robert Dupree. I couldn't get anything done without him. He's going to listen in on our conversation. I may need his help. I understand you have some technical things to discuss?"

"Why yes, sir, I do. Here's a proposal for each of you. May I show you some interesting highlights?" With that, she handed the polished documents to them and opened her remaining copy.

"You will notice first, Senator Johnson, that page one lists my first ten sponsors. Each has committed to one million dollars; so, we have a formidable beginning. I believe you will recognize these leaders as some of the most prominent leaders in Alabama. Perhaps they have been prominent in your campaigns. These astute leaders researched the merits of our project and, each independently reached the positive conclusion that we hope your analysis will reach."

"With Huntsville's prominence in America's space program, it would be fitting for Alabamians to develop the first civilian space travel opportunity. Our feasibility study shows quite clearly that with the appropriate private undertaking, and linking the capability of NASA Space Program we would mutually benefit from each other's effort in making this project happen. We believe that a joint effort would generate tremendous savings for the government. We should save significant development cost and time. I am confident that reading the proposal will excite you about our Moon City Project. All the investors are happily committed." She realized that she had rushed through the proposal leaving out much of the meat of the presentation and given him mostly fluff. She had intended not to do this, but she was mindful of the time as it had reached two-thirty five p.m.

Mrs. Sanders stepped through the door and announced, "Senator Johnson I am so sorry to interrupt but General Ragland, the Assistant to the Joint Chiefs is here to discuss some important appropriations. I don't think he has time to wait."

Senator Johnson apologized, "And I'll bet we were just getting to the good part. I am embarrassed Miss Robbins, but these matters demand priority; I'm sure you understand. Perhaps you could finish your presentation to Mr. Dupree? He will show you to his office. I will review this with him and be in touch with you."

"Yes Senator. Thank you very much for your time and consideration. If you should give your support to our project, it would help Alabama immensely, sir. Again, thank you. I will answer any questions for Mr. Dupree." The entire encounter had taken less than ten minutes.

"Thank you for coming. Please say hello to Allen for me."

On their way out the door, indeed, she met a uniformed gentleman standing impatiently. When he looked her way she made eye contact and gave her friendliest "Hello." 'If there is any hope in my project, this man might one day play a role in it.'

Mr. Dupree escorted Eileen to his office. He seemed infinitely more intrigued with the project than the Senator had been. He had questions. He hovered close to her as they studied their way through the proposal. She sensed his determined closeness. 'Perhaps, if I am close to him and he is close to the Senator, that will be fortuitous.' She allowed herself to respond to his cozy manner. Before they finished the briefing they began exchanging personal information. She was in town, alone, staying at the Willard.

"This is a very forward-thinking and impressive proposal, Miss Robbins. How long will you be in D.C.?"

"Thank you, our team is very proud of our progress. I will be leaving this Sunday."

"Please don't judge me too forward but I don't see a wedding ring. Would you be open to dinner with me tonight?"

"Actually, that sounds rather nice. Are you sure it's not an imposition?"

"Nonsense, unless you are talking about on you?"

She laughed and he followed with his own rich laughter.

"I could take tomorrow off if it suits you. I'd be happy to be your tour guide. I'm pretty good at it, according to my mother."

"You get better by the minute, but we could do that Saturday."

"Saturday can be an add on, but not an alternative. There is enough to fill both days."

"Wow I feel like I've hit the jackpot!"

"Good. I'll get tickets to a play Saturday night."

"Mr. Dupree ..."

"Bob, please."

"I feel selfish. You are being so generous and kind. I came here to get Senator Johnson's support for our project. I really have to work on his support."

"I can help, but you must understand, the Senator is very methodical, and often procrastinates with his decisions. He will ask me to study this project thoroughly. I will brief him on it in much more detail than he heard today. He will then decide whether or not to publicly endorse your project. You should brace yourself, the merits of the project won't be as important to him as the politics."

They both laughed. She knew the short wait in the Senator's waiting room was only a prelude to the real wait for his decision. 'But Dupree will be my lobbyist. I am going to be very good to him. Besides, with his handsome looks this could be fun.'

Her energy level was escalating.

Chapter 9
Excess

Returning to the privacy of her hotel room, Eileen thrust her fists skyward and exclaimed, "Yes, the Senator likes me. He likes papa. My investors support him politically. Mr. Dupree is going to help. The Senator is mine, mine, mine. We are going to Moon City. I can't wait."

The exhilarating rush was unmistakable and escalating. Eileen's mind was racing. She was sure that she had never felt better. She fantasized greatness. She wondered, 'Will they name the first space bus after me, Eileen?' She visualized it emblazoned boldly on their conical shaped bus. She would no longer be working as a CPA. 'I will be Head of Space Travel, Inc. We will have regular trips to the moon, and advanced reservations for Mars. I will travel the world over. I'll have my own suite on the moon and visit there regularly. Moon City will prominently display a life-size statue of me, Founder of Moon City.'

Eileen became aware of herself, 'My goodness, look at me, I'm dancing. Where does all of this energy come from? I only slept four hours last night. I feel as if I have had twenty cups of coffee. I am an energy machine.'

Eileen began writing her thoughts and strategies for finding other investors. She pondered ways to bind them to the project. She scribbled design ideas for best utilization of space on the bus. There were insights of reasons the military should cooperate with private industry. The space agency would be an invested party in their project. By chance she noticed the clock and was startled to realize that it was seven thirty-five.

'No problem, plenty of time.' She showered quickly, perfumed herself, applied make-up, dressed, stood and viewed herself in the mirror. She was gorgeous. Eileen mused out loud, "Goddess of Beauty," as if she were her own creation. Eileen answered the phone; Dupree announced that he was at the front desk. Her reply surprised him. "I'm ready. I'll be down momentarily."

Stepping out of the elevator she walked towards Dupree. He was taller than most and easily spotted. His distinctive good looks registered with her more than before. His build was medium to medium-large, muscular. He was six feet and two inches tall. She guessed his weight to be approximately one hundred and ninety pounds. His physical features were firm and his brow quite ample. His hair was dark, short, and lay naturally and comfortably, inviting playful fingers.

Eileen spoke first, "Hi, don't you look great!"

"No, permit me to say, you are the one who looks marvelous. You are beautiful. You could have walked right out of a movie. Move over Farah Fawcett, here comes Eileen Robbins."

Eileen did a curtsy.

Dupree elaborately performed a mock mirror curtsy and waved her toward the door. "Shall we go?"

His car was waiting. The doorman had held it for him. Dupree pushed a couple of dollars into his hand before they drove into Washington's nightlife.

Eileen talked excitedly and gushed enthusiasm. She desperately wanted to launch into further details of her project but instinctively held back allowing Dupree to be in charge. She would not usurp his lead tonight. As best she could, she bit and held her tongue on the Moon City subject. She had plenty of questions for him about everything else, the city, the people, the government.

Dupree was not disappointing. His prowess was conversation, "How did you choose the Willard?"

"It was my father's suggestion. He said it was close, convenient, luxurious and steeped in history."

"He is correct. Many Presidents have had functions there. Most have had at least one meeting there. One, Calvin Coolidge, even stayed a month there while waiting for Mrs. Harding to relocate after President Harding's death. President Grant coined the term "Lobbyist" in the

Willard Hotel. Ambassadors and VIP's from all over the world stay there regularly. Sage people seem to make wise choices for their operations base. I see you fit easily into that group."

"Thank you. You are giving me the big head."

"I'm making observations. I read more of your proposal before I left the office. It's very impressive. You have assembled some very strategic items. A good idea. A list of prominent believers. An investment adequate to fund your preliminary needs and a scientific feasibility paper that is more than plausible; it's downright exciting."

She noticed that the car was easing toward the restaurant. She recognized the name, Le Pavilion, and wondered how he had been able to get reservations on such short notice. The feel of the power gave her an energy rush. "Thank you, tell me about this restaurant." She would have plenty of time later for her project.

Inside, while waiting, she scanned everything in sight as Dupree talked with the maitre d', mentioning how great the chef, Yunnik Cam was. 'This is the life' she decided. 'I'll make sure that business brings me here often.' As the maitre d' led them to the table she felt Dupree's hand confidently press against her waist and remain there until he delivered her to her seat. 'Very nicely done she thought. No undue liberties, no swishes. Just a gentleman's chivalry.'

Their booth was slightly elevated. It felt important to Eileen. A quick look at the menu told her that steak was the house specialty.

"If you like beef," Dupree offered, "They cook it to perfection, just the way you order it, except they won't do *well done*."

"I see," she said. "I'm having the petite filet mignon. Medium rare and the mixed green salad with oil and vinegar." She inwardly knew she would ultimately eat no more than half her order.

Dupree observed, "Do you do everything right? You even order a healthy dinner. What about some wine? They serve excellent Cabernet Sauvignon that's perfect with beef. I'll get the man-size sirloin and together we can kill off a bottle."

"That sounds good," Eileen's mind remained energized and racing. She remembered Stewart from her college days. 'I need to be careful. I'll get Dupree to drink most of the bottle. I want to remember my good time. Perhaps the wine will put brakes on my racing mind.'

Without a word, like a game of charade, the wine steward made a production of presenting the selected wine. Dupree, equally dramatic, checked the aroma and the taste. He blessed it, magnifique! The wine steward poured her glass and then his. She wanted to make a toast but Dupree was raising his glass. She lifted hers to meet his. They sounded like happy miniature cymbals. "To you, Miss Robbins and your Moon City project." Eileen responded, "Thank you, Mr. Dupree, and to you also."

She could not have been more surprised at how good the wine tasted. She was embarrassed to realize that she had taken a second sip before returning her glass to the table. She wondered if he had noticed.

He did. "I told you this was good. I could drink the entire bottle, but I hope you will do me the favor of protecting me to a fifty percent limit." They shared a laugh.

Although late dinners were not unusual at the Pavilion, Dupree informed Eileen, "The maitre d' advised that we need not rush, but take our time. Let's savor the evening, the wine and the food." So they did, and as new acquaintances often do, they laughed abundantly in a fast paced conversation. They reminisced about people and politics and the Magic City of Birmingham. She enjoyed his company more each minute and with each added glass of wine. As the evening progressed, her spirits and levity escalated. Customary norms and value controls became inept in her super-energized enthusiasm. The unfolding evening would underscore this truth.

Eileen stood to go to the powder room, but her gait was unsteady. Instead of alarm she felt amused. "Uh oh!" she giggled.

Dupree catapulted to her aid.

She laughingly teased him, face-to-face, eye-to-eye, with fluttering eyelids, "You don't intend to get me drunk, do you, Mr. Dupree?" They laughed and she proceeded on to the powder room.

Dupree realized, 'She's not used to drinking very much, I can't let her become too intoxicated.'

He called the waiter and ordered coffee for each of them. When Eileen returned Dupree suggested, "Why don't we have some coffee before we go sightseeing?"

Eileen replied, "You're my guide, I'm in your trust."

Dupree drove to the mall where the Washington Monument

dominates. The clear and inviting night would render breathtaking sights.

Eileen, looking up at the sky, sensed, 'This is going to be a very special evening.' "I've never been sightseeing at night. This is actually quite exciting. Thanks for the offer."

"Thanks for accepting. This is a great city. There is so much to see and do. Then someone such as yourself shows up and changes everything. I generally do my tours during the day. This night thing is new and let's say special, just for you."

"I'm honored."

"I'm the honored one. You're so uniquely interesting. I was immediately mesmerized by you. You excite me, your gorgeous face, and awesome smile enhances even the moonlight. It's no wonder you want to go there. I'm captivated by your differences. Your beauty is like fine wine for my eyes. I hope you don't mind?"

Eileen's reply surprised herself as much as him, "Robert, my dear, if I minded, I wouldn't be here, would I?" Eileen began inquiring more about Robert. She wanted to know about his city of secular power, government and politics.

Dupree talked about the frills and thrills of the Washington scene. "There is a mystique and seduction that is inescapable," he admitted. "It's a magnet for everything and everyone, see it brought you here."

The car was now slowing to a stop in front of the Lincoln Memorial, but the sightseeing they were enjoying began to increasingly include each other. After several stops and memorial drive-bys, their conversation turned more personal and assuming. Robert boldly told Eileen that, "Holding your hand has stimulated my heart, it's racing. Now I want more. I want to go to the moon with you tonight."

"Maybe," she said, "If we are patient, we both can get to the moon." Her mind was in overdrive. 'Is it because he is so handsome and powerful or is it the wine? Or am I just having the best day of my life? Damn, what a wonderful feeling.' "Well, you promised to show me the awesome sights of the city. You did it. The night is young and I don't have to get up early. Let's go to the hotel."

The car moved faster. Robert was eager to get back to the Willard. He hoped that Eileen was signaling that the night would be awesome. They arrived back at the hotel at two-thirty Friday morning. He left the car with valet parking and walked with her to her room.

Eileen leaned against him in the elevator and down the corridor. “I'm not tired if you would care to stay awhile. I have lots of interesting schematics for Moon City that I'd love for you to see.”

“You bet, I'd like that.”

Eileen smiled knowingly. Her mind was savoring the thought. She took his hand and walked him into the room.

While Robert sat close, Eileen took fifteen minutes to show him numerous professional scale drawings including a facade elevation along with conceptual plans and some personal sketches of Moon City.

“Nice room here, don't you think? Why don't you make yourself at home, while I freshen up and change into something more comfortable?” She purposefully used the cliché.

She closed the bathroom door behind her, confident that his excitement was maximized. Each of them by now was thinking mostly of ravishing each other. Nevertheless, she maintained her ulterior motive. Her passions were dual. Her bedroom opportunity was to enjoy, but 'Mr. Dupree is signing up for Moon City whether he knows it or not.' Eileen's energy had pushed her beyond control, both in thought and action. She removed her make-up, showered and perfumed. She stretched and looked herself over. 'I am a goddess of beauty.' She slipped on the thick, white, towel robe, right side folded over left side. She left it untied and held together with her hand.

Eileen opened the door and watched Robert turn to face her. He was actually holding some of her drawings. She stepped through the door. Dupree stood up. While half way across the room she caught his eye. With her right hand, she swung open the right side of the bathrobe revealing the right half of her nude body. In a flash his eyes began to survey, but before he could focus she had recovered herself.

Dupree's attention was maximally focused. ‘This is one special, beautiful lady. Nothing in my life has matched this. Here is one wide-open, hot lady.' This night would be etched indelibly into his memory bank.

“I'm comfortable. It's your turn.” Eileen gave him the same mock curtsy that he had used earlier. This time she was inviting him into her bathroom.

Robert closed the door behind him. Eileen laughed and began to dance around the room. She became a choreographer of seduction. Her excitement was uncontrolled. She was amused at herself but also at Dupree. As she danced, she opened and closed the folds of the robe as if flashing to an invisible audience, sometimes fast and sometimes slow. 'I started the evening as a goddess of beauty. Now I will be the goddess of love. I will sell him on one thing at a time. Maybe I will take him to Moon City with me.' Unabashed, she was practicing how she would tease Dupree. In her grandiose excitement it felt appropriate and wonderful. She checked the lighting and searched the radio for mood music.

Inside the bathroom Dupree hurriedly showered. 'I haven't been this impatient since I was sixteen. She is so young and beautiful, will I be good enough? Well, let's go find out.' He closed the robe around him, intentionally, unlike her, tying his, and he knocked twice before opening the door.

Eileen and Robert held their arms out and came together. In unison, their eyes talked to each other, "let's make it the best ever." Just as their robes touched, her hands parted his and likewise his hands parted hers. Eagerly his hands found the small of her back and pulled her body to him. Her hands were locked behind him, squeezing tight. Her soft body melted against his.

Neither were patient enough to savor the moment for long. They explored each other's body with eager discovery, enjoying each find. They kissed as if passion starved. Like magic, his robe slipped off as he gently lifted her onto the bed previously prepared.

Uniqueness permeated their lovemaking. A physical and emotional rhythm evolved worthy of masterful poetry. Their eyes telegraphed to each other that they had discovered the one person who they doubted could exist.

Robert used his last bit of energy to kiss her forehead before he collapsed beside her and fell fast asleep.

It was three-thirty. Eileen bounced up at Robert's first snore. She freshened herself. She took a warm cloth and gently cleaned his face and body. Being oblivious, he never flinched.

Eileen needed no sleep. She was supercharged. 'Am I Super Woman or something?' I have just experienced the most fantastic sex of my life. I am sure the same holds for him. He is exhausted and I have tons of energy.' She remembered her plans to be a sex goddess. 'I was, but it was all natural thanks to this wonderful energy. Where does it originate?'

The experience had given her an idea. She sat at the desk while Robert slept. She used the Willard stationery to scribble diagrams for showers with two heads, control panels for mood lighting and music. These would be incorporated into the Moon City Hotel rooms.

At four-thirty in the morning, she looked over at Dupree, 'How peaceful he looks.' She eased herself out of her robe and under the sheet. She snuggled next to him. He responded before he awoke. He awakened not from a dream but to a dream. He oriented himself and was instantly joyous. Together they gleefully created more physical ecstasy. Quickly exhausting themselves, they laughed and fell asleep in each other's arms.

Chapter 10
Shopping Spree

Energy and eager anticipation of city life pushed Eileen out of bed at six-thirty a.m. She quietly dressed, then awakened Dupree. "It's morning" she said, "Time to get up."

Dupree forced his eyes open. He was astonished to see that Eileen was fully dressed. Thinking that it must be noon, he glanced at the clock and back at her. "Where do you get your energy?"

"It's natural. When you've dressed, meet me in the dining room. I'll have some coffee and read the paper." She vanished through the door.

Dupree found her well into her second cup of coffee, having devoured most of the paper. When he sat down, there was no mention of the evening before.

Eileen announced, "I feel great. I see in the papers *A Little Night Music* is playing at the Lincoln Theatre. Do you think you could get tickets?"

"I'll have the concierge work on it."

"Didn't you tell me you have taken today off?"

"Yes, it will be my pleasure to be seen all day with the prettiest girl in town." He clearly signaled continued interest in the romantic chase.

Eileen realized she was much further into the day than Dupree. She self-monitored, 'Damn, girl, slow down. Don't outrun your best hope. What's wrong with you? Contain yourself.' In vain, she tried, but the best she could do was to mix her storming energy with his typical manly pursuits. She offered a response, "How utterly charming, especially coming from, the best man in town." His smile confirmed his pleasure at the compliment. This gave her permission to continue. "I want to see it all today, Robert. The daytime recap of everything we saw last night and every other site in town." She continued, "I want to shop. I want to buy things. I want to feel good all day. Buying makes me feel good."

"Of course, everything in moderation. That's the way to go."

"Did you consider last night moderate?"

Robert, initially showed a defensive expression, but seeing her smile, he burst out laughing. "Touché, touché."

They toured until it seemed they had visited every monument, historical residence and Embassy in the district. He seemed to know everything about everything, including shops. Between stops, Eileen frequently thought of the Moon City project. 'It would be a tremendous boost if Senator Johnson came on board. Robert is so capable and he likes the project and me as well. I'll recruit him to ride with me on the first moon trip.'

"The first tour bus to the moon should be the adventure of a lifetime. I was thinking how nice it would be if you came with me."

"Now you're talking" he said. "Sign me up."

"I just did. Now it's your job to sign up the Senator."

"Is that the price of my ticket?"

"No, consider that paid in advance. You have been adorable."

Dupree took her shopping. She wanted something special to wear, sure that they would get tickets for the play. She found just the right ensemble, black, extremely elegant and feminine. She relished in escalating fantasies, but was unmindful of the possible ultimate consequences.

"I didn't expect to be escorted so formally, so I didn't bring the proper attire, so now I feel better. Oh, there's a jewelry store, let's take a look." She found a Movado watch that she couldn't live without. She began negotiating a purchase with the sales clerk.

Dupree backed off to the side and kibitzed. "I'll only be in town today. This one has some possibilities but it's not perfect. I would consider it though, for a reasonable discount." The manager was summoned. Eileen managed to purchase it at a fifteen- percent discount.

Dupree felt compelled to comment when he next had the chance. "I know you are very bright and that you do well, but please tell me you are not using any company money to make these purchases. You could get in trouble. I really would hate that."

"Of course not. Why would you even think such a thing? I am the youngest to ever be given a partnership at Levine, Randall and Smith. I am their only female partner and I have the biggest client in the firm. I am doing very well, thank you."

"Forgive me. I just like you so much and am unaccustomed to people being able to enjoy themselves this way."

"Then let me help you," she offered. "You've taken a day off. You've shown me a great time as an unpaid guide. You need a reward."

"If last night wasn't a reward nothing would be worthy."

"Oh hush. Here is a gentleman's matching watch. We will have his and hers. Here, try it on."

"Oh, Miss Robbins, I couldn't do that."

"Now don't refuse me," she ordered. "I'm not asking permission. I'm doing it. I want to and I can. Here, ma'am, please ring this up on my ticket with the same discount we just negotiated on the other one."

"Yes ma'am, Miss Robbins, happy to," the sales clerk obliged.

Dupree was awestruck. 'How will I handle this?' It was obvious he would have to wear it. 'Can I wear it to work? What will I tell the Senator? What will I tell anyone?'

As soon as they were outside, Dupree blundered again, "Eileen, I am not a gigolo." Without thinking, she slapped him. Stunned, he looked at her. He had never seen eyes like that. Volcanic fire was an understatement. Her lips were tight.

"Do you think I would buy a gigolo? Do I look like I need to resort to that? Is that what you think of me?"

"Oh, God, no. I didn't know how to express my gratitude. I don't feel deserving. I'm sorry for offending you."

As quick as a light going out, the fire was gone. Suddenly, she was serene. "Then it's settled. You'll enjoy it and I will be happy. Oh, look, they are having a furrier sale."

"Eileen, it's March, of course they're having a furrier sale."

"Let's go look. I don't have a mink coat."

"You don't need a mink coat, spring and summer are coming. It will be excess baggage."

"It's not excess baggage, if I wear it," she said.

Dupree observed more insightfully than he realized. "For us normal folk, it's excess, believe me."

Eileen retorted playfully, "I am happy to be excelling. It feels good. I like me just the way I am. Don't you like me the way I am?"

"Yes, of course, but that doesn't mean I can keep up with you."

The remainder of the weekend cemented their mutual fondness. Dupree fell completely under her spell. She was happy that he would do anything she asked.

Dupree experienced a strange sensation as he saw her off at the airport. He was sad. Already, he missed her and wanted to continue their exceptional companionship. Yet, he was tired and needed rest. She had functioned on two to three hours of sleep per night. He had been lucky to squeeze in four hours and it was a hopeless cause trying to keep up with her. It would be impossible for a working man. He wondered, 'How many people have that much going for them? Excess everything. Looks, intelligence, sexual prowess, ideas, energy, money, interest, and freedom. Does she also have excess lovers? I hope not.'

Chapter 11
Grandiosity

Flying back to Atlanta felt symbolic for Eileen. It was business as usual to catch the flight back to Atlanta. 'One day my space bus could be just as routine from Robbins Space Center to Moon City and back.'

Forced sitting allowed fatigue to catch her. She had hardly closed her eyes before she was soundly asleep.

After retrieving her car in Atlanta and negotiating through traffic out to I-20, Eileen settled in for the drive to Birmingham. She was not consciously aware of how energized she became following the one-hour nap. The two and a half-hour drive to Birmingham would be tedious because of the unfinished section of I-20 but it was great brainstorming time. Not far out of Atlanta there was no radio signal carrying anything exciting enough to compete with her own consuming mental pleasures. Her thoughts were furious and powerful, deceiving even herself with one imagination feeding the next. It didn't matter that Senator Johnson had not officially given his endorsement; he had definitely exhibited an interest and even assigned his senior staff assistant to work with her. 'That should convince some of those fence-sitters to invest in the project.'

Arriving home late, Eileen continued working on into the night until nearly two a.m. Finally she told herself, 'I must get some sleep.'

After two hours of sleep she awoke refreshed. 'Good, I'm awake and feel great. I need to get organized.' Rapid fire thoughts flooded her mind as she reconstructed her accomplishments from the weekend and her projections for the future. She was flighty. Thoughts about work encroached on her Moon City project. She found herself thinking about multiple topics at once. She could not stay with either one long enough for a conclusion. She abruptly remembered, 'This is the morning I am to meet Mr. Blackburn at eight. She had promised to analyze the potential tax consequences, if he accepted an offer to sell one of his businesses.' She rationalized, 'I have not had time to do it. I'll just have to charm him. I can do that. He likes me better than apple pie. I'll just postpone it, that's all. He will be fine with it.'

With all the important things Eileen was doing, she needed more free time. Her thinking became inventive. Levine is expecting too much of me; I need to talk to him.' She arrived at the office an hour before anyone else. She walked directly to Levine's office and taped a note to his door, "Mr. Levine, please meet me in my office at 9:00 this morning. Eileen."

Even though Levine was an early riser and always at work on time, a couple of partners saw the note on the door before Levine arrived. Skinner cringed when he saw the note. He was the most senior partner next to the three founders. Even he would not presume to leave such a note. He recognized it as a tenebrous sign. He wondered how long they would have before the storm. He thought, 'That young, arrogant, upstart is unappreciative of the advantages we have willingly afforded her. Well, maybe I begrudged the firm making her a partner, but now in retrospect, that foreboding doubt and my abstention was a sage premonition. Perhaps now they will listen.'

Her meeting with Blackburn did not go as well as she had hoped. Despite her flowery ego strokes to him, he would not be placated. He advised her that this offer had a short time frame. "My decision must be made by Thursday. If you can't guarantee to provide me with the analysis by Wednesday noon, I have to know now, so that I can ask someone else to do it." She couldn't believe that he would treat her this way.

Eileen told him she was sorry, but her meeting with Senator Johnson had required a great deal of preparation time last week and over the weekend, but indeed she would have everything ready for him by 1:00 p.m. on Wednesday. Was he sure that would be okay?

"If you have it satisfactorily prepared for me, I am sure it will." He left.

Eileen wanted to cry. It wasn't fair that Blackburn's damned ol' project was going to get in the way of her project.

Her phone rang. It was Betty the receptionist who said, "Miss Robbins, Mr. Levine says to let you know he has nine-thirty open. If you would like to see him, he will be in his office." She said, "Thank you Betty," and hung up the phone. She missed the message intended by Levine, only getting the message that he would see her as she had requested. Great, she thought, she couldn't wait to present her thoughts to him. If he had been impressed before, enough to make her a partner, he was really going to be impressed now.

At nine-thirty she entered Levine's office. Skinner, appearing unusually cheerful, was just exiting. He and Levine had been discussing their mutual concerns about Eileen's liberties and how she exceeded boundaries. They had fears of what this might do to the firm's reputation.

Eileen stepped into his office without an inkling of what the paneled walls had just absorbed from her senior partner's summit and would be hearing again in a few moments. This time from Levine's lecturing her. "Come in Miss Robbins, you wanted to see me."

"Yes sir. Thank you for seeing me. I've been thinking. I've been with LRS now for better than two years. I'm your first female partner. I'm your youngest partner ever. There are nine CPA's in our firm and I account for thirty percent of the firm's revenue. That's pretty phenomenal I think. I hope you agree, sir."

"It is quite an accomplishment Miss Robbins. You are to be commended." Sensing part of what might be coming, he added, "And I believe from your comments that you understand we have appropriately and adequately rewarded and compensated you."

"You have been most thoughtful, sir and not to be ungrateful, sir, but looking at the salaries, it does appear that I make less than half of what you make. All the partners, even though their gross earnings are considerably less than mine, make more than I do. Don't you think that is discriminatory, sir?"

"Not at all," Levine retorted. "Those partners are being paid on prior generated revenues. You are on a faster track than anyone has ever been at LRS. You should be grateful."

"It is not that I am ungrateful sir, I just believe that my earnings justify a higher compensation."

"Miss Robbins you are making a very good living."

"I am, sir, but I have many opportunities and projects. I can't stay idle. I need the economic reward for my success. It would help to capitalize my private ventures."

Mr. Levine pushed his chair back, sat upright, squared his jaw and looked firmly at Eileen, "Miss Robbins, we here at LRS are quite concerned about you and your 'private' projects. You have broken some serious rules of not just LRS but accounting in general. Professional ethics require that accountants not use knowledge of their clients to entice them into personal businesses. You've gotten old Broadman invested up to his gills in your private project. You should never have mentioned your project to him."

Eileen cut him off, "I'll have you to know, sir, I never mentioned my project to him. It was by pure accident that he found out about it. He came to me, mad as a hornet, because I had not let him in on it. I told him about the professional ethics and that we couldn't do it. He said, 'We can, goddamn, do anything we want to. Those things are guidelines, not laws. Now this seems like a good project from what I have heard from my friends and I want to know more about it.'"

"I wouldn't even tell him. I told him if he had heard about it from someone else, he should get the information from them, and that's what he did. He then came to me and insisted that he be a major investor and a Board member. He told me if there was any problem with the Ethics Committee, he would personally tell them what happened. I'm hurt that you would think I would stoop to bending professional ethics for personal gain."

Levine was surprised. He had not anticipated this answer. He began to feel that perhaps he had been too harsh and overstated his position.

Eileen, unwittingly, rescued him from his faltering backbone as she proceeded in her boundless comments. "Furthermore, I am the most ethical person you have in this firm. I have heard partners laughing at how you inflate charges, talk people into research they didn't need, stretch thirty minute conferences to an hour, call clients on the phone, perhaps as many as ten in an hour, but each one gets charged a minimum of a quarter hour no matter how short the phone call. You are just like the lawyers you complain about."

Levine's adrenaline was rising. His true color began to show a very angry red.

Eileen never noticed his color. She was on a roll. "I came in here to ask for a fair raise and for two weeks vacation beginning this Wednesday at noon and you want to lecture me, Eileen Robbins, savior of your pitiful LRS sinking ship."

Thundering, Levine shouted, "That will be quite enough Eileen Robbins, I will not be talked to like that. Not by you, not by any partner, and especially..."

Eileen interrupted him, "By a woman, Mr. Levine?"

"No, by a damn young whippersnapper that's what. Get out of here. Oh wait a minute, why don't you just take a month off. Yeah, that's what you do, take a month off starting now and if the Board doesn't vote to terminate your contract, we'll sit down and see if you have come to your senses. In the meantime you give some serious thought to this conversation, do you hear me?"

Eileen couldn't believe the turn of her situation. Except for her feeling of invincibility, she would have been devastated. She regrouped and retorted, "Who needs this crappy place?" and stormed out.

Back in her office, she thought, 'Hell, I got more than I asked for. I've got a whole month. I'll show them. I'll take all of my cases and put a note on them to Mr. Levine. He can take care of the next month's work. They'll be begging me to come back; but they can't get Blackburn's done on time. I'll take it home and do it. She stacked each one of her case folders on top of each other, gathered up her personal items and left a note for Mr. Levine, "All of these charts are timely but they can't wait a month. I'll take the Blackburn folder with me. You guys couldn't get it done by Wednesday. Good luck, Eileen." She put those with the note on Cynthia's desk instructing, "Give these to Mr. Levine." She took her personal things, along with Blackburn's chart and left.

Her energy was stratospheric and her determination so firm that she did an outstanding analysis for Blackburn. She called him to advise that she was on vacation and to ask where she should deliver the proposal. She took it to his office, flattered him, explained the proposal to him, won his approval and left his office even more convinced that she was indispensable.

Chapter 12
Delusions of Grandeur

Driving home, Eileen saw two young girls at a lemonade stand. 'Two young entrepreneurs. They need to be rewarded and encouraged.' She stopped. Both girls talked at once, "Lemonade, five cents a cup. It's really good."

"I am sure it is" handing them a dollar. She took a cup of lemonade and told them to "Keep the change. I'm proud of your entrepreneurial spirit. Keep it up."

"Wow, you must be rich."

Eileen laughed, and drank the lemonade as she returned to her car.

Approaching her apartment she saw a vase containing a dozen beautiful red roses. Many times she had received flowers before, but not often a dozen long stemmed roses. She read the card:

I have learned, roses are red
And discovered, without you I'm dead.
The relationship we began
requires seeing you again.
Love,
Robert

Eileen went inside and placed a call to Robert's home. There was no answer. 'I'll call him later. This is so sweet.'

She forgot dinner and enjoyed a feeling of the total relief of her accounting duties. 'I'm free of work, I can finish my project.' She worked the entire evening on the Moon City project. She made a list of potential investors. She felt sure that when she called to tell them that she had Senator Johnson's backing they would leap to become her new investors.

At eleven-thirty she realized 'I have forgotten to call Robert and it's now twelve-thirty in D.C. Oh, well, I'll call tomorrow.'

Just after midnight Eileen needed a break. She turned on the T.V. and began to surf channels until a sincere man's face, Brother Billy Christy, filled the screen. His eyes focused directly on Eileen. "*You* have been chosen and *you* have been washed in the blood of the Lamb of God. Jesus chooses *you*." He pointed directly at her. "He died for your sins. You have been washed clean. You are a child of God. You are being called to serve God." Eileen was spellbound. She couldn't move. His continuing rhetoric gripped her emotionally. "You owe your allegiance to the God who made you. God who provides for you. God who saved you, not to corporate America, not to worldly gods. God has given you everything. What will you give God today? Forsake everything. Give your talents to God and he will multiply them. Give that you may receive."

Eileen felt reborn. She was bolstered further when she heard Christy say, "You are anointed by God, go and do his bidding."

'Anointed' she thought. 'Yes, I have been anointed. I am His chosen one. To whom much is given, much is expected.' She did not realize that she was mixing spiritual theologies with secular visions. A new project was emerging.

Eileen methodically began thinking of what would be needed to spread the message. A Bible, yes a Bible. She went to the bookshelf and retrieved her Bible. A revelation pierced her, 'Of course, it was this Bible that I picked up and read, "Ask and it shall be given," that was when everything good started happening to me. That man on T.V., Christy, was it?, was there to remind me not to forget the true source of all bounty and all good. I must not gain riches and lose my soul.' She would need to know more about the Bible. She decided to start at Genesis and began to read and read. Genesis, Exodus, Leviticus, and on.

Eileen was oblivious to the disappearing time. The moon was fading and the sun was rising. All that was important to her was absorbing the Word. The precious Word. She remembered they had used that word about Jesus, the anointed One. 'Now I am anointed. How wonderful. How divine. I will be like a sister to Jesus. We will be a divine pair. I come to help where others have failed. I will get the word of Jesus' saving grace to the entire world. How shall I do it?' The answer will be revealed to me. I am a prophetess.'

She continued reading on into the afternoon. Eventually she had a glass of milk and a cookie, but continued reading without sleep. Exhaustion finally overwhelmed her and lulled her to sleep.

After only ninety minutes of sleep she abruptly awoke. She had been dreaming of driving with angels, singing "Jesus Saves." She shouted, "Hallelujah, thank you Lord Jesus; I see the answer."

Eileen couldn't wait. She needed to find someone with whom to share her revelations. It would have to be a man of God. She made plans to continue to learn as much of the Scripture as possible. The following morning she would get in touch with a famous and respected man of God. He would help. This would no doubt be what they had been hoping for. Rejuvenated, Eileen again read through most of the night. The next morning she prepared her list: Billy Graham, Jerry Falwell, Jim Bakker, Jimmy Swaggert, Ernest Angsley, and Billy Christy.

One by one she found their numbers. She called and excitedly explained her mission and plan, first to the operator and then the receptionist. "Hello, I need to talk to Reverend Graham. My name is Eileen Robbins. I am working on an important space program to take people to the moon. I have been anointed to help get God's message out to the world. Both these great missions will be very helpful to Reverend Graham. We will be a busload of investors, actually, angels in disguise, going to a city on the moon. We will display a mile high banner that Jesus saves and his picture will be beside it. That's going to fulfill the prophecy that every eye shall see him." Her new project and her old one had melded.

It seemed so simple to her. 'Why would no one listen?' She couldn't get past the receptionist. Each had a different but firm reason that their leader could not meet with her. None of the men of God would come to the phone for her. She knew they must be there. 'I am giving them a wonderful opportunity. They are blind just like the Sadducees and the Pharisees. They are stuck in their own rut.' It was mid-afternoon and her message could not wait. 'I have to do something.' Revelations continued for her. 'Maybe there is wisdom in not talking to national figures. After all, this is the Magic City, the hell hole of bigotry and racism, being reborn and re-tooled, as if a modern Sodom and Gomorrah, but we're being transformed into a modern Bethlehem or Mecca where every eye should look.'

She searched the Yellow Pages, running her finger down the pages of church names, as if moving a fleece and waiting for God's sign. There it was, United Fellowship Mission. By faith shall ye know them. She started to the phone and recoiled as if shell-shocked from the rapid fire rejections 'Another sign. I am to go in person.' She drove herself to United Fellowship. It was three-forty-five. She walked in the door and saw the receptionist. As Eileen approached her, it occurred to her, 'my previous approach led to nothing but rejections. I'll try something different.'

As effectively as if rehearsed, Eileen restrained her emotions and energy to become an actress. "Hello ma'am," my name is Eileen Robbins. I live close by and I am spiritually hurting and don't know where to turn. I was hoping your minister was in and could spare a few moments, I would be ever so grateful."

The receptionist replied politely, "Just a moment; I'll check."

As the receptionist stepped out of the room, Eileen stood and caught herself in the mirror. It dawned on her, she was not dressed the part of a saint or prophetess. Neither was she dressed like a woman hurting. She was dressed like a lady about to meet with a CEO. She had given it no thought while dressing.

The receptionist returned and announced, "Dr. Griffiths is our minister and he will be glad to see you now. Dr. Griffiths this is Eileen Robbins. By the way, my name is Judy."

"Welcome to United Fellowship. Won't you come in? How may we help you?" Dr. Griffiths' voice and manner were instantly calming and reassuring.

The image of Dr. Saxon asking, "How can I help you?" suddenly flashed in her mind, Eileen mused, and responded aloud, "My, how God ties everything together."

"What do you mean?"

"Oh, nothing, I was just remembering some similarities. I am here to get your help, and on a mission to save the world."

"Amen to that" Griffiths said. "We are all on the same path. We all need help and the world needs saving."

"But God has given me a plan," she invoked. "It involves you, me, lots of important people, and this Magic City we live in."

Becoming more alert, curious and suspicious, Griffiths reprogrammed his focus to make sure that he heard every word she uttered. He visualized himself standing up invisibly and dusting off one of the certificates on the wall behind him. Carl H. Griffiths, Ph.D., Clinical Psychology, Auburn University. He had previously practiced Psychology with a group, Birmingham Psychiatry, P.A. During his clinical practice he had become increasingly convinced that those who were more psychologically stable were generally those who had healthy spiritual values and adhered to them regardless of their denomination. As a result of this conviction, he felt called into the ministry as a provider of spiritual guidance.

Now this beautiful, troubled soul was bringing him a challenge for all of his degrees, learning and experience. Dr. Griffiths easily inserted himself into her confidence by saying, "I'm glad you have chosen United Fellowship. Please continue. How is it that we are to accomplish this great mission?"

"Oh, Dr. Griffiths, the Lord has been so bountiful to me. Doors are opening that have previously been sealed. I know I am anointed for this great purpose." She looked at her watch. It was ten past four. She wondered how much time he would allow for her. She needed to take this opportunity to sell the entire concept to this godly man who was willing to help save the world. She asked, "Do you have a little time? I need to tell you from the beginning?"

"Sure, we have time. How did it start?"

"I guess it started when I was given this wonderful job at Levine, Randall and Smith. It's an accounting firm. I am a CPA." She gave him her background in the firm and how quickly she had grown to partnership and prominence with VIP clientele.

By then he had calculated her IQ to be higher than average, probably one hundred thirty-five or more. He decided to give her a little latitude. Perhaps, there was going to be merit in some of what she has to say.

Eileen offered, "Sometimes my mind is like a race track. I get started and ideas just pour out. I was excited after the moon landing of Apollo XI in sixty-nine. This idea came to me. After boats were invented, they developed passenger ships. After airplanes were invented, they developed passenger airplanes. Now that space travel is invented, of course we will have passenger spacecraft. Why not be the one to get it started?"

"That's reasonable," Griffiths responded.

"I know," she said. "So many people believe in me and in this project. Within no time we have ten million dollars committed for the project. Why, just last weekend I was in Washington and Senator Johnson liked the idea. I think he is going to help us." Griffiths' peaceful demeanor was working. Her pace was slowing and her thoughts better organized.

"That's marvelous," Griffiths said.

"Wednesday I took a month off work so I could devote all my time and energy to this project. Wednesday night this dear man of God came over my television and spoke to me and anointed me. It became revealed to me that God has provided this space mission as a means to display His name, His works, and His salvation. This is the way Christ's message is to reach the whole world, "Every eye shall see Him." You see what will happen is that the people who will finance the project and ride on the space bus to the moon are truly God's chosen messengers. They will build Moon City. We will have a banner lying across the face of the moon so that everyone will see the face of Jesus and the words, 'Jesus Saves.' It will be a perpetual banner. God would have the largest billboard in the universe." She had gone into more detail than was obviously necessary, but he seemed intent and genuinely interested. She took advantage, almost as if she were presenting to prospective investors. 'He was obviously very bright, and a doctor, so naturally he should be able to understand the logic of the project.'

Indeed, Griffiths was relaxed and intrigued. He knew some of the names she had mentioned as investors. He certainly knew Johnson's record. 'These are influential, bright people. If they have signed on they have investigated the merits of her project. Still, God doesn't speak to people through televisions, at least that was my training. Otherwise, she doesn't seem psychotic but this seems to be delusional. Help me, God,' he silently prayed. 'I have to unravel this.'

"This is genius at work, Miss Robbins. You have accomplished so much already and at such a young age."

She interrupted, "Christ accomplished everything in only thirty-three years you know."

"Oh yes, but still consider the magnitude of your project and the amount of backing you have amassed already. That is formidable. Still, I am puzzled. You have come here to United Fellowship Mission. My ministry is not affiliated with a single denomination. I minister to people of all spiritual backgrounds and beliefs; even to those who profess no religious beliefs. And yet, you say this message came directly to you."

"Don't you see, Dr. Griffiths, the revelations just keep coming? That's why all of those big name evangelists wouldn't talk to me. God was directing me to you because His love is for all of His children. This is for everyone. Maybe the message should read, 'God Loves You.'" Her expansive thinking quickly and unconsciously incorporated his ideas into hers. "We need to think and pray on this to determine exactly how we should get the message across. I am so glad God has directed me to you."

Griffiths asked gently, "You obviously have bountiful energy for this project. Have you been losing sleep over it?"

"I've dozed off an hour or two here and there over the last week but God has given me the energy to just keep going. I don't know how else to explain it."

"I have lots of friends who are medical doctors. They tell me when a body pushes too hard this way, there can be a total collapse, even death. Sometimes God turns us on by turning up our chemicals but it is up to us to get them under control. Your thyroid may be too high for example. I wouldn't want an important project like this to get scuttled because we overlooked your health."

"You're so smart. I never thought of that. Can you check my thyroid?"

"No," said Griffiths. "I have friends who will be happy to help. It is six-thirty now. Suppose you try to get some rest tonight and come back at nine in the morning. Bring some of your drawings with you so I can see more detail. I will call one of my doctor friends, and see how we should go about getting you tested. By the way, have you had any family members who had thyroid problems or chemical problems?"

"No. Unless you mean drinking too many chemicals. I have had a few that drank too much alcohol and, oh, I had a brother that killed himself. We never figured out why. My mother made me go talk to a shrink about that."

"Oh, who was that?"

"Dr. Saxon."

Griffiths' face lit up. "Dear old Sam. He and I are good friends. In fact, before I came into this ministry, he and I were in the same group."

Eileen had been too busy telling her story to read his credentials. She said, "The world gets smaller every day."

"Indeed it does," Griffiths agreed, "As a matter of fact that same group has some M.D.'s as well. Some of them have a family practice background. They specialize in my favorite field, which is psychology and psychiatry. I find them real easy to work with. They listen to you psychologically as well as medically. In fact, I might call one of them."

"You sure seem to know a lot."

"So do you. Maybe that is why God is putting us together so we can work collaboratively for everyone's benefit."

That night after her shower she read the Bible for a while. She slept for four and a half-hours.

Griffiths left his office thinking, 'I really must put on my clinical hat in addition to my minister's hat. I see delusions of grandeur, flighty thought patterns, reduced need for sleep, expansive thinking, high energy levels, multiple projects, fragmented attention, infectious enthusiasm. She is high achieving and bright, with a family history of excessive use of alcohol and at least one suicide. There can be absolutely no doubt that she is Bipolar and in a manic phase.'

At least he had not seen paranoia or hallucinations. 'She also quickly incorporated my thoughts into her schemes. Perhaps indeed, she will return in the morning and I will be able to get her in for psychiatric evaluation.'

Chapter 13
Label and Lock

Eileen arose early the following morning. Her four and a half hours sleep had refreshed and energized her. Before leaving to meet Dr. Griffiths she organized her drawings and prepared an elaborate outline. In lieu of breakfast she ate an apple en route to United Fellowship Mission.

She arrived five minutes early. The office was open and Judy was in a cheery mood.

"Good morning, Miss Robbins. How are you? Dr. Griffiths is here. Would you like some coffee?"

"Yes, thank you, Judy."

"Good morning, Miss Robbins, I am so glad you're here. I see that you have brought some work with you. Won't you come into my office?"

"Good morning, Dr. Griffiths, I am grateful to you for helping me. I have some of my drawings for you." Eileen accepted the coffee from Judy though she eventually drank no more than one or two sips. She rushed into explaining her project to Dr. Griffiths, especially how the two of them would save humanity from its ungodly ways. "Isn't it wonderful how prophecy works? Civilization develops at just the right pace to achieve the fulfillment of prophecy. Until now there was no realistic manner to affect every eye seeing Him. It's so exciting to be anointed and working God's will."

Dr. Griffiths found it more difficult to interject himself into the conversation than he had expected. He was hoping to convince her to meet with a psychiatrist. He realized that the momentum of her energy would require his strongest authority and determination to redirect her. Looking at his watch he stated, "Oh my. It's nine-thirty, we don't have much time. Let me tell you, I prayed last night for guidance on our project." Griffiths prayed often for guidance, but felt a special need in Eileen's case. "I am convinced that God works through his people in wonderful ways. He guides us so that we look out for each other. I see clearly, praise be to God, that we must take care of your health before you completely exhaust yourself. You are giving too much of yourself."

She interjected, "I feel great. I slept all night. I haven't felt this good in weeks."

"That is a trick of your body. Don't you see? You will continue to push until you completely drop and the project will be lost," Griffiths pleaded.

"You mean the devil, don't you? The devil is trying to trick me. I didn't even think of that."

Griffiths allowed a half-hearted agreement, "If you will."

"I spoke with a friend of mine, Dr. Lavoy. He can see us this morning. He makes rounds at the hospital every morning. He told me that we should meet him at around ten a.m. If we leave now, we can just make it. Dr. Lavoy said he has seen cases similar to yours, and yes, there are chemical imbalances that cause energy and exhaustion. It would be prudent to get yourself checked. Shall we go?"

"Would it be okay to leave my papers here? I wouldn't want to lose them." Eileen was completely unaware of the eminent life changes awaiting her.

"Of course you may. They will be perfectly safe and undisturbed. I will make sure of it."

He escorted her out to the car. It took only ten minutes to drive over to Brookwood Hospital and another five to get from the parking deck up to the seventh floor where the psychiatric unit was located. The elevator opened and they entered the reception area where she saw the sign; Brookwood Behavioral Health. Although it registered, she made no comment.

"I'm Dr. Griffiths; we are here to see Dr. Lavoy."

"Yes, Dr. Griffiths, he is expecting you. Please have a seat."

Within a few minutes Dr. Lavoy entered the area extending his hand,

"Hello, Carl, it's good to see you again."

"Hi, Tom," Carl began. "This is Eileen Robbins, the lady I spoke to you about. I have informed her that you have seen other hyper-energized patients who did indeed have chemical imbalances. I told her that you can check her for possible imbalances and stabilize her if need be. I am quite concerned about her."

Eileen said, "Why, Dr. Griffiths, I'm not unstable." Laughing, she extended her hand and said, "Hello, Dr. Lavoy, it is a pleasure to meet you."

"Hello, Miss Robbins. It's my pleasure. Carl has had some very nice things to say about you. If you will come with me, we have a small interview room where we can sit and talk. Carl, will you please join us?"

After taking seats in the interview room, Dr. Lavoy began the interview process. "Carl tells me you have an exciting project, and fortunately you have had great energy to devote to it. He is concerned that the energy is beyond what most of us mortals can muster. Therefore, your chemicals may be turned up a notch too high. If that is the case, it could lead to devastating results with you crashing and having difficulty finishing your project. It's possible even to become physically exhausted and damaged thereby. Also, we need to understand that excess energy can push us a little beyond what is reasonable." He was taking a chance to add that last comment, but after all, Carl had been with her a couple of hours already.

"My energy level is fine. In fact, I am better than I have been in weeks. I am in perfect control, and I have been able to accomplish a monumental task. I have most all of the project completed as far as the paperwork. I even have many financial backers. The difficult part is ahead of us. I'll need energy for that."

Dr. Lavoy agreed, there was no doubt of the diagnosis, Bipolar Affective Disorder, Manic Phase. He was witnessing the symptoms Carl had mentioned to him. If he outpaced her, she would refuse treatment. He commented, "Yes, we have seen people who let the energy push them too far. You have an important project. We want to make sure that your health is never compromised. Carl and I both think your chemicals probably have become ratcheted up a notch or two and it would be to your advantage to let us check all of that for you. Indeed, if they are high, there are things we can do to bring them back into balance."

He continued with routine questioning. Some of them were familiar to her by now because of Dr. Griffiths' questions the evening before. She was not requiring as much sleep. She was excelling in her efforts. She was developing important and major projects, and she even felt special, in fact, anointed by God to carry out his mission to save the planet or at least the people of the planet.

Dr. Lavoy continued, "Eileen, I've seen people with similar histories allow a pattern of high energy to drive them past their peers. Have you noticed that you may be excelling or exceeding the performance of your peers?"

Eileen eagerly agreed, "Of course. They are the tortoise and I am the hare, only I won't lose."

Seizing the chance to use her own analogy, Dr. Lavoy commented, "It's our job to make sure that your energy stays sufficient, and that you don't fall down at the end of the project. We try to coordinate all of those things. You have worked diligently and exhaustively on this project." He was trying to suggest to her that she was near exhaustion. "It would be a shame to let your chemicals overpower you and then be unable to complete your quest." He was careful to not use the word fail as it was not in her vocabulary.

"Oh, I'll succeed. I should say, 'we' because Dr. Griffiths and others are helping."

Dr. Lavoy continued his line of questioning, "Have you, by any chance, had any unpleasantries or run-ins with any of your peers or supervisors?"

"No," she answered. "Well, there was this little encounter with Mr. Levine. He's the founder of our firm. You see, they are all jealous of me. I am their youngest partner and their only female partner and I have more business than any of them."

"What kind of encounter?" Lavoy asked.

Eileen felt this was a little too personal and more than what she wanted to reveal, but she had mentioned it, so it would be up to her to finish it. "Mr. Levine showed some anger because I found it necessary to point out to him some professional and ethical improprieties by the other partners."

"That takes a great deal of courage for a junior partner to tread on such controversial issues. Sometimes high energy can stretch one beyond their normal finesse and diplomatic skills." He was gingerly suggesting that perhaps 'you are out of control.'

"Oh, he had it coming," Eileen retorted. "He knew all along that they were outside the boundaries. Yet, he accused *me* of breaching boundaries."

Sensing that he had pushed too hard, Dr. Lavoy decided to shift to persuasion to try to get her admitted to the hospital.

"I do hope you will let us perform a work-up and determine exactly what your chemistry status is. I sincerely believe it is higher than is safe. If so, we can make adjustments and you will be able to proceed as you see fit with your projects but without the risk of exhaustion."

She restated her position. "I don't think I will be exhausting my energy because it is God given. To those whom He gives much, He expects much. He has anointed me to do this work. Dr. Griffiths is going to help. I'll have the energy."

"I have no doubt you will have the energy. I am concerned that you might have too much energy. That could truly be disastrous, believe me. Let's get you checked out. Unfortunately, it is not a simple blood test. It is a matter of full evaluation and that will take a few days. You could stay here. Our unit is much more comfortable than other hospital units where you have to stay in a room and stay in bed. Here you have the freedom to be up and around, and to participate in activities, and even continue your work if you like."

Eileen for the first time was silent to the point that Dr. Lavoy and Dr. Griffiths could see her cognitive wheels turning before she spoke, "Let me get this straight," she said, "You are asking me, an anointed deliverer, to be admitted for a work-up? I am not some mental nutcase and I don't need to be locked up here."

"Miss Robbins, you came right off the elevator and we have walked around freely. You can see others are walking around freely. This is a much more comfortable place to have your check-up than anywhere else available. I would strongly encourage you to do it now. If you should have an adverse chemical event, a reversal, the circumstances of your evaluation might be in far less comfortable surroundings and with less personal control. We understand your needs and can work with you."

"This is interfering with God's work. You can't do that. Who are you to get in His way?"

Dr. Lavoy said, "God helps those who seek Him. We are not at cross purposes. The reason Dr. Griffiths has brought you here, he being a strong man of God, is because of his experience and our long friendship. He knows that this is the way to coordinate secular and spiritual projects; through healthful and methodical cooperation between us all."

Carl spoke up, "Dr. Lavoy is right, Miss Robbins. The quicker we can accomplish this, the quicker we can move on with what we need to do. May I strongly encourage you to follow his advice? I won't desert you. We will continue to do our work. I will keep things safe and in just a few days we can more confidently move forward." Dr. Griffiths disliked encouraging a delusion but it seemed appropriate at the moment.

Eileen interpreted that to mean that he was not as confident as she was about the project. Her mind was churning. She felt 'teamed up' on, even 'trapped.' Finally, she asked, "Suppose I let you do this evaluation and you think I am out of balance, what kind of treatment, what kind of chemicals?"

Dr. Lavoy answered first, "The thyroid. It is possible your thyroid could be overactive. If so there are two or three ways we could treat that. It is possible your sugar could be out of balance. That would, of course, be treated in a different way. It is possible that other chemicals that have to do with nerve transmissions could be out of balance. One of the chemicals we use for that is Lithium."

Eileen became incensed. "You think I am manic-depressive? You don't believe what I am telling you. You think I'm psychotic. You will have to answer to God for this. If you think this is being sick, don't cure me. I feel great. God loves me!"

"Hold on, wait a minute. Nobody has mentioned manic-depressive. That's an old term and people think of that as an untreatable mental illness. We now prefer to use the term Bipolar Affective Disorder. It is a very treatable condition but if it is untreated it can be life-altering. We don't know what your evaluation will determine but you should not take unnecessary chances."

Not waiting for a yes or no, Dr. Lavoy told her that Sanquetta, the unit secretary, would assist her in the admission process. "Dianne, my assistant, will meet with you to ask you some further questions, please be as specific as possible in your answers. She will particularly ask about your family history."

In the minds of Dr. Lavoy and Dr. Griffiths there was no question that her diagnosis was Bipolar Affective Disorder. Eileen would not like that label.

Later in the afternoon, she attempted to catch the elevator to go to the gift shop but learned that in order to call the elevator you must have a key. 'Damn, I'm locked in. I've been betrayed. They think I'm crazy. This is not fair.' She mumbled to herself, 'Oh, God, don't let Robert find out.'

Chapter 14
The Unit

Sanquetta, the unit secretary, was very pleasant. She had treated Eileen in a normal manner throughout the entire admission process. One quickly learned that she was to go-to person for answers about the unit. Eileen would later learn and be pleased to know that Sanquetta had been awarded the Employee of the Month Certificate of Achievement.

Despite Dr. Lavoy's assurance to the contrary, Eileen conjured up visions of the Cuckoo's Nest. She expected Nurse Ratchet to materialize any moment. On finding the accommodations to be reasonably comfortable, her anxiety partially abated. Though the rooms were double occupancy, privacy curtains were provided, along with comfortable single beds, a worktable and adequate closet space. Also, the unit included a small, common kitchen area and an exercise room.

Nurse Spargo met with her for the customary nursing intake assessment. Eileen assessed him to be a kind and gentle man. He instructed her on the various activities of the unit. He explained a morning community meeting where unit concerns or problems could be discussed. The doctors generally made rounds during the morning and met with the patients one-on-one. Group activities started at ten a.m. Some classes were didactic; others were more interactive. Yet others were for personal work and were process oriented. She was cautioned to talk first about generalities rather than specific problems that might be embarrassing. She should be advised that, while everyone was advised to keep all information confidential; it was possible that another group attendee could be related in some way and pass word along to friends or family. The staff tried to control this, but there could be no guarantees. Depending on your doctor's treatment plan, you may also attend a relaxation group led by Linda. We also have music therapy. Dr. Lavoy had ordered medicine for her. If she had a headache, Tylenol or aspirin were available. A sleeping pill had been ordered in case she had difficulty sleeping.

Eileen thanked Spargo and went to the day room where she had spent only a few minutes. She previously observed people there who appeared quite troubled. These warranted a closer look. Eileen recognized her own curiosity, but without personal insight. It emphatically registered with her as, 'look at them.'

Eileen walked to the corner of the day room for a panoramic and clear view of every person in the room. This was unfamiliar territory. She needed to prepare herself for anything that might happen.

Sara P. was a patient whom she had briefly met. She continued to sit in the same chair and position where Eileen had previously met her. She was sound asleep with her head hanging over the back of the soft chair. Eileen presumed her to be "zonked out" on medication.

Andrew T. was another patient appearing around thirty-five years old. He was disheveled, sitting at a table, alone. He was talking aloud to himself or someone that only he could see. Eileen could distinguish only a few of his words. She noticed that his sentences often were incomplete, garbled, and meaningless.

Morris O., also a male patient of roughly fifty years old, was endlessly pacing. He made repetitive motion with his hands. She wondered what the significance could be and with a mental shoulder-shrug, thought to herself, 'probably nothing.'

Doris S. and Pam C. were two women patients sitting at another table, one had coffee and the other had a soft drink. Later, she would hear Doris, who was in her late twenties, talking with conviction about being the mother of Jesus. Eileen thought, 'how absurd, they have me here with these nuts.'

When bedtime came, Nurse Lola offered a pill to Eileen. "What is this for?" she inquired.

Lola said, "It is something to help you sleep."

"No, I mean, what is the name of it?"

"It is Thorazine."

Eileen shot back, "Thorazine? That's for crazy people. I'm not crazy."

Lola soothingly reassured her, "No, you're not, but you're wide awake. Dr. Lavoy said it is important for you to sleep. This works very well in your condition to help you sleep. It will be worn off by morning." After a while, she persuaded Eileen to take the pill. Lola watched to make sure that it was swallowed, not cheeked. About forty-five minutes later, Eileen gave in and found her bed. She awoke after five hours of solid sleep, even though the sun was not yet up. Her roommate continued sleeping soundly. She pulled on a heavy robe which Judy had been kind enough to retrieve for her from her apartment. She preferred Judy's help rather than allowing her parents to learn of her admission. Eileen went to the day room where she found a man of about sixty-five sitting alone. He was drinking coffee, but his head was low and his expression sad. He avoided eye contact with everyone. He looked absolutely pitiful. 'If I could only give him some of my energy. 'Why not' she thought. She sat at the table with him. He barely acknowledged her presence.

"Hello," she said. "I'm Eileen Robbins."

Begrudgingly he offered, "I'm Keith Shores."

Eileen pushed, "You don't look so hot. You feeling bad today?"

"I feel great." Thick sarcasm attacked her.

"What's wrong with you?" Eileen asked, and then to soften her question, she added the old cliché, "Did you lose your best friend?"

Keith mumbled, "More than that. I lost my job, which was my whole life. I lost my family. They don't care about me, why the hell should I feel good? My life is over. Yours is just beginning so you go ahead and feel good."

"You haven't lost everything. You haven't lost God. Jesus Christ cares about you. He loves you. He will save you. Whatever you ask, he will do for you."

With irritation, Keith asked, "What universe did you come from? I don't see God giving me my job back or my family. He made me old. The only thing left for me is the cemetery."

Stunned, Eileen began a new awareness of this much different world. She had never heard anyone talk in this manner before. 'I wish Dr.

Griffiths was here to help me pray for Keith. I don't know how to help him. I don't even know how to pray with him. This is really frustrating.'

She felt relieved to see Nurse Lola coming over to sit with them. Lola commented, " Opposites attract. One with too much energy and one with too little. Both of you are up early this morning."

Eileen commented, "I felt so good I couldn't stay in bed."

Keith said, "Hell, I felt so bad I couldn't lie there. I had to get up. The coffee ain't helping either."

Eileen began to orchestrate rescue strategies; 'I need some way to help these people, they are so miserable. There are many generous people in the world, they just need to be organized, we could help them with jobs, clothes, therapy and medication. I wonder if Dr. Griffiths would help me with it. On no. I'm doing what they said. I'm jumping from one topic to another.'

There was commotion at the nurse's station. She heard a patient, Elise W., demanding and yelling that her doctor better give her "the shot." She would sue him and sue the hospital if she didn't get a shot for her headache. She complained that she was admitted voluntarily and she could leave anytime she wanted to. Eileen couldn't hear what the nurses were saying. The staff seemed calm and quite unfettered by the event. She saw someone come through the door and the nurse pointed to Eileen. The lady came over and said, "Hello, I'm Dot and I'm here to get your blood."

"Get my blood?"

Dot explained, "You know, to stick your arm to get some tubes of blood for the lab."

"Oh, to check my chemicals?"

"Sure, that's right. Why don't we go to your room?" Dot drew out four tubes of blood, then applied pressure at the venipuncture site. Dot advised Eileen to hold firm pressure for a few minutes and thanked her.

Eileen wanted to know, "What all is he checking?"

"I don't know, I just draw the blood, but he must be checking you for everything, huh?" They shared a laugh. Eileen's being the weakest.

Eileen attended several classes that day. Her mind however, was busy on her personal projects more than the content of the classes. She managed to catch something about an over-achieving personality, but no details. Someone told a joke that neurotics build castles in the sky, and the psychotics lived in them and the psychiatrists charged rent on them. It seemed obvious to her that they were referring to her because of Moon City but, 'How do they know? I haven't told anyone.' Overall, the day had not been as boring as she had anticipated.

Eileen began her first patient education class with preconceived ideas. 'First of all, I don't need to be here. Secondly, it is highly unlikely that I will learn anything meaningful.' She felt, "*above*" her "*peers*." 'Their backgrounds are so different from mine. My reason for being here is different. Maybe *they* need to be here. I am only getting my chemicals checked out.'

Education class Instructor, Nurse Dean, welcomed the group and introduced the day's topic as medication compliance in treatment. She elaborated that while she would mostly be talking about compliance with medication, it was equally important with other forms of treatment such as regular appointments with her psychiatrist or therapist or attending aftercare classes.

Eileen's thoughts were already drifting back to Moon City. 'Surely time is wasting with me being here. I need to be out there with my investors, keeping their enthusiasm up. I need to keep the project moving forward. I need to keep everyone focused. I need to get out of here.'

Ms. Dean continued with the didactic information, essentially spoon feeding them before trying to discuss it. Hopefully, they would digest it later.

Ms. Dean lectured; "Most of the illnesses, symptoms and problems faced by our patients are readily controlled through treatment with new and improved medications. The skills we teach here in the classes are also important."

'Why doesn't she mention balancing the chemicals?'

When Griffiths came to visit that evening, Eileen implored, "Carl," appealing personally, "You have to get me out of here. These people are nuts. Some of them are absolutely whacko. I need to help them but I don't know how. I'm sure together we could figure it out."

Dodging, Griffiths replied, "Eileen I had to call in a favor for Dr. Lavoy to see you. I promised him that you would stay and get the entire work-up and treatment, if you need it." She interrupted, "But I don't need it."

"Your evaluation is not complete. What have you learned so far?"

"They just drew my blood this morning so I haven't heard anything."

"Be patient. I remember him saying it will take several days. It has only been one."

"One and a half," she corrected.

"Sorry, that's still not enough time and we agree on that. I need to talk with you about something, Eileen."

"What's that? You're not bailing out on me, are you?"

"No, not at all. I'm getting further enmeshed. I have been studying your drawings and outlines. They are absolutely fascinating. I can't wait for us to discuss them more.

"That's great," Eileen bubbled.

Eileen spotted Freddie, one of the patients. She called out to him, "Freddie, come here, I want to introduce you to someone. This is Dr. Carl Griffiths. He is the man of God I was telling you about, the one who is helping me on my project. Carl, this is Mr. Freddie Freeman who saved my life earlier today."

Mr. Freeman was a huge black man who towered six feet, seven inches tall and weighed two hundred and seventy-five pounds, with not a hint of fat. He looked as if he could indeed have saved her life. His deep bass voice resonated as if it came from the bottom of the Grand Canyon. "I didn't do that."

Eileen corrected to Carl, "It sure felt that way to me. I was cornered by Mr. Casanova, who was trying to paw all over me. I couldn't get away. I kept trying to push him off. I noticed that Mr. Freeman was watching us and I mouthed, 'Help me' and he immediately came over and stepped in really close, almost separating us. He looked down on Casanova and demanded, 'Man, don't you hit on this lady.' Casanova responded, 'Butt out big boy, this is private. Me and the lady are having a little fun.' With that Mr. Freeman took a step, placing himself between us. He placed both hands on his hips, making of himself a huge wall. He told Casanova, 'You want to have some fun, come on.' Casanova dropped his head, turned, and walked away mumbling, 'Party pooper. You ought to mind your own business. We were just having fun.' Mr. Freeman stepped aside and gave me room to breathe. He told me if I had any more trouble just to call him. Since then, I have been staying very close to my new friend."

"Mr. Freeman tells me that Dr. Lavoy is also his doctor. He's now been here about ten days. He was having trouble sleeping and thought people were after him. He works with the power company. At work, while installing a new line, he began to think that his co-workers were trying to trick him into an accident with the back hoe. He thought they were going to sell his body parts. His co-workers called their dispatcher and obtained permission to bring him to the hospital. He told me that this has happened to him twice before. Both times he was treated at another hospital with Haldol. They diagnosed him as having Paranoid Schizophrenia, but Dr. Lavoy said his paranoia is part of his Bipolar illness. Dr. Lavoy is treating Freddie with a combination of Prolixin and Lithium because he has a chemical imbalance. At first he needed Thorazine to sleep, but now he sleeps fine without it.

Eileen remembered asking him, "Freddie, how did they find out you had a chemical imbalance?" Freddie answered, "I think the doctor can just look at you and tell. Anyway, he must be right because this is the best I have felt since before the first time it happened. This time I feel like the monkey is off my back."

Picking up the opportunity, Carl led Freddie with a question, "Mr. Freeman, you are now feeling much better I take it? So, will you be returning to your job? Do you feel like getting back to work?"

"Yes sir, I can't wait to get back to my job. I've got a big family to feed and I don't want to use up all my sick time. Fact is, I will be going home tomorrow and back to work the next day. The doctor says I got to wear a hat and long-sleeved shirts because the sun might burn my skin with the medicine I take."

Knowingly, Carl added, "I've even known people to have to wear sunglasses, Mr. Freeman."

"Is that a fact? I'll do what it takes because this medicine has done me right."

Again, Carl added, "I'm sure the nurses and doctor have told you how important it is to take your medicine as directed and to not stop taking it."

"Yes sir. We even had a class on how important it is. I'll be taking it."

Visiting hours were up. Carl left feeling smug in his oblique instructions to Eileen. Freddie and Eileen talked more and exchanged phone numbers.

The next morning before Freddie checked out, he and Eileen chatted a few minutes. In a brotherly manner he instructed her, “Miss Eileen, it is important that you listen to what the doctor says. Whatever he tells you, you do it. You're a smart woman. One day you are gonna be real important and I want to ride that space bus with you. If you have any trouble, you call me. I'll be home at night.”

Instinctively Eileen hugged him. Freddie was easy to like, but she had come to appreciate him equally. She told him to “take care of yourself.” Her mind raced ahead to wonder if he would eventually join Dr. Griffiths' mission?

Later Freddie was discharged and departed for home. They had bonded and she was sad to see him go. He was a friend in a time of need. She would not, nor could not, forget him.

Chapter 15
Family Conference

During Dr. Lavoy's visit with Eileen, he suggested that she invite her parents to meet them the following morning for a family conference. Eventually she would need to let them in on her situation. They would appreciate being included sooner rather than later. It would be okay to tell them that he was running tests on her and that hopefully enough of the tests would be back by the following day to have a clear picture of what needed to be done.

"What do the test results show?" Eileen wanted to know.

"Nothing as yet, except normal routine blood count and urinalysis. More results should be reported tonight."

That night Eileen was given a stronger dose of Thorazine, ensuring a full night's sleep. She awoke refreshed and had breakfast. She was groomed and ready by the time her parents arrived at a quarter 'til nine. She had not seen them since her trip to Washington. Although they knew about the Moon City project, they had not shown interest, so she had not exercised a great deal of effort to keep them up-to-date.

"Hi, Mom. Hi, Dad. Thank you for coming. I'm here getting some tests. Dr. Griffiths and Dr. Lavoy seem to think my chemicals might be too high."

"Dr. Griffiths is helping me with my project and he said it's important to get my chemicals checked out." She was repeating what she had told them on the phone the previous day. Mr. Robbins wanted to know how Dr. Griffiths fit into her Moon City project.

"If you have faith, miracles happen. All things work together for the good of the Lord." She explained that she had come to realize that her space transportation company had been revealed to her as God's plan to emblazon his message across the face of the moon. "We will have world peace and harmony, all in the name of God. I am so fortunate to be the one chosen for this mission."

Mr. Robbins being pragmatic said, "Honey, aren't you biting off more than you can chew?"

"You don't understand, Dad. I was anointed by God to do this. The man in the television told me."

Mr. and Mrs. Robbins looked at each other and tightened their hand grasp which was under the table, hidden from Eileen's sight. It symbolized their heartache. Neither knew what to say next.

Dr. Lavoy's timely entrance was an answer to their silent prayers.

Introductions and greetings were exchanged. Mrs. Robbins explained that they had received a call from Eileen; in fact, they had tried to reach Dr. Lavoy. He acknowledged being aware and hoped they understood the receptionist's message. "Without a patient's consent and permission we do not divulge whether or not we have a particular patient. We refrain from discussing privileged information. In this conference, Eileen has given her permission for you to sit in to learn what we are doing, much of it at the same time she will be learning it." He turned to Eileen, "Do you have any concerns about discussions in front of your parents? If there is anything you do not wish me to discuss we will step outside so you can inform me, but I truly don't know of anything that you have disclosed to me that you should be concerned about your parents knowing."

"I have no secrets from my parents. They can hear everything. That's okay with me. Did you get the tests back?"

"Yes, as a matter of fact, I do have them. Let me give your parents some background. With the kind of heightened energy, expansive thinking, and pressured speech Eileen has been exhibiting, we began to think that very likely there are some chemical imbalances that need attention. When the chemicals are, shall we say, raging, a person will feel on top of the world, even invincible. They function physically and mentally at a faster pace than the rest of us. We will seem slow to them by comparison. They feel extra-well and extra-special. They often incorporate into their thinking some mechanism to improve the feelings and status of others. It appeared that Eileen was doing this, so we needed to test her. We tested for various things, including hyperthyroidism, sugar imbalances, liver function, vitamin deficiencies, the blood indices such as hemoglobin and hematocrit. We further checked the blood and the urine for foreign substances including known drugs of abuse, both those that are prescribed and street drugs."

"You didn't tell me you were going to test for that. I could have saved you the trouble."

"I guess as a matter of fact," Dr. Lavoy said, "We didn't name everything that we would test for, but I am happy to report that tests for all those kinds of drugs were completely negative, as we expected them to be."

"What about my thyroid and my sugar?"

"They were normal."

"Well, what about that Bipolar chemical you were talking about?"

"The researchers are still searching for ways to check that one," Dr. Lavoy explained. "Years ago before we had means of checking the hemoglobin and hematocrit, we would look at a persons' nailbeds and their lower eyelids to glean from the level of pinkness or paleness whether or not the person was anemic. Eventually, when the correct blood tests were invented we could quantify exactly how much anemia they had, even the type. We are at a similar stage now where we look for clinical ways to *identify* the Disorder. We are searching for the chemicals of the Bipolar Disorder and ways to measure them. For now we rely on clinical evaluations rather than blood tests. You have all of the signs necessary to make the diagnosis. In addition to the ones I mentioned to your parents earlier, we consider that your thought pattern is flighty, and that your expansive thinking incorporates the thoughts of others and embellishes them. The good news is that this is very treatable. The medicines we use today bring the chemistry down to a normal level allowing you to function with appropriate energy and with creativity but without exceeding normal boundaries. Many people who don't check their chemistry begin to exceed their character boundaries and overspend or overextend themselves financially or even in personal relationships. We wouldn't want that to happen to you."

Eileen protested, "But I tell you I feel great. Who wants to be treated for feeling great?"

At this point Mrs. Robbins reached over to pat Eileen on the arm. "Now, now Eileen, let's hear what the doctor has to say."

As Dr. Lavoy had calculated, her parents would help him to keep her under control long enough to hear her diagnosis, treatment plan, and prognosis. An advantage for him was that he only needed to explain it once. They could not manipulate what was or was not said. Separate meetings often lead to triangulation.

"The treatment is with a natural chemical, an element that we retrieve from the ground. Its unique electric properties cause it to slow the nerve impulses when they are too fast and to speed them along when they are too slow. Bipolar Affective Disorder means a person's mood swings from normal to alternately high or low. The element, Lithium helps treat both poles of the illness, though it appears to work best on the manic side. You see, Bipolar Disorder is the illness we previously called Manic Depressive Illness. I think it quite ironic that when we had Manic Depressive Illness we didn't have adequate treatment. Now that we have changed the name to Bipolar Affective Disorder, we can treat it quite effectively. It was a coincidence that the name was changed when the treatment was found," said Dr. Lavoy.

"Most people can take Lithium with no difficulty. A few people suffered kidney damage, but they had taken excessively high doses. Those doses aren't necessary and we check your blood levels to make sure that your level is appropriate. If your Lithium level is too low, it doesn't help. If your level is too high it can cause toxicity. One might develop a tremor or confusion or develop brain or kidney damage."

"Does that mean I have a Lithium deficiency?"

"In your case, I will say yes. In general, if we checked everybody in the unit we wouldn't find measurable Lithium in anyone here, except those taking Lithium. In Lithia Springs, Georgia and in certain areas of Texas, you would find Lithium in people's blood stream because that's where it is found in ground deposits. It shows up in the drinking water. People who live there have some natural control for this disorder. Most people require about three tablets a day, some less, some more, but after you have taken it a few days, we check your blood and then a few days later, we check it again. After a few tests, we know how your body assimilates and handles the Lithium, and thereafter, we don't have to check you very often. Most people should be checked every three to six months. There are certain conditions that would require us to check you more often. For example, if you had high blood pressure and were taking antihypertensives, or if you were taking diuretics, or for a person who perspires a great deal such as people who work in the sun. When you lose too much sodium, your Lithium level goes up. When we keep your Lithium at the therapeutic level, you should function at a much more even keel."

"I don't want to be labeled a fruitcake. People won't respect me."

Dr. Lavoy pleaded, "Listen to me, Eileen. The treatment works. We have only had it a few years. We have been able to use Thorazine and Haldol for the extreme highs but we haven't had anything to use for maintenance. Lithium is a great maintenance medicine. As to respect, let me name a few people who have had this Mood Disorder before there was any treatment for it. They managed to gain respect, despite episodes of depression or mania. Abraham Lincoln, for starters, but also Winston Churchill, William Faulkner, and Ernest Hemingway."

"I suggest that you stay in the hospital a few more days, until you have fully returned to normal. You are fortunate that your normal level of function is much higher than the average person."

"Yes, but it doesn't feel this good."

"I know, but a continuation in this state will lead you into ultimate danger and difficulties. Also, often, when the high goes away the person becomes extremely depressed and during the depressions the person feels just as much despair, as you feel exhilaration in your high. There are no boundaries to the highs or the lows and some people even suicide.

"Are you telling us that's what happened to my brother?" Eileen displayed a sense of shock as if this was the first insight she had grasped.

"In all probability, Eileen, Bipolar Depression is what happened to your brother. He had no way of knowing, just as you had no way of knowing. The depression is a totally hopeless and helpless feeling. People feel there is no way out of their extreme misery. That's why they don't seek help or tell anyone. You are lucky that your first major episode is a high. You have experienced some moderate lows previously, but were not treated."

"It's important that you and your parents understand that this is a natural illness. It is inherited in the same manner as diabetes. Our chemical systems do not always work properly. It is not a neurotic habit because of some poor or poisonous interaction between you and your parents. Sometimes a disorder will be unexpressed in parents. At times we fail to find it anywhere in the family tree; but usually we do. I believe we see it in your brother. You have told me that several members of your family drink excessively. Alcohol often is a mask for Bipolar illness. Many people who have Bipolar Disorder are so uncomfortable that they turn to alcohol looking for something to numb or control their emotions. Often, they become addicted to alcohol and consequently that's what people notice about them. With your parents' help we may be able to trace the family lineage of this disorder. We may not find it, but we should try. In general, what one can expect genetically, is that when one parent has the disorder, one out of four children will inherit the disorder. So, if a family has four children, the odds are that one will have it and three won't. But just as any calculation of chance there would be some families where all four have the disorder and others where none have the disorder. It's only when you add them all up and divide, it comes out to about one out of four or twenty-five percent."

Continuing, Dr. Lavoy added, "There is one more thing that you should know at this early stage. There is a phenomenon called the *kindling effect*. Think of it as kindling a fire. Basically, if you have an illness, whether it is Diabetes or Bipolar Disorder, and you leave it unchecked, the illness grows and becomes more damaging to you and more difficult to treat. Most people with Bipolar Disorder have mood swings. They might have an episode of depression or mania. They could even have hypomania which means being high but not of manic proportions. Usually they will remit to a normal state which we call euthymia. For all practical purposes, each time that a person has an episode, the illness grows. Such episodes will be apt to happen in a shorter interval and at a more intense level. In fact, the illness may progress to a rapid cycling stage. The highs and lows can be very close together or even mixed with symptoms of each at the same time. Arresting the episodes by diligent treatment is essentially tantamount to arresting the illness. Don't forget this. It's a warning worth remembering and a caution that demands adherence."

"Events that most often trigger an episode are stress-related. Stress results from both good and bad influences. Yours have been mostly good. Things have been going extremely well for you from what I hear. You have taken advantage of them to grow by leaps and bounds, nevertheless, this is stressful. The loss of sleep is a frequent inducer of a manic state and conversely a manic state usually produces loss of sleep. Likewise, depression often causes sleep disturbances, such as difficulty sleeping well, waking up early and being unable to get back to sleep."

"And one other warning. Alcohol tends to precipitate episodes and should be scrupulously avoided. If you ever drink it should be minimal. You should never use street drugs such as marijuana or LSD, mescaline, Angel dust, or anything that is not prescribed by a doctor who is aware of your disorder, and prescription medicines should be used only as prescribed."

"The nurse will have your first dose of Lithium ready when we finish the conference. I hope you will start it and get used to it while you are here. Most people have no side-effects but a few people have nausea or diarrhea. A few others have problems with edema or their food might taste metallic or they may gain weight. These are small percentages of people, but if you should notice anything unusual, call me and discuss it with me."

"Eileen, when you leave the hospital I want you to attend a self-help group. It is called the Depressive Manic-Depressive Association of Birmingham. It is a chapter of a national organization. You will be able to get support and insights and reciprocate. As part of your treatment I want you to go for at least three months as part of your ongoing responsibility for self-care and help. I hope you will continue it indefinitely."

"There are also weekly aftercare meetings provided by the hospital. There is no charge and you should attend for three months."

With continued conversation and genealogical quest it seemed likely that the paternal grandmother and an aunt likely harbored the Bipolar gene and suffered its consequences though neither had been formally diagnosed. Both had been moody and made suicide attempts and both overused alcohol. So it seems reasonable to believe that the gene came from the paternal line: They were counseled that family members should be made aware of the potential so that mood disturbances could be detected early, and hopefully further tragedies could be prevented. When the meeting was over Dr. Lavoy suggested that the parents stay for further conversation with Eileen to help them get comfortable with each others' concept of an ongoing disorder that would be her lifelong companion. Dr. Lavoy would wait until another session to deal with the misguided guilt that parents often feel about unwittingly carrying an unknown gene. He would counsel that we can only be responsible for that which we are aware. We should be responsible for what we know and declare our health and our shortcomings, including genetics, to our potential spouses and potential partners for our children."

Chapter 16
Stigma

Eileen's first hint of being stigmatized as a "mental patient" came from her own prejudices. She was jolted to hear Dr. Lavoy say, "You are improving nicely. You should be well enough to go home in a few days." The word "well" derailed her attention, throwing her into a tangential thought process. 'If I am getting well that means I have been sick. I am in a mental ward. He is telling me I am mentally ill.' She defended her sanity to her own self. 'I will not wear that label.'

'I am not mentally ill. I am Eileen Robbins. I have the best list of clients in Birmingham. I am respected. I am sure to be on the prestigious list of "Top 40 under 40" this year. If I get labeled as mentally ill there goes my career, my life. I can't let that happen.'

Unaware that she had missed the last few sentences by Dr. Lavoy, she blurted out, "I've always been well. I didn't come here because I was sick or needing to get well. I came here to get my chemistry balanced, so I wouldn't exhaust myself, I believe that is the way you put it, Doctor."

Dr. Lavoy interrupted her, trying to head off her energized fury, "You are correct. We are both correct. You were overexerting yourself and you were headed for exhaustion and it could have been disastrous if left to its natural course. In medicine, we call anything that is unhealthy a disease. Disease is an *unwell* state. But we say get well, rather than get healthy or get rebalanced. You will agree that your level of energy remains very good and allows you to be quite productive, yet you are at a safer level than when you were admitted."

It was now Eileen's time to interrupt. "But if you label me mentally ill, do you realize that you will be ruining my career, not to mention my future or my life!"

Dr. Lavoy had been through this exercise before. It is often difficult to persuade someone to accept their unwanted diagnosis. With some, it was even impossible. For example, cancer, Diabetes, mental illness, Multiple Sclerosis, etc., are not welcome diagnoses. Each would mean personal emotional anguish with life-altering, albeit, necessary changes. He knew that some patients would accept their diagnosis and treatment recommendations and do their best to be compliant in treatment and good partners in their own healthcare strategy. Others would resist, and in their noncompliance, therefore allow their illness to run its own unchecked and destructive course. That would be tragic with anyone, but it seemed all the more tragic with those who were indeed gifted and apparently destined for great accomplishments. Unfortunately, these would often be the most resistive. Their minds, being sharp, would be more creative in their attempts to deny the illness and attempt to beat the odds. They must learn that playing against the house rules is not smart.

"Please hear what I say. We are here to help you understand your own make-up. Everyone's genetic make-up markers are as different as everyone's fingerprint. Some will grow taller or shorter than others. Some will have blue eyes. Some brown. Some will be extremely bright like you, and others not quite so bright. Others will develop Diabetes in varying degrees of severity. Others will develop what you have, Bipolar Affective Disorder, again, in varying degrees of intensity. As physicians, it is our duty and privilege to help you understand exactly what you have. Also, we help you to understand your genetic lineage as well as the prognosis for yourself and your children. We do that by teaching you about your illness. You must learn what is good for you and what is not. For example, alcohol is not good for you. Steroids can likewise precipitate or exacerbate your illness. Undue stress and lack of sleep can cause exacerbations of your illness. You need to guard against those things. You are not a Bipolar person or a manic depressive. You are a person, an individual. You are a very fine individual *with* Bipolar Affective Disorder. You have been born into an era in which there is reasonable treatment. You are the first generation to be offered a maintenance treatment. Just a bit more than twenty years ago we had no treatment. Our first medication for psychiatric illnesses came in nineteen fifty-three, Chlorpromazine or Thorazine, which we have used with you to help combat the mania and promote sleep."

Lavoy continued, "Being labeled should be no more ruinous for you than for Abraham Lincoln who had repeated depressive episodes. Winston Churchill, likewise, had repeated depressive episodes, which he called his "Black Dog." We now know both of these likely had the same genetic Bipolar gene. Fact is, these people are widely known for their great works, but their mood disorder is not well known. Diligent historians discovered their lifelong struggle with depression. Your own attitude, and the way you respond to these challenges will mean more than the way others look at you. It might interest you to also know that this same gene also affected Emily Dickinson, and Cole Porter. Let me paraphrase something Eleanor Roosevelt once said. The power of the words of others is only empowerment by the listener. How true that is."

"Be assured, Eileen, we do not tell people that you are our patient nor do we give out information about you. The insurance form does have the diagnosis on it but the insurance company also maintains confidentiality. During this time of hospitalization you were already on leave from your work. They may not even know that you have been hospitalized and may not find out. If they do, they still do not need to know the details. Since you have been out on personal leave rather than sick leave they should not even require a doctor's release to return to work. You should plan to go back to work, as if nothing ever happened."

Eileen listened intently, but rejoined with her doubts, "That's easy for you to say. I'm going to feel self-conscious. I'll feel like they are watching me, waiting for a mistake so they can get rid of me or laugh at me."

"That's unlikely," explained Lavoy. "Consider your importance in the firm. How much you produce as opposed to how much you take out. It will be to their advantage to do everything possible to help you rather than cause problems for you. Don't lose sight of your value."

Eileen's mind continued to race ahead to new questions, "Are my children going to have this, this, thing? Will I have to tell my fiancée? If I tell him will he turn and run? Tell me, who is going to marry a manic depressive?"

Continuing the persuasion, Lavoy offered, "Many people with Bipolar

Disorder marry quite well. I have already given you several examples. There are many more. People fall in love with the person, the character and the personality. If total perfection and total lack of disorders were the criteria, I'm afraid no one would or could get married. Also bear in mind, we have good treatment today and it is improving constantly. By the time you are married and have children that are old enough to manifest the disorder, the treatment will be substantially better than it is today. Eventually, science will neutralize it."

Eileen could almost see Dr. Lavoy give a sigh of relief when she commented, "Okay, so I've got this disorder. It's inherited. It won't go away. It will get worse if I don't do as I am told, but I'll have a good chance at a decent life, if I'm a good girl. So, doc, tell me what I've got to do and let's get on with life but don't expect me to stand at the lectern and be your poster child. 'Hey world, my name is Eileen Robins and I am manic depressive.' No sir, it's not going to happen, at least not yet." This marked the seminal moment of Eileen's acceptance of her diagnosis and of her commitment to personal responsibility in her treatment. She understood that her first step was only one of many that would be necessary.

At the Robbins home Eileen's parents were having an unusual protracted extra cup of coffee following their breakfast. The topic was the recent developments with Eileen. In retrospect they recounted her moody ways, particularly as a teenager. They had never considered that she might be manic depressive. During their deliberations, they resolved what should and should not be said; definitely the term manic depressive would never be mentioned. If there had to be a proper reference, it would be Bipolar Disorder, but for practical purposes they would try to simply say chemical imbalance. It was nobody's business but their own. They found unity and agreement in their discussion as to how they would protect themselves and Eileen from gossip and stigma. Though on this morning there would be no finger-pointing; it could be predicted that after ascertaining genetic lineage, there would be strong accusations. "This is all your fault. You should have told me that your genes were faulty." There would be the counter-claim, "At least we had brains and knew how to work and get things done." Eventually, they would call a truce to their self-imposed, mutual destructive debates.

For now, they looked outside the family and decided to tell no one, not even their closest friends. They looked inside the family and decided to tell only those with a need to know. Currently that meant no one. They would be a self-appointed observation committee of two. If they noticed suspicious behavior they would, together, consult and decide whether to say anything, and if so, what and how much. They considered the possibility of belated understanding and recrimination as parents if they let people know of the true underlying reason for their son's death. They still could not say suicide. They knew some had blamed them for pushing their son too hard. Ultimately, they decided that since it had now been nine years, they should not open old wounds. Besides, they could not predict with certainty how people would react. Likely, family members would deny or would not want to believe, because they might then be vulnerable. They did not want Eileen, and vicariously themselves, to become the mentally ill branch or the black sheep of the family.

Chapter 17
Reconnecting

Mrs. Robbins drove Eileen from the hospital to her apartment. She expressed grief over Eileen having Bipolar Disorder. She offered constant and complete support and reiterated hope of good present and ever-improving treatment.

Eileen, in the privacy of her own apartment and the protectiveness that a daughter only feels from her mother, burst into tears, "I don't want this Bipolar. I hate it. Just when my life is going so well. I thought God liked me. Why me? Why Brad?"

"Why anyone, dear?" Mrs. Robbins offered.

"I know, but the timing is just so bad. I have all of these investors, my project is going so well, Dr. Griffiths is a wonderful man. He is helping me. Senator Johnson likes the project and his assistant, Robert Dupree is a true prince and he likes me and my project. Last week I had so much energy nothing could stop me. Now look at me. I'm just like anyone else."

"Honey, you're not like anyone else and no one else is like you. You're special and you should never forget it. Ninety percent of the people in the world would gladly exchange places with you. You still have all the energy you had before, only now you have it regulated better."

"Do you really think so, Mom? I hope you're right. I can't let this ruin my life."

"Good. That's the spirit!"

"It's just that right now I feel so disconnected. Thanks for being here. It does help. We've reconnected. Now I have to call Dr. Griffiths and call

Robert. I'll call Cynthia at the office just to chat a moment. I'll call Mr. Broadman. He needs to know about the meeting with Senator Johnson. I'll call the engineer. I have to reconnect with life. My tears are gone. My eyes are dry. Thanks Mom, you're a lifesaver."

"I love you. Dad loves you. We'll be home. We'll be there anytime you need us, okay?"

"Okay. Thanks again. Bye."

"Bye-bye."

Eileen was able to reach Robert at work. "Hello, this is Eileen. I hope I'm not interrupting anything. If you're going to be home tonight I can call then and we can talk more. I tried to call you to thank you for the beautiful roses and the very sweet poem. I echo your sentiments. I tried to call that same night but missed you. Since then it has been an absolute whirlwind here and I have been so busy I haven't had time to do anything but thank goodness things have settled down now. There is so much to catch up on. Can we talk tonight or tomorrow night?"

"I'm so glad to hear from you. I was worried that perhaps something was wrong, that you might be sick, or you might have decided you didn't want to hear from me again. Sure. I'm going to be home tonight. Why don't I give you a call?"

"That would be wonderful. I'll look forward to hearing from you."

"Sounds good to me. Probably around nine my time, eight your time?"

"Just right. Have a good day."

"Same to you. Love you. Bye."

'He said "Love you." I didn't say love you. Are we in love already? I'll have to think about this.'

When Robert called during the evening he showed no concern for how long they talked. He was definitely solicitous of her affection. Though there was no one else in her life, she coyly held back claiming, "You're so likable and it is tempting, but that's a little premature."

Robert disagreed, "I've looked a long time to find someone to capture my commitment. It's not premature."

"Oh Robert, how lovely. I'm sure it is going to work out fine. Just give me a little time okay?"

"Sure, but not much time." Actually, Dupree was confused. It seemed to him that the roles were reversing again. Usually she was at the forefront of decisions, now she was holding back. He concluded that he couldn't understand women's thought processes.

"By the way, Senator Johnson has some business in Montgomery and Birmingham that will be coming up shortly. I'll be coming with him. We don't have the exact time yet. May I call on you while I am in Birmingham?"

"Robert, that's great. I will promise to keep my calendar open just for you. Just let me know when."

"Well that's a start. I really am looking forward to seeing you."

So far her reconnections were going better than anticipated.

Eileen sought out Missy, "Can we talk?"

"Same as always, what is on your mind?"

Eileen sobbed and poured out her worries about her new diagnosis. "What will become of me? Should I not tell Robert or even see him anymore?"

Missy never failed to be the support that Eileen needed. She seemed instinctively to say the right things, but she had her own worries; could she herself ever find Mr. Right and true love.

Eileen effortlessly returned reassurance for Missy.

Chapter 18
Maintenance

Nurse Spargo was very thorough when discharging Eileen from the hospital. He went over prescriptions and told her how important it was that she take her Lithium, three hundred milligrams, three times per day. She should get her blood level tested in two weeks. She was to take Thorazine fifty milligrams one or two tablets at bedtime as needed to ensure adequate sleep but should not take it if she was able to sleep without it. She was not to drink alcohol. She should eat a balanced diet and maintain good health habits. It was also recommended that she take a multivitamin with a meal containing a small amount of fat such as milk or buttered toast.

An even more specific instruction was for her to attend the maintenance after-care group. It was led by a social worker from the hospital. Eileen equated the group with Alcoholics Anonymous and instinctively did not wish to participate. Her rationale was that she was not addicted to this chemical imbalance. She certainly had no need for support from fellow sufferers, but rather had an imbalance which she needed to keep in line by taking her Lithium. She skipped the first meeting. There was no call from the hospital. The services were offered and provided but not mandated. She was not a legally committed patient. She was free to make her own decisions.

On her first visit to Dr. Lavoy he ascertained among other things that she had not been to the after-care session. He strongly encouraged that she begin attending. "It is so easy," he said, "to become complacent and think you have nothing to worry about. By keeping in touch with others who contend with Bipolar, you will see the insidiousness of relapse. Just when you think someone is doing well, you will hear at the next meeting, 'Did you hear? Jane or John Doe is back in the hospital. They did this or they did that.' It helps you to maintain a perspective that you don't need to lose. Please promise me you will go. I will see you every two weeks for these first couple of months. If you are not going to go to the after-care group then I would prefer to see you weekly." He also encouraged attendance of the DMDA (Depressive Manic Depressive Association) self-help group.

Eileen thought that was overkill. "I'm not unstable. I'm not crazy. I'm taking my medicine. What more do you want?"

"What I just described, weekly after-care, DMDA meetings and bi-weekly visits with me, only for a short time. Three months for after-care. Our visits will be stretched out as soon as feasible. Your Lithium level by the way was zero point nine. I just need to clarify that you took all three doses the day before your blood test and that you did not take Lithium on the morning you had your blood test and that your blood was drawn between seven and nine a.m."

Eileen confirmed those facts.

"Good," Lavoy commented. "If you didn't take the Lithium correctly or if you took one on the morning of the blood draw or if you had the blood drawn later in the day, the accuracy of the blood level would be affected. For example, if you missed a dose the day before or if you did not miss a dose but did not have your blood drawn until mid-afternoon, the level might be artificially low. If we didn't know the reason and consequently increased your intake you might develop a Lithium toxicity. We checked your thyroid during the hospitalization. Although its functioning was normal, you should have it rechecked after six months and then yearly while you are on Lithium. Occasionally, Lithium appears to influence the thyroid level, driving the level down and causing hypothyroidism."

Eileen attended the very next after-care program. She pulled her car into the parking lot beside the education building. As she was walking to the front door, a maroon sixty-nine Chevrolet pulled up. She noticed a hand waving at her from the passenger side. She recognized Freddie, and walked toward him to speak. In the driver's seat a pleasant, plump woman said hello as Freddie introduced them. This is Miss Eileen and this is my wife, Alma. His children, Freddie, Jr., eight, Wilma Jean, six, and Mary Jo, two, were in the back. They also were introduced. All had pleasant dispositions with quick smiles, and like Freddie exuded friendship. They were eager to meet one of his fellow students as he had told them he was going to a class, so this made her Freddie's classmate. Eileen was bemused at herself at how much she enjoyed the short chat with the children and Alma was an absolute delight. 'What a family' she thought. She then remembered that Freddie had the same diagnosis as hers. It hasn't stopped him from having a fine family. Already, going to after-care was sending a positive signal, and she was not even in the door.

A Master's level Social Worker (MSW) gave a prepared generic, didactic, short lecture before asking for comments and discussion. General questions and conversation ensued. Most seemed to do with Depression and Anxiety or Panic Disorder.

Eileen was bored. She had no questions to ask and was daydreaming about her Moon City project more often than not.

She wondered, 'How long did Dr. Lavoy say I have to do this? Maybe the DMDA meeting will be more in tune with my needs.'

Chapter 19
Family Discord

Except for the ritual holiday meals and the once a month Sunday lunch at the country club it was unusual to be invited to an evening meal at the parents' table. Consequently, Eileen was suspicious of a hidden agenda for this dinner. Try as she might, she could not discern a plausible topic. 'Are they just interested in my current state of health and demonstrating their emotional support?'

As always, when she let her guard down, she would get a jab to the heart. As their plates were being served, her mother observed that Eileen was not yet back to work. 'This must be it already,' Eileen became tense and anxious. She snapped as her defenses were much less checked at home than in public. "I've taken a month off. I needed the time to work on my project. There is only so much time in a day. My project won't wait."

"Are you sure that's all there is to it?" her mother probed.

"Did you invite me here for forty questions or for dinner? Please Mom, get off my back!" Eileen was furious.

Mrs. Robbins, following the familiar script, began seething and retorted, "Get off your back. What do you mean? You're our daughter. You are our life. Don't you understand how much we care about you and how much we love you? We only want what is best for you."

"I hear criticism and doubt, not caring."

"Maybe I don't know how to express myself properly. Or maybe you don't know how to listen appropriately."

"Whatever."

"We need to know what is going on in your life."

Mr. Robbins, always uncomfortable in these situations, knew that he would have to rescue them from their battle. He broke his silence, "The thing is. We are a family of three. We were a family of four. Your mother and I have likely become excessively frightened. We have lost a son. We have seen you hospitalized with this imbalance and we know it can go both ways. We want to be close enough and make sure you don't..."

Eileen interrupted, but just before she was about to blurt out, 'Blow my brains out?', she visualized her brother and quickly changed her statement to, "Follow my brother." Her father said, "Well, yes. Looking back over your mother's heritage and mine, it appears I'm the one at fault for giving you this gene. I am so sorry. I would not have done it intentionally."

Eileen sharply and quickly threw a double entendre to them, "At least you gave me brains." As soon as she said it, she regretted it.

Her father, again rose to the rescue, "You are fortunate from both of us on that count."

Eileen meekly retreated, "That's what I meant." Her mother knew otherwise.

Eileen relented. Her father seemed to always calm her. Of course, her parents cared and would be supportive. She agreed to keep them posted on her affairs and would most assuredly feel comfortable on calling on them for any needs. They had reached an uneasy but acceptable truce.

Eileen's mother had other concerns. She would not resist bringing these up despite them having reached an amicable interlude.

"Have you heard anything from your cousin Thomas?"

Eileen had no idea where the question was headed. Thomas was her father's younger brother's son and he was a freshman at Auburn this year. "No I haven't heard anything except that he is at Auburn. Why do you ask?"

"Well, we hear that his senior year of high school was very difficult. He was moody and stayed in his room a lot and now down at Auburn he seems to be drinking a lot. The doctor said that drinking was bad for this gene and since he is your father's brother's child, well, I just wonder." Eileen spoke up, "Well, have you told Uncle Richard that it would be a good idea to have him checked?"

"Well, there is no certainty at this point. We wouldn't want to be, you know, premature." Eileen again interrupted her mother, "You mean in exposing our family flaws, don't you? How will you feel if you wait until it's too late Mom?" She was furious that to preserve pride they would risk her cousin's life. It was only an hour and forty-five minute drive. She would drive down there and meet with him. Who better to help him understand than her?

Eileen resolved to take care of the matter herself. She asked them to just drop it. She would visit Thomas.

Her mother continued ticking off her agenda, "Since your father has the same chemical, does that mean that he is going to have problems? I have to be afraid all the time that either one of you might lose control."

The father spoke up, "For heaven's sake, Rachel, it's not that God awful bad. For Christ's sake I am 48 years old and I have not had any problem. At least we now know something about it, and I am perfectly prepared to immediately get help if I have a problem."

"Well, okay, but what would they say?"

"Who gives a damn?"

"Get over it, Mom. It's not like the old days with leprosy."

"You just can't be too careful about your reputation and your image."

Mr. Robbins opined, "I'll just stick with character, to hell with reputation and image."

"Well said, Dad."

As Eileen was leaving she reminisced that home had basically been a fun place. Now, every time she came home, she became tense and defensive, as if she had chosen some disgraceful lifestyle. She had always felt that she was her mother's protege, her vicarious image. The feelings even intensified after her brother's death. By inference and reflection, the more perfect the child, it should be obvious to everyone else, the more perfect the mother. Eileen had worked hard and felt she had been proven worthy. But she knew her mother would never cease pushing her expectations. At the moment Eileen was unaware that in her critical analysis of her mother she was also reflecting herself as well.

The following Saturday she arrived at the spacious and beautiful Auburn University campus, "on the plains" in Southeast Alabama. She had been there before. Although there was unsurpassed rivalry between

Auburn and her school, Alabama, she could nevertheless appreciate the lovely setting of Auburn.

Eileen drove to Thomas' dorm. She had left word with his roommate that she would be arriving around noon, hoping to take him to lunch.

Thomas was even more of a college partier than Eileen had been. He had no idea of the purpose of her visit. He had been trying to sleep off the late night party and his subsequent early morning headache. He had barely finished dressing when the knock on the door announced her arrival.

"Come in," called Thomas without going to the door. Eileen opened the door and walked in. This was definitely a male's room and barely reminded her of her college dorm days. She noticed the odor of musty clothes.

"Hi Cuz, how've you been. Glad to see you."

"Hi Thomas. Let's get some fresh air and lunch."

"Sure thing."

Eileen asked if Toomer's Corner would be okay with him. She knew it to be a favorite of the Auburn students. It was not a major game weekend, so Auburn wouldn't be boasting one of its many wins by "rolling Toomer's Corner." Not that it would matter, they would eat there anyway.

The two had never been close, but certainly were solid family. There was no need for a great deal of family chitchat, so Eileen pressed her subject fairly early into the lunch. Despite interruptions of fellow students speaking and asking who the cute chick was, she kept the conversation focused.

"Thomas, let me be straightforward. I'm hearing things that concern me. Because I care about you I'm here face-to-face to fill you in on some things you might not know."

"Cuz, if you are here to lecture me I have heard it all before. I'm nineteen and I can take care of myself. I'm passing all my subjects. I don't want to be a doctor or lawyer or scientist. I just want a degree then I'll go home and work with my dad. I'll marry Sue. We'll have three or four kids. Life will be just hunky dory."

Eileen interrupted, "So, that's your pat answer, huh?"

"Look Cuz, I've been through this, with Mama, with Daddy, with Sue and even with her dad. If I had known this was your reason to come I could have saved you the trip."

"Then you've only heard half the concern, half the risk, half the opportunity. I'm going to ask you to do me a favor. Don't tune me out. Don't close me out, just hear me out. I'm going to do some risk-taking here. I suggest you do the same. Our family has a chemical imbalance that nobody knows about. It killed my brother. It drove me into the hospital."

Thomas couldn't contain himself, "Yeah, I heard you went nuts. Well, I ain't nuts, you hear?"

Eileen was stunned. This was the first time anyone had called her nuts. 'I am here to help this insolent, stupid, ungrateful little know-it-all, even buying him lunch. I asked him to hear me out and he has the impertinence to insult me. If he knows about my Bipolar and says it to my face, how many others are talking behind my back? Damn. What will Mom think?'

"Shut-up," Eileen snapped at him. "I was not nuts. My chemicals were high. I was working on too many projects and I became exhausted. Anybody could do that."

"You said we had a chemical problem in the family."

"Correct. Under stress such as college and drinking too much, the chemicals can get triggered to go up or down. If they go down, you may wind up like my brother. If they go up, you might wind up in a hospital having to have your chemicals pulled down or balanced."

"Not me. There ain't nothing wrong with me. If you are down here trying to get some sympathy, forget it. Get a grip. My life is going just fine, thank you. Thanks for lunch but I'm through and you can go back to Birmingham."

Straining with all the control she could muster she said, "Thomas, I'll go back to Birmingham, but I'm also doing great. You should at least do yourself the favor of speaking to a counselor and let them know about this chemical gene that is in the family."

"Look, I'm no different from the rest of the guys down here. I'm having fun. I'm passing my classes. If you and Brad got screwed up because of Aunt Rachel and Uncle Hershel, then that's just too bad, but don't try to drag me into it. My bad moods were always because there was something bad going on in my life, but that never stopped me. So, no thanks for your chemical excuses."

Walking to her car alone, hurt, emotionally bruised with tears streaming down her face, she wondered, 'What was I thinking? I have never seen him this way before. He is blind, defensive, hostile and obviously in denial.'

Back in Birmingham she was again crying when she relayed the encounter to Dr. Lavoy, who listened patiently and offered support.

"That was a rather brave thing to attempt. Self-disclosure to protect your cousin who has no clue."

Eileen said, "And stupid, too."

Lavoy explained, "Not stupid, perhaps naive. There is a parallel to new converts in religion. They are the most zealous, but the least experienced in teaching, or sensing when others would be receptive to hearing new information. Your cousin is just not ready to hear you, but I agree with you that his signs and symptoms indicate imminent problems. Heavy drinking, erratic hours, erratic eating, irritability, defensiveness, anger, hostility, denial, avoidance of responsibility, and I believe even projection are all strong indicators of an underlying problem. At least you have planted a seed. Hopefully, when his time of need is urgent, he will recall your message. If so, he might call you rather than anyone else. You need to be prepared, there is a good chance you will get that call."

Eileen said, "So, you think he has the gene?"

"The signs and symptoms fit."

"Should I tell his parents?"

"Are you a glutton for punishment?"

"Yeah, you're right. They're probably the one's who told him that I'm a nut case, right?"

"Quite likely. It's fairly common for people to try to find a family member or unit to identify and cast as the unsavory side of the family."

Eileen also discussed the encounter with Dr. Griffiths who confirmed the comments of Dr. Lavoy. He wanted to add however, that families and individuals only lean further away from spirituality by looking too hard at the secular issues; answers, problems, faults, cures, and pleasures. For example, the cousin clearly was addressing his own ego and health, and his control over his life. He seemed to have no doubt about his ability to direct where he wanted his life to go. Furthermore, he seemed quick to condemn her for what he viewed as loss of control of her own life. It was clear that he had no concept that nature might throw him a curveball, similar to the one she and her brother encountered. Nor did he have any compelling need for spiritual nurturing. He was completely satisfied at the moment with youthful hedonistic pleasures. Dr. Griffiths reassured Eileen that she had matured beyond that point by seeking deep, spiritual meaning in her life and in her work.

Eileen was grateful to hear his counsel and thanked him. Lately she had not felt so close or even anointed. She felt dejected and wondered, 'If God might be mad at me and punishing me. Have I not been pleasing to God? Am I doing something wrong?'

Dr. Griffiths asked her if she had reported those feelings to Dr. Lavoy. She stated she had not. She hadn't felt them important, as she was mainly concerned with her cousin during her last session with him. Dr. Griffiths stated, "You need to make him aware of this. It could be that the chemicals are reversing."

At eight fifteen Eileen called Robert. Her sluggish and muted voice tipped him off that something was amiss.

"What's wrong?"

"Nothing."

"I can't hear your smile. Who is bothering you?"

Eileen related that her cousin Thomas was too wild at college and that he might get into trouble.

Robert reassured her, "He's only an immature college kid. Everybody does it. He'll be OK."

Eileen elected to thank him and dodge further dangerous personal conversation.

That night she had difficulty going to sleep. She was worrying about her cousin, her parents, her project, her illness, her future, her job. She could not turn her mind off. Around two a.m. she remembered the Thorazine and took one. Forty-five minutes later she slipped into sleep.

Chapter 20
The Damnation of Mental Illness

On the third Sunday of the month, Eileen dutifully attended the Depressive Manic Depressive Association (DMDA) meeting at two p.m. She knew no one except Freddie who introduced her to Gerald, the President of the group. Gerald welcomed her and was solicitous of her membership.

Eileen felt out of place. She experienced an unusual awkwardness being a new member. It became apparent that many of the members attending this support group and others like it were often there because they had so little support elsewhere. 'Most of them seem worse than me.' She chose a seat next to Freddie.

Their custom was to open the meeting indicating that it was a support group for depression and manic depression. The meetings were confidential. Members were there to help each other and should not talk about each other's problems outside the meeting. Gerald explained that they would go around the room with each person introducing themselves using first names only. Each person should tell what their diagnosis was, the medications they were taking, and how they were doing.

Always, when there was a new person in attendance, Gerald would say that the meetings were from two to four p.m. The first part of the meeting is social with refreshments and the second part was business and the third part or the second hour they would generally have a speaker. Usually, the speaker would talk twenty-five or thirty minutes and then would offer time for questions and discussion.

Gerald explained that the group had a medical sponsor who was a psychiatrist. Different psychiatrists would volunteer for this position and serve until someone else volunteered. The current sponsor was Dr. Lavoy. He would generally meet with group a couple of times per year. He was always available in an advisory capacity.

Everyone introduced themselves. Eileen told her name and then said she had a chemical imbalance and that she was taking Lithium and Sinequan and sometimes Thorazine for sleep.

Eileen was quite surprised at the amount of discussion the members put forth on every topic.

During the business portion of the DMDA meeting it was customary to consult with the general membership to obtain topics of interest. In this way, the program coordinator had guidance from the group.

Sonya uncharacteristically spoke up. Only last Sunday from the pulpit her minister denounced mental illness as a consequence of sin, or as God's punishment for human disobedience. She recalled to the group how just a couple of years ago she asked her primary care physician to refer her to a psychiatrist because of unbearable mood swings. Some of her lows had been frightening, even causing thoughts of suicide. Her doctor had rebuked her, telling her to go to church and pray for forgiveness. He told her that "when she got right with God" all of her problems would go away. She recounted being extremely hurt as she was a faithful believer and church goer. He had not even bothered to inquire about her spiritual status. He had only made assumptions. She recalled contacting Dr. Lavoy and imploring him to take her as a patient without a referral. Upon seeing him, she had requested that he not communicate with her primary care physician. As Sonya was talking others were nodding their head in painful understanding that she was expressing a prejudice still prevalent. The task of education and of ridding society of the negative myths remains a monumental task. Sonya suggested a discussion on religion in mental illness.

Joy spoke next. She had always thought how ironic and dumb of her parents to give her a name such as Joy when her life had been anything but. Her highs had practically destroyed her financially and socially and her lows had literally stopped her heart with an overdose on one occasion, and dropped her into semiconscious stupors on several others. She seconded the unofficial motion and stated she was tired of being sent to Hell by some preacher without a medical degree.

Gayle spoke next stating how true that was. She wanted though to remember and give thanks for the good ministers who soothed their souls in time of need. Her minister had been especially helpful following her diagnosis. He counseled with her and her parents, helping them to accept her illness. He encouraged them to take her to a psychiatrist and ensure that she took her medication.

Gerald, without waiting for a formal motion, asked the group to give some names of local ministers for consideration. He thought it indeed a good suggestion to have someone from the clergy come and speak with the group.

Mary spoke next recommending Bishop Goodman. She thought how appropriate and fortuitous that a truly good minister could have started life with the name Goodman. Her opinion was that he was a good, understanding, kind man, and she thought he would be appropriate as their speaker.

June asked what denomination or faith Bishop Goodman was. Learning that he was Morman, she stated that since she was Church of Christ she was concerned that a Morman would not be open-minded to anyone outside the Morman faith. It was her opinion that Mormans felt that persons of other religions were following a false path and could not make it into Heaven.

Mary almost retorted, "Well, isn't it the same with the Church of Christ? From what I understand you believe only those of your faith can make it to Heaven."

Gerald reminded the group that this was not a theological debate. "As a group we want someone from the clergy so that we can get an overall understanding of the clergy's interaction with the mentally ill. Also, we want to educate the clergy regarding the spiritual needs of the mentally ill." He reminded the group that it was up to the members to remove the barrier and stigma. "We have to do it by involvement, dialogue, and interactive education of the non-mentally ill."

At that point, Joan spoke up, complimenting Gerald on keeping the members focused. She wanted to recommend Reverend McCants of the Episcopal Church. She personally had been to many different churches and found this church and this minister to be the most open and receptive of any she had attended. She admitted that she had no idea if this was representative of the greater Episcopal Religion. At least she had been quite comforted, and felt he would make an excellent choice. She further felt that Reverend McCants was the type who would take up a cause. He might even be willing to champion some of their needs in terms of public relations.

Immediately, there was a motion and a second that Reverend McCants be invited to speak. It carried unanimously and a tentative date was set pending his availability.

On the appointed date Reverend McCants arrived promptly. His talk was far better than any had dared to hope.

After being introduced by Gerald, Reverend McCants began by graciously thanking the group for the invitation. He dispelled any concern that he might be there to preach or proselytize. He welcomed the opportunity to meet with persons of various spiritual backgrounds and paths. He realized that he was in a group of persons who, through no fault of their own, had to deal with results of mental illness, either within themselves or their family members. He understood that it was human nature for people to react to personal adversities in their individual manner. He knew that afflictions of all types affected peoples' spiritual lives. It left profound questions for the deepest of thinkers. There was even a book addressing such questions, When Bad Things Happen to Good People by Harold S. Kushner. When God Doesn't Make Sense by James Dobson is another good book. The books didn't have all the answers and neither did he.

"However," Reverend McCants continued, "All truth seekers were on the right path because they were identifying their own path to spiritual truth, which can only come from God. We may take different turns and streets but we are all headed to the same city of spiritual peace. Most of us call this Heaven.

Interestingly, Reverend McCants stated his awareness that there might even be atheists in the group, certainly within the acquaintance circle of the members. He implored compassion and understanding of all people. He noted that good can come from humanists with conscience. Many of them are good people and do good works for society. However, he offered some pity for the humanists as they could only expect the fruits of one life and no afterlife bounty.

In the discussion period, group members wanted to know why some clergymen felt that mental illness in particular was a punishment or a curse from God, and that devout belief and faith would cure the person, and that therefore, the ill were undoubtedly unbelievers. Reverend McCants assured the group that this was not his belief nor was it the belief of most of the clergymen in his acquaintance. He acknowledged that there are some who hold such beliefs but it was his opinion that these were in the minority. He believed they were the less enlightened, and that as science further unravels the mysteries of illness, particularly the genetic and organic causes, that we will see these beliefs fade from popularity. The scientific community as well as the alliances of the mentally ill, such as these groups: The National Depressive and Manic-Depressive Association and the National Alliance of the Mentally Ill are making good educational efforts helping the general public to understand mental illness. He stated it was regrettable that we were still far behind the understanding of the somatic illnesses such as cardiac disease, diabetes, cancer, etc. He encouraged the group to not be dismayed and to continue the effort to destigmatize the mental illness diagnoses and therefore the people carrying them. He suggested more personal dialogue with ministers of all faiths.

Interestingly, Reverend McCants then urged members not to forget the power of the media. He pointed out that negative news coverage is the standard. When someone with mental illness or who has been treated by a mental health professional becomes involved in a crime, the media will mention that the person is a mental patient or has been treated for mental illness or has been under psychiatric care. We never see in the press or in the media that someone who has done something great has a mental diagnosis or has been treated for a mental illness. Neither do we see in the print that a criminal is a former heart patient, for example.

Reverend McCants highlighted the differences in mental illness and character flaws. Behavioral aberrations can be from characterological weaknesses or from mental illness. Manic behavior, at times, leads to excess spending, promiscuity, etc., but weak character can cause it without mania.

There are many people who do great works and who also have mental diagnoses, but who choose not to let themselves be an open book to the public. Those who are open with their diagnosis are helping to demystify and destigmatize the illness and the treatment. He pointed out that we must do better in those regards. Some have come forth but not nearly enough to make the necessary public impact. How many know, for example, that Charles Schultz has severe depression. He does much of his "Peanuts" work in his depressive phases, thus forever endowing the world with the phrase, "Good grief!" We must propagate this type information, he intoned.

Freddie responded, "Good grief. I never heard that before."

Reverend McCants stated that he wanted to be clear, that from his perspective, prayer was important for everyone: the healthy, the physically challenged and the mentally challenged. The group was impressed with how well read and knowledgeable he was. He knew that many of the mental illnesses are simply a different form of physical challenge because a number of them are physical or biological or organic in origin. He stated his strong belief that prayer was individually powerful and collectively even more powerful. He emphatically stated to the group, however, that proper treatment should be rendered and that non-treatment of diabetes is foolish and irresponsible. It is no less so for mental illness. In his opinion it was proper, appropriate, and incumbent for ministers to arm themselves with factual knowledge. Only then could they properly minister to all people - the healthy, the wealthy, the sick, and the poor. He emphasized his personal belief that God had answered prayers of those in need by providing us with the technology and resources to develop advanced medicines for our various illnesses. Surely he would intend for us to use them. He stated that the less one knows about their parishioners, the less effectively they will be able to minister to them. He thanked the group for having him and acknowledged that being invited had refocused his thinking and concern for the mentally ill. He pointed out that this was part of what groups such as this needed to do.

The group members were uplifted and inspired by Reverend McCants and the information he shared. They especially appreciated the fact that he understood. Unfortunately for most in the group, the enthusiasm would leave with Reverend McCants. It wasn't the nature or the training of most members to believe that they could make a difference individually or collectively. Simply being a member of the group was a big step for many of them.

Eileen was unusually quiet, reflecting on Reverend McCants' insightful talk. She was surprised at some of the names she heard of famous people with mental illness. She thanked her lucky star or maybe her guardian angel that she had been led to Dr. Griffiths. Indeed, he had been a lifesaver for her.

Chapter 21
Good Deed Repaid

The following Tuesday night Eileen's ringing phone awakened her at eleven-thirty. Freddie was on the line. "Miss Eileen my baby, Mary Jo, is sick. Please talk to Alma."

Eileen, hearing urgency in Freddie's voice, willed herself into full alertness. "Alma, what is wrong with Mary Jo?"

"Well, Miss Eileen, she is running a high fever."

"When did it start?"

"Yesterday, but today it has been getting worse. I've been giving her Tylenol. It just keeps going higher. I've sponged her with cold water but nothing seems to help."

"Have you given her an aspirin?"

"No."

"Then don't. Stick with Tylenol. Have you contacted a doctor?"

"No, we just thought it was a cold and would go away."

"You need to take her to the emergency room."

"That's just it. The car won't crank. I just thought you could tell me she would be all right."

"No. I can't, but I will get dressed and be right over. You get her ready and we will take her to the emergency room."

Eileen hurriedly dressed and drove to their house. On her approach to their house, Freddie, Jr., stood outside to make sure that she didn't drive past.

Eileen went inside and felt the baby's forehead. "Wow, she's burning up. What's her temperature?"

Alma said the thermometer was broken so she didn't know. One by one the entire family loaded into the car. Eileen was imminently introduced to unexpected intercultural differences.

At Children's Hospital emergency room Mary Jo was checked in efficiently and soon seen by the staff physician. Blood tests and x-rays were done. There would be a wait before the diagnosis could be confirmed, but it appeared to be pneumonia. Alma stayed with Mary Jo.

Meanwhile, Eileen waited with Freddie, Freddie, Jr., and Wilma Jean. They talked about family importance, and the fright that illnesses cause. They discussed the difference in the public's perception of an acute medical illness, such as the pneumonia Mary Jo was experiencing versus the chronic mental illness that Freddie and Eileen experience.

At three a.m., they were informed that Mary Jo had bilateral pneumonia and would need to be hospitalized for a few days.

Alma made sure that Freddie would get the older two children off to school the next morning before he left for work. She wanted to know how he would get to work and expressed her appreciation to Eileen for bringing them to the hospital and agreeing to take Freddie and the kids home. She, of course, would stay with Mary Jo.

Freddie was effusive in his appreciation and stated that he would have no problem the following morning. He would also get one of his brothers to help get the kids to school and get himself to work. After work, a fellow worker would bring him home and he would get his car taken care of and then go back to relieve Alma for a few hours.

Driving home, Eileen reflected on the Freeman family bonding that she had just witnessed. The closeness was abundantly evident, even to the point of the children staying up late and missing sleep, having to sleep in uncomfortable waiting room chairs. But to them family meant togetherness. A lot of us could learn something from the Freemans; the experience had made her feel almost like family.

In describing the night's event to Robert the next day Eileen remarked, "I felt as if I were physically transported from my universe to one unknown. There, an unspoken language told me clearly what family connectiveness and love really is. It's a night I won't forget. In fact, the experience was a gift."

Chapter 22
Threatening Preview

It was the first Sunday in the month of June. Eileen contemplated not going to this support group but the word "compliance" pestered her. Her project work could wait the two hours it would require to attend the meeting. 'Besides,' she thought, 'if we don't support each other, how can we expect others to be supportive.' Without knowing it, she had just formed the kernel for future advocacy leadership. She was a maximizer by nature, *get the most out of everything,* could have been her motto.

Gerald started the group in the usual fashion. Speaking last, the new attendee introduced himself as Ted Waterman. Immediately, after the introductions, Gerald, with uncanny empathy, turned to Ted and addressed him directly, "We are glad you came today, Ted. As you know, we are a support group, we help each other in times of crisis and trouble but we also help each other to understand our illness, our treatment and sometimes our family and friends. By the way, for confidentiality we try to avoid last names."

Eileen was intrigued at how delicately Gerald had invited Ted to be on the spot. She also noted that Freddie was sitting next to Ted. She recalled Freddie had been talking to Ted the entire time prior to the start of the meeting. That was characteristic of him. Always helping, always making others feel comfortable. Gerald was continuing, "Sometimes it helps to hear other people's stories. When I was in my early twenties I became convinced that I was to go to Boston and help spread the gospel. This thought consumed me, it energized me. I had so much energy I didn't feel

I needed anything else. Even though it was in the wintertime, I left for Boston with little money and few clothes. Thank God for my supportive, caring, giving stepmother who tracked me down and brought me home. I was diagnosed with manic depressive illness and treatment was started. I stay pretty balanced now, but I take my medicine every day and I see my doctor regularly. Would you care to share anything about your life or treatment with us?"

Eileen had never heard Gerald self-disclose. She wondered what prompted it. It reminded her of herself, but of course, hers was different. She felt quite sure there was a true connection for her evangelical work for God, but she wouldn't dwell on that for now. Still it was interesting to hear the parallel. Later, she would learn it was not an unusual parallel.

Ted thanked Gerald for his personal anecdote.

Eileen perked up. She could already tell Ted was not the village idiot. He was likely intelligent.

Ted continued, "I'm not accustomed to public speaking, and I'm not keen on self-disclosing. In the past, I have been forced to attend rehab treatment programs. This is the first time I have been politely invited and with such a promise of support."

Gerald interrupted, "That's the way we are, but don't think of this as public speaking, think of it as a family sharing with each other around our common table."

"Actually, that's a bad analogy, Gerald. If my family were more supportive, I might be at their table and not at this one. I am an only child. I grew up in Vestavia. My family is well off. Materially, I had everything a kid could want. Grades came easily, but I was bored. My parents had active lives. They told me they loved me and sent me out to enjoy, well, whatever I wanted to. I was good at everything. I was popular, and enjoyed plentiful friends, girls, boys, even the teachers liked me. I constantly tried hard to make everybody like me. If I ever felt slighted or left out I would get really funky. My mood would drop like a rock."

"In one of those blue moods my best friend offered me a beer. After a couple, I felt pretty good. So, I put two and two together. Two beers equals feeling good. From then on if I felt down, I found a couple of beers. Before long it took three. I didn't realize it was happening but before long a six pack was nothing. I started smoking pot. It was easier to hide, but I didn't stop drinking. I could do the Mary Jane before school or sometimes, if the conditions were right, even at lunch. My grades fell away from my usual straight A's."

Ted continued, "My parents complained. They blamed it on my friends. They told me I was ungrateful. They pointed out how much they had given me. They said I had everything anyone could possibly want. They specifically said I had no excuse for not being happy and not making good grades."

"I tried to tell them I didn't always know why I was unhappy. Sometimes for no reason I would be unbelievably happy and at other times feel nothing but doom and gloom. I didn't understand myself. I assured them it was not my friends. I reassured them that in fact my friends made me feel better. I even told them that at times maybe at a friend's house, I would have a beer or two. I didn't tell them the extent of my drinking and I didn't tell them about the other things, the pot and so forth. It was easy for them to believe me because it was convenient for them. They threatened me with loss of privileges and the use of my car, if I didn't obey the rules to not drink too much, and I was to pull my grades up. But somehow, I kept doing my thing and they continued doing theirs."

"I totaled my car. My best friend got a concussion and a broken arm. My grades fell to mediocre. It didn't seem to bother me. My parents threatened harsh punishment but they didn't do anything substantive. I was unable to get into a major college and decided to enter a smaller college. I was sure I could pull my grades up and transfer to a major college."

At Montevallo it was easier than ever to drink without my parents knowing it. Acid and PCP were abundant. I spent all of my money and most of my time chasing beer and drugs. I never even gave any thought to my grades, only to where I could find more Acid or alcohol. Finally my parents were exasperated. I was spending their money and failing most of my courses. I stayed high or drunk most of the time. They called Dr. Richard Ince who had seen me when I was in high school. Dr. Ince suggested that I had progressed beyond outpatient treatment. His recommendation was that they call The Brookwood Lodge and set-up an intervention. They had not previously heard of "intervention" but it sounded good to them. An intervention specialist came from the Lodge. I was unaware that anything was about to happen. I had only planned to be at home for one night. They actually woke me up the following morning. My parents were there, the counselor was there, my cousin and my best friend. They teamed up on me big time. I used every technique I knew, but they did everything but put me in a straight jacket. At any rate, that's how I got sent off to the Lodge. I told them it was all their fault, of course. They had neglected me, provided me with the money to buy all the drugs and alcohol. Besides, they drank also, so what was the big deal? It didn't work. I was gone."

Eileen was listening intently with her analytic mind. She collected information and connected it to her previous knowledge base. 'Every time I hear a story where parents are involved, it is always different. Yet, a common denominator nearly always points to the parents blaming the child and the child blaming the parents.' Projecting ideas ensued, 'Perhaps there is a message here for me and my family. Perhaps there is even a message for the public at large.' Ted's monologue recaptured her attention.

"After the family sessions I became very depressed. It was different. This time I felt hopeless and helpless. In my situation, I had lost control. I was locked up or at least if I ran away I might become lost in the woods, and who knows what was out there. I was unable to get to a fix with alcohol, coke, or marijuana; nothing was available. I felt that if life has to be this way I saw no point in it. I told a buddy that I was going to pretend to be a perfect patient and get out of this preachy place. I planned to commit suicide. I would try not to embarrass my parents. I would just have an accident. My buddy told me to just go get a bottle instead and drown my sorrows. We laughed about sharing a bottle as soon as we got out. I thought we were in tune with each other. That afternoon I was called to the counselor's office. There I learned my buddy had snitched on me."

"What's this business about getting out of here and committing suicide?" the counselor asked.

"You been talking to Wiley?"

"We have our sources."

"Well, Wiley and I were just horsing around. We were talking about getting out of here and drowning our sorrows in a bottle. Life wasn't worth it without a drink. If he wants to say that is suicidal he's just trying to get brownie points. You gonna believe what he says?"

"Tell you what, Ted, I'm going to believe what Wiley said. When you leave, there are two gentlemen outside the door. They will load you in a van and together ya'll are gonna take a little ride over to Brookwood Hospital and you will be admitted to the psychiatric unit. We don't take kindly to our patients committing suicide, it hurts our reputation, you know, not to mention your life."

"Well, just supposin' I don't want to go to this psychiatric unit?"

"Don't matter. You should go voluntarily, that way when you talk the doctor into lettin' you go, you'll be free. You can go involuntarily and that way you'll have a harder time talking your doctor into dismissing you because he will also have to convince the judge to drop his commitment order."

"Well you sons-of-bitches. You just got me trapped here, don't you? You can do anything you want with me. Whatever happened to life, liberty and the pursuit of happiness?"

"That's just it Ted, you are pursuing death not life. We are the ones pursuing life for you."

"What's life without liberty and happiness?" He then walked into the waiting arms of the two attendants.

Ted continued, "To my surprise, things at the hospital were friendlier after I got over my anger. I was told about depression and chemicals and placed on a treatment regimen including Sinequan, an antidepressant, which to my pleasant surprise made me sleep much better. I started to feel better after a few days. After about ten days I was feeling pretty good. I got out of the hospital and continued taking my medications. I was glad that I could get back to a few beers at night. Over the next two weeks I felt better every day. In fact, I felt so good I didn't need sleep for two, maybe three days. I was back to drinking lots of beer and doing coke but it was only because I wanted to, not because I needed to. I felt wonderful. In fact, I felt so confident of myself and my abilities that I planned to drive up to the University of Tennessee in Knoxville and talk to Coach Bill Battle about a scholarship to play football. If I couldn't get a scholarship I would just walk-on. When I told my parents of my plans they immediately wanted to know if I was "back on drugs." I felt so invincible that I confessed, 'Sure I'm taking a few drugs, but it's not like before, I don't need them now. I only take them because I like them.' My parents reminded me that I couldn't play football on drugs. 'No problem. I will stop when I get to school and practice starts.'"

"My parents insisted the problem was bigger than I thought and that I needed to immediately get off the drugs. Then, if I wanted to go play football it would be more reasonable. They insisted on seeing the counselor at the Lodge. I thought that since I hadn't been on them for long this time it would only take one or two days to get off them, and then I could go up to Knoxville. I agreed and they drove me out to the Lodge."

"I was admitted for detox. The next day when the counselor assessed me, he realized that I was hyper. He asked the psychologist, Dr. Jerry Anderson, to test me. Dr. Anderson recommended that I go back to Brookwood because I was likely Bipolar and that my chemicals were too high."

"First they tell me they are too low, now they tell me they are too high. Why don't ya'll make up your mind?"

"Voluntarily this time, I agreed to head back to Brookwood. When the psychiatrist interviewed me he told me that the pattern was now complete and the diagnosis was upgraded to Bipolar Affective Disorder and that I was in a manic state. I was treated with Thorazine and Lithium and was taken off my Sinequan. After stabilization, I was discharged and told that I should come and be part of this group. So, that's my story and why I am here."

To Eileen, it was as if she had just been threatened by a preview of what could be awaiting her cousin Thomas, or even herself. Eileen silently thanked God that she had never had a problem with drugs and alcohol. But her worry about her cousin Thomas only intensified.

Gerald was wishing the Medical Director was in attendance. He had heard him discuss on several occasions that alcohol frequently masked the disorder of Bipolar. As he was contemplating what to say, Lillian spoke up, "Ted, we are so glad you came. Your story is not unusual though it may seem so to you. Bipolar is an inherited disorder as you probably know by now. It affects our moods. We are often quicker to be moody and turn to unprescribed drugs, alcohol or chemicals before we learn what our true disorder is and how to properly treat it. Unfortunately, many of the street drugs such as alcohol, coke, and marijuana are addictive and seduce us into further problems rather than help. They give us a false sense of happiness. The temporary relief deludes us into believing that what we are doing is okay. Alcohol is often our tranquilizer or sedative to help us sleep when we are depressed or hyper. When it is used frequently or for very long, most people will become dependent on it and many will be addicted to it. It is an addictive substance. The body becomes dependent. The mind becomes addicted."

"As one becomes consumed by addiction, they become more visible to friends, family and others. Frequently, the underlying Bipolar is obscured, if not invisible. The addiction gets the attention. It's understandable but the underlying mood disorder, the Bipolar problem is often missed until we are detoxed from the chemicals. Often, we then have an overt manic or depressive episode."

"So, don't feel singled out, Ted. You have gone the route of many before you. You are lucky to find this out so young in life. You now have a chance to learn about your entire self, your Bipolar Disorder, and your drug and chemical dependency. Treat them both with equal respect. Both can seduce you. The penalty of ignoring either can be as bad as death or an entire life of discord, unhappiness, unfulfillment, disconnectedness, depravity, and becoming bankrupt financially, emotionally, socially, and spiritually."

"Just one more thing and I'll be quiet. Parents can be warm and nurturing, in fact, many are. Others may also be lousy and unnurturing. In fact, too many are. But in the final analysis it's up to us, the individual, to mature, become an adult and direct our own destiny."

Spontaneously, a soft round of applause arose for Lillian. It was her first time to take the floor in a teaching role. One could safely surmise why she knew so much on this aspect of Bipolar illness.

Eileen was alert to this new information. Somehow, it seemed personally important hearing one member of the circle tell another. This was compelling rather than boring. Once again, her mind raced beyond the group into the public at large. 'We have to come out of the dark recesses. We must stand in the light. We have a duty to take this knowledge and understanding to our silent constituency, the unsigned members. When we learn about ourselves, take charge of our fate, organize and promote our cause, we will have a chance. We need understanding from our family, friends, employers, insurers, and the government. As it is, no one treats us as equals. We must become more assertive for our needs. We are in a battle. Battles inflict damage. Everyone loses. The winner is only the one who suffers least. We need a strategy to avoid and prevent conflict. We need to gain respect, promote research, find better treatments, and educate everyone.'

She had no immediate idea as to how this should be accomplished, but the idea was being neatly assimilated into her repertoire of knowledge for future reference. Maybe Rogene Paris would have some helpful thoughts; Eileen had been very impressed with her at the Alliance of the Mentally Ill (AMI) meeting.

Freddie spoke up, "Hey, everybody, we been buying the wrong cookies. Its Ted's family that makes the Waterman cookies." He was alluding to the local "Butterman Cookies" that were part of today's refreshments. Everyone in Birmingham knew of the Waterman and Butterman rivalry through their advertisements pitted against each other much like Pepsi and Coca-Cola ads.

Eileen spoke up, "Great information, Freddie. Waterman Bakeries are known everywhere for great cakes, cookies and pastries. Maybe Ted can get us a tour of the factory with samples."

Eileen wanted to personally meet Ted. Though he was younger than she, it was likely that their parents knew each other and they possibly have other things in common. When the meeting ended she maneuvered closer to him. She took the opportunity to speak with Freddie and to check on the health and status of Alma and the kids. She was delighted to hear they were doing well. She always enjoyed seeing Freddie. He never failed to give her a broad, genuine smile. He truly liked and appreciated Eileen, which she knew, felt and reciprocated.

Eileen's brief conversation with Ted failed to uncover any family ties. Usually in Birmingham you could find mutual ties within a few short minutes. She guessed, 'Surely, later we will discover some mutual link one way or another.'

Gerald thanked everyone for coming as he collected unused plates and cups signaling that participants should begin leaving. Gerald was visibly upbeat following what he perceived to be a productive meeting.

Chapter 23
Not the Same Person

Eileen learned more than she had bargained for or even wanted to know by attending the support group and the aftercare program. These were horrid stories. She abhorred thinking that her life could be like those. It troubled her that some of the members had been bright and well-educated. Her assumption that her intellect and education would be a safe buffer, had been decimated. Over the next few days she began feeling anergic. Where had her energy gone? Also, she had difficulty falling asleep. She worried about herself, her illness, her future, her ability. Even whether God had forsaken her. She awoke early feeling unrested. She felt completely exhausted. Mornings were unbearable. The blinds remained closed. The phone and doorbell were frequently unanswered. Her Moon City project languished, unattended. Her grooming deteriorated and irritableness replaced usual cheerfulness. She incorrectly reasoned that the Lithium had brought her too far down from the high, so it seemed reasonable to discontinue it. She decided not to call Dr. Lavoy. She increased her Sinequan without telling him. She planned to discuss it with him on her next visit. She let her housework go.

Eileen had not realized that this was the week that Robert Dupree would be coming to Birmingham with Senator Johnson. The Senator had an important event that required his presence. They both would use the opportunity to stay in Alabama for a few days. The Senator would rekindle some ties while there. It was a perfect opportunity for Robert because he wanted to be with Eileen again.

Dupree phoned Eileen on Thursday morning. She answered after the eighth ring. Initially, he surmised that he had dialed the wrong number because her voice was so slow, low and different.

"Is that you, Eileen?"

"Yes, who is speaking?

"This is Robert. Robert Dupree."

"Oh, Robert how are you? What's up?"

"I'm in Birmingham with Senator Johnson. We have some business to attend. I was hoping I could see you."

"Oh, Robert I'd love to see you, but I must be sick. I feel so bad."

"Do you have a cold, the flu, pneumonia, what's wrong?"

"Oh, I don't know. I just feel so, so empty and hopeless. I can't get anything done. I can't get organized."

"You can't get organized? There *is* something wrong with you. I'm coming over."

"I'm not dressed. My house is a mess."

"You're my girl. I'm coming over."

Dupree's mind scanned all the scenarios he could dream up as to what might be wrong with Eileen. He had never heard her sound so down, pitiful in fact. It was nearly lunchtime so he picked up lunch on the way. He would get to the bottom of this and find out what was wrong with her.

Eileen lay in the bed another half-hour dreading to see anyone, or to have any conversation. She couldn't even think. She caught a glimpse of the clock. She was startled to see that it was eleven fifteen a.m. 'Oh, my God, he may be on D.C. time.' She forced herself out of bed, pulled on slacks and a blouse, and freshened up.

Although devoid of excitement, her manners pushed her unwilling body to answer Robert's first ring of the doorbell. Eileen opened the door and greeted him with affected pleasure. "Hi Robert! Come on in." With some last minute energy she had managed to apply her make-up.

Dupree had prepared himself to be greeted by, as he thought, 'Not the same woman.' He even planned to keep a poker face. To his delight, she looked quite well. She had presented herself much better than she had sounded. He noticed that she had lost some weight, a few pounds maybe. She was moving less fluidly than he remembered. 'Where was her fire?' He leaned to kiss her but her face did not tilt up for him, as if there were no energy or interest. He kissed her forehead.

Robert had decided to surprise her with lunch. He brought one Burger King hamburger and one cheeseburger. Also, fries, one cola and one vanilla shake. He suggested they eat while it was still warm. She chose the burger without cheese and the soft drink.

Dupree was puzzled at the change in her. It was necessary for him to initiate all conversation. He wanted to ask, but didn't, 'Where has all your spunk gone?' Instead, he gently asked if she knew what her problem was. When she denied having a problem, he wanted to know if she had seen a doctor. On learning the answer was yes, his curiosity pushed him further, "Are you taking medicine?"

"Yes."

"What kind? Maybe you should go back to the doctor and get your medicine changed."

Eileen answered, "Perhaps." But she thought to herself, 'It's the medication that's the problem. After all, I've left off the Lithium and my energy might be rising.' She assured Robert that she would revisit the doctor if she was not okay in a couple of days. She offered the universal excuse, "It's probably just PMS."

Dupree, determined to revitalize Eileen, decided to shift the topic of conversation to her favorite subject, Moon City. He asked enough questions to sound legitimate, such as, "How long, realistically, would it take to develop a shuttle bus to the moon? Was she sure that it would be affordable enough to make it a feasible project? Had she fine-tuned the projections well enough to know how many passengers would be allowed on each trip?" Even in her dulled state she recognized the importance of the next question. Robert had set her up and she felt all his other questions were merely a prelude to this last one. It told her that he was genuine and the Senator indeed had an interest. "Since you are asking for government cooperation and assistance, would there be complimentary seats for government personnel and would there be age limits for the travelers?" That indicated the senator wanted a ride.

Eileen could not answer questions such as this without Board approval so she did the best she could. "I believe the Board would have an interest in working out some type of arrangement early on in the project. It likely will hinge on how much it would cost. Do you think the Senator is ready for another meeting?"

"I do believe we are getting closer. I'll work on it." He thought he saw some spark beginning to rekindle. "I love it when your eyes sparkle," Dupree told her.

"So do I," adding, "You're a help."

"My pleasure" Dupree told her, "I have a totally ulterior motive you know, hope you don't mind."

With a hint of a twinkle, she told him, "Not at all." She was even surprised at herself by the sincerity of her comment. Was she ready to "wake up?" Was she coming out of her dull cocoon? Could she be the beautiful, colorful butterfly again?

Dupree told her that he and the Senator were going to a fund raising event in Montgomery that night.

Eileen did not take her medicine all day that day except for doubling up on the antidepressant during the morning she assumed that it was perhaps because of leaving off the Lithium that her energy was returning. She would continue to leave it off tonight and see how she felt tomorrow.

Chapter 25
New Moon

Eileen had trouble sleeping again that night. Her mind raced in every direction, concerned about everything, including wondering if tomorrow would afford her some new energy to get back to her beloved project. How different from last night when every thought was pessimistic and foreboding. She dropped off to sleep around three-thirty in the morning.

At six a.m. Eileen bolted awake. Her arms and legs were alive again. Her mind was reaching out into the day, organizing the morning, prioritizing the afternoon, and anticipating Dupree's call. For dinner, she would suggest Michael's Steakhouse with supposedly the best steak and potato in Alabama. Dupree would appreciate the sports memorabilia plastering all the walls. 'You can't leave Birmingham without saying you have eaten at Michael's.'

Eileen, The Exuberant, was back as if she had never been gone. Her mind gave no thought of yesterday. Just as the dark moon gives way to the new moon, glitter and promise were shining through. The full moon was coming; she could feel it. She was enthralled with the spirit of adventure. She rescued her work papers from the coffee table where she had hastily placed them to give the appearance that she had been working on the project. When she spread them on her desk she was appalled at the disarray and began sorting and organizing them. This evolved into her becoming absorbed in her project. She was adding thoughts of new designs and new schemes to an already expansive Moon City project of monumental proportion. In her heightened state of energy and grandiosity she dreamed and counted them all as probable, scarcely even considering them as merely possible.

By mid-afternoon Eileen's energy level had reached full throttle. In her mind she had explored the moon's surface and added to the design of Moon City. It now boasted a fitness center complete with the design in mind necessary to compensate for the much lower gravity. She wanted to add a swimming pool but lacked the technical knowledge to consider it. She made a note to discuss it with the space engineers. She added a media center complete with a movie theater.

'I have to make sure that tonight Robert promises to deliver Senator Johnson's support.' She changed the bed adorning it with her special occasion linen. She rubbed her hand across it feeling its silkiness and smiled. She left it turned down. The message was as apparent as an open invitation.

Dupree rang her doorbell half an hour before their dinner reservations. He saw two sparkling eyes and a beaming smile. "That's my girl" he said, "Welcome back." He drew from behind him a dozen red roses. It was obvious that he hoped the relationship would flourish. Eileen could not fully read his thinking. 'If I could settle down with her I would be ecstatic,' he thought.

Eileen was impressed. 'Another dozen roses in so short a time.' She opened the card.

"I've missed you a lot,
but a poem I have not."
Love,
Bob

Robert's romantic style was sublimely effective; until now she had Dupree comfortably niched as part and parcel of her grandiose scheme. Personal feelings could endanger the project. She was in fact, taking him for granted through intention and thought, but her heart was out muscling her brain and warming to his clever solicitations.

Dupree did not think or feel like he was being taken for granted. In fact, he now felt he had resumed his rightful leadership role. 'I pulled her out of her funk. I made her whole again.' Typical man, he was planning far into the evening, but so was Eileen.

Eileen had taken the roses to the kitchen where she diagonally cut the stems, placing them in a vase. To his amazement, she then poured a third of a can of 7-up into the water.

Dupree asked "What's that for?"

"It will help keep the stems from sealing so that they will absorb the water for a longer period of time," she explained.

"What else do you know?" asked Dupree.

Eileen said, "I know it is time for our reservation; we better be going."

"We are going to Michael's. You're in for a real treat."

Dupree rebelled, "Treat hell, I'm treating you tonight. You're my date."

"I wasn't offering to pick up the tab; I meant you are in for a real meal treat."

"I am trying to hold on to some control in this relationship."

The comment was a revelation to Eileen. She had been inadvertently insensitive to his needs. 'What an idiot. I must remember these male egos, especially his. I could win him over and then lose him by beating him at a chess game. I can play this game,' she said to herself. 'I must be careful.'

Michael's was an unassuming corner building on Twentieth Street, diagonal across from the University of Alabama Medical Center. When they walked in the door the thick aroma of good food being prepared was the first impression. Steaks must be cooking. It would only get better from there. A gray-haired, seasoned hostess matter of factly escorted them through two rooms where two rows of booths hugged the walls. They were seated at a big wooden table that separated them. After a few minutes, a waitress, appearing to be roughly the same vintage as the establishment decor, greeted them. She likely was one of the originals, working there since the opening of the restaurant. She had long since lost her figure, perhaps from eating here too often. There was no attempt at charm, just efficiency. For her good service she would expect the customary fifteen percent reward.

When Dupree saw the menu he encouraged his appetite to think big. Eileen ordered a petite filet mignon, medium. Dupree ordered the house specialty, the man-sized steer butt steak and a baked potato, "Load it with everything," he instructed.

Eileen thought, 'He doesn't know what he is in for, watching this should be fun.' First came a basket of rolls, white ones plus gooey succulent cinnamon ones. Dupree couldn't wait. He quickly sampled a cinnamon roll. "Divine," he said, "These are great." Next came their house salads, scrumptious in taste and full sized. Dupree protested unconvincingly, "But we didn't order these."

Eileen was laughing inside 'I knew he would love this place.' "It's a Michael's thing," she said. She ate a third of a white roll and half her salad. Dupree finished his second sweet roll and one white roll and all of his salad.

Much to Eileen's surprise when the huge steak and potato came, Dupree joyfully devoured all of each. She worked diligently consuming less than half of hers. He had eaten unashamedly with the passion of new discovery. He finished with an unmistakable radiance of saity and contentment.

When they returned to her apartment, Eileen remembered that he needed to feel in control but she nevertheless, needed to get the Senator's promise out of him tonight. She felt that the best time to do that would be during the anticipation phase of the evening. She decided to flatter him and play to his needs. "Robert, you are such a dear. You've come and pulled me up out of a dark hole. You brought me roses, and you made me feel special and wonderful. How can I repay you?" As Robert started to open his mouth, she looked at him and interrupted, "Don't say it. Don't even think it." They both laughed.

Eileen wasn't through with her cunning yet, "Tell you what dear, I need your help with a little something. I'm willing to play double or nothing?"

"Now you're talking," said Dupree. "Gambler extraordinaire, that's me. I can open jars, change light bulbs, park cars, what's your problem; I'm ready."

Eileen said, "Oh, nothing like that. It's just with this Senator thing, several of my potential investors know that I went to see the Senator and they are anxious to know what he is going to do. I shouldn't have mentioned going to see him, but I felt so sure that he would like my proposal. Anyway, I've learned my lesson, but do you think you could get him to say something positive? Perhaps he could take a look at my latest drawings. When you asked me those questions, I realized the Senator wants to have a ride to the moon also. Maybe we could name a seat after him."

Dupree sat beside her on the sofa. She waited to show her new drawings to him. He put his hand on hers and said, “Eileen, honey, let me tell you about politicians. They will say plenty about how proud they are of you *after* you accomplish the fact. He is not going to make a public statement for a project that's still in its infancy.”

Eileen sounding crushed, “Then I'm doomed with the 'Tuscaloosa Trio' and the 'Decatur Duo.' I was counting on about five million from them plus an in-road to their friends in other states.”

“Well, hold on,” Robert pitched his voice up. “We don't have to be Senators to have a few tricks. Let me teach you one. First of all, the Senator genuinely is fond of you. Second, he likes your project. He thinks it's a natural coming from an Alabamian, with Huntsville Space Center being here. Third, I'm sure he would very much like to have a trip to the moon, but he is realistic enough to know that his age may preclude him from the trip; so, here's what I propose we do. “

“What's that? Let's hear it!”

“You should have the most influential person from the 'Trio' and the Duo to call me at the Senator's Washington office. I will sell the two of them and they will sell the others. Here's how I propose to do it. I will tell them how excited the Senator is about the project and that he is sure you are the one to get it done. He's personally met you and been fully briefed. He likes the project. He thinks it is workable and he is going to quietly work behind the scenes to help get the government's cooperation. The Senator hopes to be on the first bus. However, at this time he thinks it would be more harmful than helpful if he's publicly pushing it. He is afraid they will accuse him of pork barreling a pretty face so he is letting me do all the work for him.”

Eileen’s gaze was fixed on him as he explained his plan. Eileen speculated “I think it will work. I believe they will go for it. We’ll do it, set up a time for them to call so that you will be in the office.”

Dupree draped his arm around her, and pulling her close he asked, “Does that sound like a double?”

Without missing a beat, Eileen said, “Sure does.” Gentle kissing commenced, igniting stored passion. Before long he carried her to the bedroom. When he stepped through the door and saw the bed adorned and turned down invitingly, he almost dropped her. Thoughts ran through his head. 'Was she ahead of him again? Has she taken control?' Her arms were around his neck and pulled him down for another kiss. His doubts melted as they glided into the bed. They enjoyed each other deep into the night.

Chapter 25
Surprise Betrayal

Eileen awoke disoriented with the telephone ringing. She answered, "Hello" while still looking to see the time, nine-thirty a.m.

"This is Cynthia, Miss Robbins, from the office, you know."

"Of course Cynthia, how are you?"

"Oh, I'm fine, but we need to talk. You've always treated me so nice. I don't like some of what I am hearing and I just think you ought to know."

"What on earth are you talking about Cynthia?"

"I can't say anymore on the phone." Sounding secretive, she continued, "We could meet for lunch. I've got thirty minutes, but if we go between twelve and one p.m. ten more minutes won't be noticed."

Eileen stated, "That's fine." They agreed to meet at Brittlings.

They met at a quarter past twelve. As they were nearing the end of the cafeteria line Eileen noticed Horace approaching with his famous smile.

"How are you, Miss Robbins?" Horace inquired, surprising her by remembering her name. "I'll get you a place up front. I will be back to get your tray in just a moment." He came back and related that he had just cleaned a booth up front. Eileen and Cynthia found their booth, glad for the privacy it afforded.

Eileen began, "It's good to see you. You look great but don't be so nervous. What is this all about?"

Cynthia was anxious and didn't try to hide it, "Oh, Miss Robbins, I feel like such a heel. I'm in the middle of this awful situation, but I just couldn't be quiet. You have to know."

"Know what, Cynthia?"

"You know I have been with LRS for nine years. I know everything about that firm. I type all of the important letters and all of Mr. Levine's legal opinions. I know how they think."

Horace was approaching the table with one tray. He gently sat it down on the empty table close-by and piece by piece placed everything in front of them, getting everything right for each of them. Then came his signature question, "What else can I get for you, ma'am'?" Eileen answered, "That will be all, Horace. Thank you, very much," as she placed a tip in his hand. "Thank you ma'am'. Have a nice day," Horace then left them to their meal.

Eileen observed out loud, "It's beginning to sound as if maybe I should be the one who is nervous."

Cynthia volunteered, "Miss Robbins, you have been the most exciting thing that's happened to our firm since I've been there. You're like, alive. You're nice. You work hard. You treat everyone so well. I like you. If you ever go out on your own, I hope you will consider taking me with you."

"Why would I want to go out on my own, Cynthia?"

"Well, I mean if they didn't treat you right or something."

"What are you leading up to Cynthia?"

"It's just, I overheard Mr. Skinner and Mr. Estis. Mr. Skinner sounded so negative. He sees everybody's faults, but you'll never hear him giving any praise."

"Is he finding fault with me?"

"Yes, ma'am. Of course, but others are also, oh ma'am, this is so hard to say. He told Mr. Levine you had been in a mental hospital and that kind of information was going to leak out and ruin the firm's reputation. He said it would cause a mass exodus of clients if they knew that. He was recommending that the Board take some type of action."

Eileen became incredulous, "How could Skinner say such a thing? I had some tests done and he is making a big deal of it."

"Mr. Skinner's neighbor's mother was a patient there and she told her son and he told Mr. Skinner."

"Oh, my God!" Eileen said out loud. Her mind was racing. 'That's all supposed to be confidential. This has to be illegal. It's illegal for them to use that kind of information. They aren't supposed to know this. What happened to all those assurances? Cynthia isn't supposed to know this. This is devastating.' She realized that Cynthia was reading her stunned silence.

"Listen, Cynthia. You're not to say a word about this to anyone. Do you understand? I'll have to think about what to do. I'll let you know, and yes, if I go out on my own I hope you will come with me. Don't breathe a word of this to anyone, please."

Back at her apartment, she alternately paced the floor or sat at the desk tapping it with her pen. She struggled to figure out what to do. She had been betrayed. 'That snitch at the hospital had no right. LRS has no right. They didn't like a woman coming in there anyway. This was just their excuse.' She had to think this through very clearly. What did she remember about her conversation with Cynthia? Skinner got his information from a neighbor. That's only hearsay. Cynthia was positive that Skinner, Levine nor Estis had known that she had overheard their conversation. She knew that Levine had become sympathetic to Skinner's cause. Eileen needed an ally. Who could it be? Who was strong enough to give her the support she would need to fight a powerful firm like LRS, if there was to be a fight? She decided to sleep on it. She was glad that Robert had left for Washington on the morning flight.

When Eileen awoke the next morning, her familiar energy surge remained with her. She would need it to face the matters at hand. She considered Cynthia. 'What a brave lady to risk her job to give me bad news. On the other hand, they don't know she came, so she hasn't risked anything. If the firm has problems, she has a possible out with my new firm. Smart lady and on my side too, I like that.'

'Who can be my ally? Who do I trust enough to open up to? I have no choice. It has to be Broadman.'

Eileen was concerned that the pressure of this threat and of having to discuss it with Mr. Broadman could trigger an untimely episode. She reluctantly restarted her Lithium.

Eileen called Broadman: "Mr. Broadman, sir, something has come up and I need some serious advice. Would you mind letting me bounce something off your experience?"

Broadman sensed that she didn't want to say what it was over the phone. He wondered, 'is there some mistake in my trust work? Was there a problem with our Moon City project that I and my friends are heavily invested in? Or, perhaps, was she seeing the light and wanting to get out of that stodgy old firm she was in. At any rate, the sooner the better. This time I'll take her to The Club.' There, high atop Red Mountain, they could have a delicious and leisurely lunch and overlook the city of Birmingham which now solidly filled the former Jones Valley. Not bad for a city only 100 years old.

The maitre d' showed them to an elevated window table with an excellent view. He had barely turned away when Broadman took the lead, "I come to this place to enjoy beautiful people and to share good news. I know I'm right on the first count. I hope I'm right on the second count." Eileen said, "Oh, it's nothing like that Mr. Broadman. It's just you and I make such a good pair. We do such good work together. I want you to know more about me. Nothing bad you understand. I just think if you know me, you can be more comfortable with me, and I might need your help. I don't know yet, but the more you know about me, the more comfortable I will be in asking for help if I need it."

"You're not in any legal trouble are you?"

"Of course not. It's some of the people at the firm. They are jealous of me. I think some of them would like to see me go."

Broadman sensed the lack of her usual confidence and decided she was going to need some soothing and encouraging. "Well, that's just human nature. The one out front is shot at first and most often but don't you worry your pretty head; you're smarter than the whole bunch of them. You can dodge anything they can throw at you, and hell, if you can't, I'm indebted to you more than I can ever repay you. Together, there's nothing we can't beat. Now, why don't you tell me the details and let's work out a little plan, okay?" Broadman had been suspicious that there was more to her time off than what Betty had told him about her needing a few weeks to work on her project. It didn't fit because she had now been out over three weeks and she had not contacted him or any of the other investors regarding the project. He had frankly begun to wonder why the let down! He had gotten used to her action-packed, fast-paced, take-charge manner. Broadman continued, "Just why do you think they might want to see you out of there? Do you have anything specific?"

Eileen was trying to figure out the best way to proceed. She didn't want to say more than she absolutely had to, but she had to say enough for him believe her, and be in her corner. Her calculations were keeping her silent, and his questions were going unanswered.

Broadman wanted to know, “Is one of the partners after you?”

Eileen thought, 'How perceptive and he has opened the door. I can be honest about who is after me.' She revealed, “I have it on good authority by one of the staff that trusts and likes me. Cynthia tells me that Mr. Skinner told Mr. Levine that I'm nutso or something like that.”

Broadman's face became crimson. Eileen read this as a sign of how emotional he was about her. It meant he liked her more than she might have guessed.

Broadman, surprised her with his forceful cursing, “Well, that little son of a bitch. We belong to the same country club. I’ve seen him cheat at golf. He also talks about people. He’s a back stabber and it’s not right; especially to someone as deserving as you. Miserable ingrate, that's what he is.”

Eileen was emboldened by the fierceness of Broadman's defense for her. Her guard dropped, so she revealed more than she had planned.

“Yes sir,” she said, acceding to his power position. “You see, back in nineteen sixty-five when my brother took his life, it put a cloud over our family. Some people try to take advantage of that. I've never had any problems. In fact, if anybody wants to live life to the max, it's me. I've worked hard and earned everything I've gotten. I don't think people like Mr. Skinner work hard or study hard. They take up space on the ships of life chartered by the rest of us. They complain when they are not treated royally. Anyway, he told Mr. Levine that I was in the nut ward and that it would cause an embarrassment to the firm and they should get rid of me before that happens. They would concoct some sort of plot to entice the clients into staying with them. I could have been out on my ear before I knew what happened, except my friend Cynthia came and told me all about it. They are unaware that she heard them talking; more like plotting my ouster.”

“Good. That'll make our job easier. We don't have to worry about protecting her, but we will if we need to.”

“What are we going to do?”

“Don't know yet. Tell me the rest of it. Is it true? Were you in a nut ward?”

Now, Eileen's face became red. She felt herself blushing and knew he wouldn't miss it.

Broadman noticed it, but didn't let on. His natural lie detection sensors were now on full alert.

Eileen was fully aware that everything she said must be believable or all hope with him would be lost. She started, "Well sort of, not really. Well, it's like this."

"One of the people that is helping us with the Moon City project is Dr. Griffiths. He is a very fine man. He is also trained in counseling and while we were working on the project he commented that he thought my energy level was too high. In fact, he thought that if I continued at that level, you know, working so hard without enough sleep that I might become exhausted. He persuaded me to see a medical doctor friend of his that specializes in chemical problems. He would be able to check out all of my chemistry. So, yes, I checked in, really not realizing that it was on the psychiatry unit. He told me I was not nuts or crazy, but he did say my chemicals were too high and he has balanced them. I'm fine now."

"Well, you certainly seem fine to me except maybe you're a little worried about this LRS thing, but we will be taking care of that."

"My job means a lot to me. I can't believe they would try to take it away from me. Where's their gratitude?"

"They can't even spell gratitude, let alone show it. I knew that the first day I met them. How did they find out about your hospital stay? Did you tell them?"

"Of course not. It was all supposed to be confidential. I was told no one would know."

"So, how did they find out?"

"Simple enough, Skinner's neighbor's mother was there with depression. She told her son who told Skinner. Skinner has blown it all out of proportion."

Mr. Broadman's wheels were spinning rapidly now. 'So there was at least enough in the story for Skinner to make something out of it; so I'll need to know for a fact that she is not going to go nuts before I stick my neck out too far. She is already my accountant. I have invested a million dollars in her Moon City plan and now I am about to go to battle with one of the most respected firms in Birmingham. I would be a fool to get into a shouting match with someone as smart and experienced as Levine without knowing the facts. I may not have them all at this point, so I have to know for sure.' "Eileen, listen to me, you have worked hard, they can't do this to you. The way we win, is to be completely prepared. Here's what we will do. You set up a meeting with you, me and your doctor. He will prepare us with the words and knowledge we need. We don't know how much they know. We have to assume they know a lot. We've got to know enough to neutralize anything they have to say. Don't you worry. I've got a plan. We'll slaughter their asses."

Eileen should be reassured, and she was; but yet she remained anxious. 'Why did he want to meet with Dr. Lavoy? Will he probe and find out that I am Bipolar? Would Broadman hear, manic depressive; then turn and run? Would that be the last of my best support? But what choice do I have, I opened the door; he walked in and backed me in a corner. Now I might lose my job and my Moon City project.'

Eileen asked Dr. Lavoy about a joint meeting. He suggested that as an alternative perhaps it might be preferable for him to prepare a short explanatory letter. She agreed and wished that would work, but she knew that would not suffice for Mr. Broadman.

Understanding the urgency Dr. Lavoy scheduled the meeting for ten a.m. two days later.

Mr. Broadman and Eileen were on time for their meeting with Lavoy. Eileen knew from her private call to Dr. Lavoy that he would handle the discussion with Broadman as gently as feasible.

Broadman, ever the take charge person, spoke first, "Hello, Dr. Lavoy. I'm John Broadman. It's kind of you to make time for us, but Miss Robbins and I are in a predicament. It seems a fellow patient has broken confidentiality and told her family about Eileen's hospitalization. It has gotten to her employer and they are claiming that she is nuts and needs to be discharged. I want to help her but I'm in the dark, and that's why we are here. We need your help. If we go in there without knowing the lingo and what information they've acquired we will be at a tremendous disadvantage. I am going to help her through this but we need to be fully prepared."

"I quite understand."

"Hopefully we won't bother you for too much of your time, but just tell me, if you will, about this chemical imbalance that Miss Robbins has. Did it make her, well, crazy? Why was she on the psychiatric unit? Was she in any danger to herself or anyone else? Was she out of control with her judgment? Well, you know the things I need to know."

"Yes, I think I do," Lavoy replied.

"No, she was never a danger to herself or to anyone else. She was not crazy. So far, her judgment has been good. She had an episode of excess chemicals, as we say. This made her have excess energy. To the rest of us she would seem hyper. We would have difficulty keeping up with her. Her mind and her thought process did become expansive, creative, imaginative. Perhaps she was even slightly grandiose in her beliefs and discussions with her employer. But, all in all, she has stuck to facts as she understands them and has always worked with someone to help keep her on a balanced path. For example, she sought out Dr. Griffiths and he has worked with her in that capacity. In fact, he is the reason she came to the psychiatric unit. With her chemicals being high she needed to be checked out. We do that best on the psychiatric unit."

"On the unit, the person is able to be up, active, and interactive learning about themselves, their chemistry, their coping techniques and things of that nature. Eileen, while not believing that she needed any of that, nevertheless, applied herself diligently and has learned the appropriate information to help her deal effectively with her chemical imbalance. We use medication for balancing, and the education helps her to avoid the things that might precipitate the imbalance."

"Should I know what those things are? I have a pretty good investment in this young lady's project."

"Miss Robbins has given me permission to be fully open with you, so the answer to your question is yes. She should not consume excess alcohol, preferably none. She should not excessively use stimulants such as coffee, tea or stimulant medication. She should be mindful of using steroids. She should be cautious to get plenty of rest. Lack of sleep can trigger episodes but the reverse is also true. She should monitor her stress levels, both the good and the bad. If she is feeling overly stressed she should modify something. These are the things that can precipitate an episode of either a high or low mood."

"Doctor, you are mentioning mood, that calls to mind manic

depressive? Are we talking about manic depressive here?"

"We certainly don't prefer that term Mr. Broadman. We use the current nomenclature of Bipolar Affective Disorder, which means, it is a mood disorder that swings to both poles, alternating highs and lows. Fortunately, we have very good treatment for Bipolar. Research is ongoing and new treatment is imminent. We are very fortunate today. In the old days, yes, it was called Manic Depressive Illness and it was essentially untreatable because we had not discovered the medicine that would affect a treatment response. Nowadays with maintenance medication such as Lithium we don't have near the mood swings we had in the past, either in frequency or intensity."

Dr. Lavoy added, "You should probably also know this is an inherited illness. Inherited in the same manner as diabetes and other inheritable illnesses. Only about twenty-five percent of the offspring of an affected person will inherit the illness. When treated, we don't expect the illness to progress but rather to stabilize. The affected person should be able to have a very normal life. We ask that they monitor themselves for mood swings and if they notice a mood swing higher or lower than comfortable they should contact us. It is important for you to know this because close friends can be part of the monitoring network. You might, for example, notice that she is high or low prior to it registering with her. If that happens, you should simply mention it to her. She should trust you and contact me. That essentially is what you would need to know to be able to discuss her case with anyone at her employment."

Eileen was relieved the session had gone so quickly and innocuously.

Broadman was reassured. He felt more confident to proceed in setting up the meeting with LRS.

'Broadman is a wonderful man. I'm so lucky to have him and Robert there for me.' Eileen called Robert and they nurtured each other for nearly an hour scarcely giving a thought that the connection was long distance. She elected to withhold this news from him for now.

Chapter 26
Showdown

Eileen thought Broadman's plan was bold, but it was typical Broadman and she trusted him implicitly. It was nearing the end of her thirty days leave. Cynthia had not been able to get full information on what Eileen should expect but she was positive they had something dreadful planned for her, maybe even termination.

Eileen tried to set her meeting with Levine for Thursday. However, he insisted that it be Friday at four p.m. Eileen and Broadman both were familiar with the management strategy of setting bad news meetings for late on Friday. Hatchet men always seemed to believe that anger, hurt and vengeance would be diluted over a long weekend.

Broadman assured Eileen that she should not worry. LRS was in for a big surprise.

When Eileen arrived at LRS. She was prompt at one minute until four p.m. Betty seemed pleasant enough. Eileen told her that she was there to see Mr. Levine. Betty dialed Levine to announce Eileen's arrival and was told to "Have Eileen come on back to his office and, oh, by the way, since things were pretty slow it would be okay for her to leave early as soon as she got things tidied up a bit."

"Oh, thank you Mr. Levine," Betty said. Eileen wondered 'what Levine could possibly have said that would get a thank you from Betty' but she dismissed it and nervously proceeded to Levine's office. The door was open.

Levine was smiling, "Hello, Eileen. Come on in. Good to see you.

How have you been?"

"Fine, sir. Hope you are doing well," trying not to show any suspicions, she spoke amicably to Mr. Skinner and Mr. Randall who flanked Levine.

Obviously Mr. Levine was in charge and leading the conversation. "Won't you have a seat, Miss Robbins?" he said, signaling that the informality was finished and business had begun. "You have now been with LRS nearly three years. We feel we have helped your career immensely. The opportunity we have given you here has been unparalleled in this city and you have made good advantage of it. It has been good for you and for us. We think that in the future though it might be better for you, and for us, if you went out on your own. Of course, we would help you get started if you stay here in Birmingham, but we thought you might want to, uh, move on up, maybe to one of the big eight firms. We could get you in a firm over in Atlanta. We wouldn't have to tell anyone over there about your Moon City project and how you let your position of influence in the firm get big name investors to put their money into your dream. You know that was wrong, Miss Robbins, no matter what you say."

Eileen bit her tongue. She desperately wanted to interrupt their diatribe, but her instructions were to not say a word. She should listen first to everything they had to say. Mr. Broadman and his friend would also be listening. Her purse had been outfitted with the best electronic listening device available. They were in the parking lot waiting for the right moment to enter.

"Oh, I forgot to mention," Mr. Levine continued, "Mr. Spellman is having an amended federal tax return filed. Seems you made a little error in preparing his report. Fortunately, Mr. Skinner went over your work and found the error, so Mr. Spellman won't be embarrassed by having the IRS find an error in his return."

"Also, there is one other matter. We are aware that you have a chemical imbalance that disturbs you and others in your family. For your own good, you don't need to be in a high stress situation such as we have here at LRS. We wouldn't want to feel responsible for bringing on any unhealthy imbalance."

Eileen was sure that she saw a subliminal smirk on Skinner's face. Randall appeared quite uncomfortable with his jaws clenched tight.

"Now we want this whole thing to be amicable and we want to treat you right. We are prepared to give you a thirty-day separation time. Of course, you won't have to be here to do any work; and if you relocate to Atlanta, or somewhere outside of Alabama, we'll throw in a ten thousand dollar relocation fee."

Levine was pleasantly surprised at how much better this was going than he had anticipated. Having expected her to "throw a fit" he surmised they must have her 'dead to right.'

Randall thought, 'something is wrong here.' He wondered if she had a pistol inside her purse. He was uneasy. He hadn't been for this, but was outvoted and forced to be a witness and thereby appear as if he were part of it. Everyone knew that he and Eileen had been close. This would give her the illusion that he had turned against her. He was bitter about it.

Mr. Skinner laughed inside. She had shown him up more than once. Now it was his turn. Besides, with her gone he would receive monetary benefits from her residual collections; and oh how sweet and ironic, her efforts would be a source of a Christmas bonus for all, including himself.

Eileen wondered, 'What else can they do? When will Broadman show up?'

"Oh there is this one other little thing, 'We have prepared a letter, in fact, two letters, you don't have to decide today, but we would like to know by Monday which one you prefer that we use. They both say about the same thing, except one states you will be opening your own solo practice here in town, whereas the other says that you have decided to take a position out of state. The letter just states that by mutual agreement with the partners in the firm you have decided that you would prefer to either be more independent or move to a new area. That way no one will be asking questions. Uh, speaking of questions Miss Robbins, you've been very quiet, do you have any questions?"

Eileen never said a word she only bit her lip more tightly until the door opened. Mr. Broadman walked in and behind him a prominent well-known and powerful attorney Mr. Wyatt Steel. Everyone but Eileen was shocked. Levine demanded, "Broadman, what are you doing here? Wyatt, you can't come in here like this."

Broadman countered, "Like hell we can't. We're here, aren't we?"

Levine offered a weak response, "We are having a private meeting with Miss Robbins. What's your business here?"

"Miss Robbins is our business. So, let me tell you something."

Levine pled, "Wait a minute. If you've got a lawyer in here, I've got a right to have my lawyer too."

Broadman ordered, "Stuff it, Levine. You are a lawyer. Deal with it. What we talk about Wyatt won't mention to anyone. You bring more lawyers in here, first thing you know, everybody in town is going to know about this meeting. Now, you don't want that to happen, do you?"

Levine knew he was trapped. 'Broadman was right on all counts so far. What did he have in mind?'

"My friend Wyatt has a few words to say to you gentlemen. I suggest you listen very closely, because if you don't listen today, you are apt to hear them repeated in a public arena."

Wyatt Steel never went to any meeting unprepared. He studied background, learned the details and meticulously prepared his plan and surmised the opposition's plans as well. He knew the answers before most could formulate the questions. He called Levine by his first name, "Jack, you know what you are doing is illegal. Miss Robbins is a minority in your firm. She is a woman, for God's sake. You guys are ganging up on her? She's your highest producer. I don't know if she made a mistake on Spellman's income tax or not." Everyone was shocked that he knew about that. They all looked at each other. "But if I were you, I'd take a good look at it. She's caught Skinner here in quite a few mistakes, so you want to make real sure it's not him that's made a mistake instead of her. Otherwise, you could all have egg on your face. By the way, she has a right to see the alleged error and to defend her position or to admit that she made the mistake. Hell, everybody makes mistakes. If that is the only one you can find on her, I dare say none of you have a better record than that. As far as you using her chemical imbalance, that's cowardly and downright lowdown of you. I am ashamed of you, Skinner. Was that the only way you could get the best of her? Well, it didn't work. And what of you Randall? Miss Robbins thought you were a trustworthy friend; are you a Judas?"

Tears were running down both Randall's cheeks. He was quietly thinking 'this is my worst nightmare. The greedy bastards are bringing about everyone's ruin. There will be nothing left for any of us by the time Steel is through with us.'

Steel continued, "You've totally misjudged Miss Robbins. She came in and asked for a couple weeks off. You forced her to take a month. It has been a hard month for her but she has learned a lot and matured a lot. She is in control of all her chemicals. Perhaps you have lost control of yours. Seems you're the ones with the faulty judgment. I'll tell you this. Since you're in a negotiating mood, why don't we finish the negotiation before we adjourn? I've heard your offer; now I'll tell you what's acceptable. Miss Robbins will take that month that you've offered her but contrary to last month she will have full rein of her office. She will come and go as she pleases. She will choose what work she wants to do. She will leave the rest to you. We've looked over her figures; she brings in at least four times the revenue of the salary you *generous* guys are allowing her. So she is going to take a twenty-five thousand dollar bonus to help her forget this little meeting today and then starting tomorrow, which I believe is the first of the month, her salary doubles. And by the way she will leave your firm when she is so inclined. You might get unlucky and it could be sooner than you think. There will be no letter. There will be no further character assassinations on Miss Robbins, and you, Mr. Skinner shall have only thirty days to find new employment. You sir, must leave the firm, and if you ever smear this good lady's name again, you'd best make very sure that you can back it up."

Mr. Skinner, now bleached white, uttered not a word. He knew not to speak without an attorney.

Mr. Steel continued, "These demands, if you will, are the beginning point of our negotiation. They are also the ending point unless you choose not to meet them. In that case, the stakes will be much higher for the firm and for everyone in it. It won't be in a closed room like this. We'll see you in court. I believe I heard you say Monday would be okay for the final word? We'll expect an answer by ten a.m. Monday morning."

"Oh, and there is one other little item, Mr. Broadman has spent about four thousand five hundred dollars to date on private investigators, learning about you guys, and a little bit on my fee. I hope you will consider reimbursing him all of that. After all, it is a small fraction of what he's paid the firm. And you know what, he never sat down and checked on the actual hours you bill him, but he could, you know."

Eileen followed Broadman and Steel out the door without saying a word.

When they reached the outside, there was no back slapping, hearty 'Guess we told them' conversation, only a business-like, "We'll see what Monday morning brings." Eileen was now trembling. Broadman had been right, just like always. Steel was awesome. She was grateful he was with them.

Chapter 27
It's Not Fair

Eileen arrived early for the DMDA meeting. It was two p.m. on the third Sunday. She had taken a seat just to the right of what would be the head of the table. She was sipping regular coffee, whitened by copious Creamora but with no sugar. By now she was a regular. She watched as each member arrived. Early or late? Outgoing or withdrawn? Eating or not and where each sat and by whom? Then, as if self-analyzing, she wondered; 'What does all this mean about me? Nothing.' she decided, and resumed observing others.

Jerry came in. She remembered him from two meetings previous. She had thought that he was both shy and sad. He had made almost no eye contact and had said nothing except his name. Immediately after the program he left without making any acquaintance. He missed the preceding meeting.

This time Jerry surveyed the room briefly, walked directly to the refreshments, picked up a canned Pepsi and a couple of cookies. He went to the far end of the table which was unoccupied, and sat on the opposite side from her.

Jerry sat down and glanced directly at Eileen. Her meeting his gaze appeared to surprise him, and he instantly looked away. She knew that he was different today than he had been four weeks ago. His state of agitation was obvious.

The topic for the day was genetics. Dr. Morgan Jones gave his prepared speech. The message was repetitious for her.

At the conclusion of the talk, Jane asked if she should have children. There was discussion from the other participants, and the speaker, as to the variables to be considered by an individual seeking their own answer. How prepared was she to live responsibly with her illness. This would be necessary to be an optimum mother. How prepared was she to accept that one or more or all of her children might have the Bipolar illness? How prepared would she be if the children did not respond favorably to treatment, or even allow treatment once they were of age?

Throughout all of the discussion, Jerry was quiet, but fidgeting. Eileen correctly perceived his inward seething with something that needed release. Intuitively, she spoke to his need. “Jerry, we haven’t had a chance to get to know you. We are all in this together. We are here to help each other. I have a sense that you are hurting. If you will share with us, we will share with you. Are you in pain?”

Jerry looked at her with cold and accusing eyes. He unleashed an inward turmoil, “Yeah, I’m hurtin’; you sit around this table and talk about this damn illness like it’s a philosophy course, well, it has just ruined my life. I would rather be dead than have this curse.” He glared at Jane, “Why the hell would you want to have a child? Look at me; would you want to have a child like me?”

Eileen said, “Jerry, we are all like you.”

Jerry shot back, “Like hell you are. Which one of you is going to share my .38 special? No, you are not like me, you have all deceived yourselves. You sit around in your smug little lives, but you don’t know what is going on with me or for that matter, with the person next to you, and you probably don’t care.”

Eileen pleaded, “Listen, Jerry, if we didn’t care and we weren’t aware, why would we offer to share and ask you to share? We are here to help each other. That includes you. When you were here a month ago you looked more down than you do today. At least today you are talking and feeling, you didn’t appear to even be feeling a month ago.”

“Oh, yes, I was feeling. I was just so depressed I couldn’t move. I couldn’t think. Now I am doing both.”

The speaker expressed a truism, “That’s the way it goes Jerry, when you begin to get better you can see things you couldn’t see before. You can feel things you couldn’t feel before.”

Jerry interrupted, "That's just too bad isn't it, because now I know it is not worth it. Life's too screwed up. There is no way out. Just three months ago I was a schoolteacher, loved by my students. I taught math and coached football. I thought life was wonderful. I was married with a two-year-old boy, now I don't have anything. My job is gone. My wife and boy have gone to Florida to her parents. My future is gone. My life is over. Am I supposed to live like some sort of freak, and watch my kid grow up, wondering if he has this damn gene? I probably cursed him with this illness. Maybe I should take him with me and spare him the horrors of this life."

Eileen spoke directly to Jerry in an obviously compassionate voice, "You know Jerry, we all know, it's not fair is it? For you, for us, for anyone but giving up makes it more unfair."

Freddie spoke up, "You want to talk about fairness, let me tell you. I'm big and clumsy and I've got this illness and I try to do everything just like my momma says. My brother, he's tall like me, but he's trim and handsome. Everything goes his way. Nothin' goes my way. He's popular and everybody likes him, but he won't listen to our momma. He got messed up on drugs, got himself in jail, cost my momma all her money just to get him out. I had to quit school, get a job, and help my momma. My brother never said thank you. I've been in the hospital four times with this illness, but you know what, man, I'm glad to be alive. My wife loves me. My children love me. My job waits for me, and I found out these people right here in this room love me and you know what else man, we will all love and help you too if you'd let us." "Oh, Miss Jane, go ahead and you have all the children you want."

The speaker offered more points, "Jerry, earthquakes aren't fair, lightning strikes aren't fair. Being handsome or ugly is not fair. Being tall or short is not fair. It's called life."

Jerry said, "Yeah - and death."

The speaker said, "That's a poor choice. There are many other choices. We can help you find them. You can learn how to control this illness. How to live life to the fullest despite the illness. How to overcome the adversity of unfairness, just as many other people have. I have several patients with this same illness who are very much in control of their lives and families and are doing very well. One is a healthcare professional and planning to write her own book when the time is right. She is not yet public with her illness.

Jerry said, "But they didn't get hurt as bad as me. I can't climb out of this hole. It is too deep."

The speaker continued, "I look at you, and how much you have accomplished already. You are an educated person. You are bright. You are attractive. So, you have this gene. It can be controlled. You might have lost a job; you can probably get it back. So your wife and child have gone to the in-laws, you will likely get them back. Don't bury yourself and your talents in the sand or a grave. Realize your potential and let these friends and your doctors help you find and enjoy your potential."

Gerald had been nervous about this entire exchange. Sitting in the President's chair he was compelled to do something but had not figured out what it should be. Perceptively, he asked a question to the point, "Where's your .38 Jerry, do you have it with you?"

"No, it's at home," Jerry answered.

Gerald, relieved, continued, "Good, then you don't need to go home. Who is your doctor?"

"Dr. Moore."

Gerald said, "I have seen him at Brookwood. He practices there doesn't he?"

"Yeah, I was there a few weeks ago."

Gerald continued, "Well, it's time to go back there. I'll take you. Who can go with me?"

Jane offered for the group, "We'll all just go with him. We are a support group. Next month you can come back and thank us."

"I don't want to go to the hospital. I didn't ask for any help."

The speaker reassured, "No, Jerry, you didn't consciously ask for help but subconsciously you have laid your soul out in a group of acknowledged helpers and supporters. Yes, you are asking for help. Now give in to it. I am extremely proud of this group for hearing your call for help and answering it in such a direct way. This night should be the turning point of your life, Jerry."

Group members began to assemble around Jerry as if to enclose him in a protective circle. The speaker pulled Gerald aside and instructed, "When you get him to the hospital, it is up to you to make sure the doctor knows that he is suicidal and should be admitted, even if it is against his will. Make sure they contact his doctor and that the doctor knows about his very explicit suicide threats and his mention of homicide to his child. Here's my answering service number. If they have any trouble getting him admitted, call me immediately."

Gerald was grateful, "I will; thank you very much."

Eileen, processing the events, noticed Freddie, standing a full head taller than Jerry. Freddie locked his arms with Jerry as soon as he stood up. His characteristic concern and caring was always in his action.

Several in the group caravanned to the hospital emergency room. They stayed with Jerry until he was safely admitted.

Eileen wished she could call Robert and tell him about the meeting. She couldn't do it.

Instead, she called Alma and told her how proud she was of Freddie.

Chapter 28
Monday

Promptly at ten a.m. Eileen's phone rang. "Good Mornin' Eileen," this is Jack Levine. "Is this a convenient time for us to talk?"

Eileen said, "Well, of course."

"Uh, the Board took some time and did a lot of thinking and talking over the weekend. We feel like everything really got out of hand and we don't know how we let it happen. We figure we owe you an apology and we ask you to forgive us. We wish you hadn't done and said some things, but we forgive you of those. So, we can just all get back to business as usual, if that's okay with you?"

"Does that mean you accept all the terms of our counter-offer?"

"Well, we are prepared to meet you half-way."

"Well, Mr. Levine, I am prepared to stay where I am; why don't you call Mr. Steel? When ya'll reach an agreement, just give me a call. I am ready to come back to work, but it has to be on Mr. Steel's terms. I'm going to follow his advice."

Levine had not wanted anyone in the room with him when he talked to Eileen. He wanted to minimize any chance of being personally embarrassed by this situation and especially by Eileen. After the conversation, he summoned Randall and Skinner to his office to discuss her response. Levine had told them in the preliminary discussions that Steel would not play games. Still, it wouldn't seem right to immediately accede to his demands. They should at least try for some concessions; but thought their best chance would be through Eileen. However, she had proved stubborn. She was doing exactly what attorneys tell their clients to do, let the lawyers talk. Stay out of it. They must decide if their game plan would continue to be the same. They would discuss meeting Steel's demands, and be willing to meet him halfway, but salvage Skinner's position with LRS. All three agreed this would be the negotiating plan. Levine would do the talking, lawyer to lawyer.

Levine went back to his office to call Mr. Steel, "Uh, good morning Wyatt. How are you? Did you have a good weekend? This is Jack Levine."

"Morning, Jack, of course, I had a good weekend. You know me, I work all the time. Most of my weekend was right here at the office working. What you got for me this morning?"

"Well, Wyatt, you drive a hard bargain but there is no reason to put a stake through our heart. We understand that we were hasty and didn't adequately think things through for Eileen. You made some good points. We appreciate you bringing them to our attention. We spent some time going over things and want to make amends. Skinner was just trying to think of the firm...really didn't realize he was overstepping his bounds but he understands that now, and won't do it again. You were right we could have been paying Eileen more than we were. She is doing a helluva job for us, so we think it is appropriate to give her the raise you asked for. We don't mind reimbursing Broadman for his expenses including yours, of course. Eileen could still enjoy her work here and she has a good future with us. We would ask her forgiveness, give her an apology and of course, no hard feelings. If she has legitimate outside interests, so be it; we shouldn't be concerned about that." Levine knew that Skinner and Randall would be appalled if they heard this supposed negotiation. He knew he was capitulating on every point, except trying to save Skinner's job but he could sense from Steel's demeanor that he was not in a giving mood.

"Uh, so if that suits you. Eileen can just come on back and we'll keep the firm going right along. Everybody will be just one happy family again."

Steel inquired, "Everybody?"

Levine was pleading, "Well, Wyatt, everybody is entitled to one mistake. Skinner has been with the firm a long time. Just wouldn't be fitting and proper to kick him out. He said he's learned his lesson. You can at least give us that, can't you?"

Steel, without hesitating, "By the way, Jack, did you happen to look over that Spellman IRS form? Was Skinner right or was Eileen right?"

"Uh, hum, funny thing about that, it was a new reg that Skinner had overlooked, so Eileen was..."

Steel interrupted, "Eileen was right?"

Levine conceded, "Yeah, she was right."

"And you still want to keep him? Don't you realize he will keep on making mistakes? Don't you know he doesn't keep up with things? Don't you see that he is a backstabber? Don't you know you'll be next if he ever gets the chance? I'm doin' you a favor, Jack. You don't have the balls to get rid of him yourself. You got an excuse now. You got a reason. Do it while you can."

"You think so huh?"

"Jack, you know me. I got no axes to grind. I'm tryin' to help everybody here, even you. Oh, I would tell you this though, if Skinner has any severance pay coming I'd stretch it out as long as you can, and make it contingent on his silence. If he breathes a word of this anywhere, he loses all his severance pay and delayed compensation."

Levine began his acquiescing, "Now that is a good idea. I appreciate you offering it."

"My pleasure. We got a deal Jack?"

"Deal, Wyatt."

"When do you want her back at work?"

"Why don't you just tell her to come when she wants to?"

"Sounds good to me."

Steel called Eileen. When she answered the phone, he informed her, "Well, young lady, you got everything you asked for." One would have thought from his comment that she engineered the entire scenario and pulled it off all by herself. He had a way of making people feel good about themselves.

Eileen said, "Everything?"

"Absolutely."

"When do I go back to work?"

"Jack's words were, 'Whenever you want to come back, you're welcome. Just come on. Take your time. If I were you I would give Skinner a day or two to get his things packed and out, and oh, by the way, he was wrong on that Spellman IRS tax return that he was beating up on you about. You were right all along."

"Oh, thank you, Mr. Steel. It is all so unbelievable. You've been wonderful. I'm glad Mr. Broadman knew to get you involved. Ya'll are just so smart. Even to get LRS to pay for all the work ya'll did."

"Well, I don't know how smart we are, some people say we are but we are experienced. You take care and call me if you ever need me. I'll be right here at the office."

Off the phone Eileen was exhilarated, energized. She had to share this with someone. She phoned Dupree. To her amazement he was in. "Robert, you won't believe what has happened with me." Up until this point she had not filled him in. "Everything always goes so well for me. I feel guilty." She gave him a brief but fairly telling synopsis of her recent ordeal. He was enthralled. Eileen focused on jealousy issues and withheld any reference to illness.

"That's fantastic. I can't believe they tried to do you that way, but then, of course, I see stuff like that all the time. What I don't often see is outcomes like this. We need that guy up here in Washington. How quick can you pack his bags and bring him up here? I want to see you anyway."

"Do you really, Bob?"

"I really miss you Eileen. I'm not the same when you're not here. I am like a run down battery. How soon can you come? I'm working but we could have evenings together and some lunches."

"Would I have to stay at the Willard again? I mean, I've seen it. We could save time, if it wouldn't be too much trouble, I could just stay with you."

"Trouble? No, I'd love that."

"Well, I do have time off from work. Why don't I see if I can catch Eastern's whisper jet on Wednesday? I could stay until Saturday or Sunday." They happily agreed on the plan.

'Oh, what a Monday. I must be the luckiest woman in the world. Everything is going my way.' She was beginning to mentally arrange her traveling wardrobe for Washington. She was eager to see Bob again. She felt good when she was with him. She wanted to know more about what his future plans were. She wondered if he would come to Alabama or maybe she thought, she might go to Washington. 'Time will tell, I guess.'

Eileen reflected, 'What a week. The best Monday of my whole life and Tuesday is just icing on the cake and Wednesday will be the cake.'

Chapter 29
The Big Question

On Wednesday morning Eileen called Jack Levine. "Mr. Levine, I'm excited about getting back to work. Would it be okay with you if I begin next Monday? I plan to use the first week to catch up and ease into a routine, if that will be okay with you." She informed him that she would be out of town until Monday, but would check with Mr. Steel and him on Monday morning to confirm that the paperwork was officially signed. If so, she would come by the office. She would check with him regarding any special assignments, etc. She said that she had been missing the work, her clients and the people at LRS. Even to Levine, it sounded genuine. He resolved in his own mind to make sure everything was ready by Monday morning.

Later that morning she flew to Washington.

Dupree met her at the gate, "Eileen, you look great! I'm glad you're here."

"Me too," Eileen's eyes and smile reflected the mutual joy. They retrieved her luggage and drove to his apartment. He gave her a quick orientation. So far it had not been much different from checking into a hotel. She scanned, with interest, the obvious masculine theme, deciding that it had been done with little, if any, help. She managed to keep her comments to herself. If she were going to be there for an extended stay she would exert a personal influence.

Dupree offered her a drink. They both settled on colas and sat at the breakfast table. He told her how excited he had been anticipating her trip.

"You are full of surprises, you know. Nothing could have surprised me more than when you told me you were coming this week, except that when you said you would stay here. You're a real trip. You are always talking about a trip. A trip to the moon, now this trip to Washington. I think I'll just call you, 'Trip,' Yep, you're my 'Trip.' That's what you are. I'll tell you something, I'm enjoying the ride."

"Oh, Bob you are so sweet. I've never had anyone give me a nickname before. 'Trip,' huh? Maybe that's symbolic. Perhaps we'll get to take that moon trip together. Fly me to the moon."

"No. Fly us to the moon!" Dupree replied, "That's one trip I'm eager for, my dear. We'll work on it together."

At that moment a tacit but tender moment enveloped them. She looked into his wide, revealing eyes. She saw and felt his yearning, needing, wanting and yet it was different than the previous lustful encounters they had shared. His hand was gently clasping hers as if to measure her essence and keep her near. Her gaze stayed fixed, searching deep through his wide pupils. What else was there; she was curious to know. As if on cue to her inner question, Dupree spoke up, "I enjoy being with you. You are special to me. I feel good when I'm around you. Thank you for coming."

"Thank you for having me. It's great to be here."

His hand pulled away as he looked at his watch. "It's about five-thirty. We have reservations at seven. I want to take you to the 1789 Restaurant in Georgetown; it's one of my favorites. I hope you will like it."

When they arrived at the restaurant, Eileen instinctively joined Robert's comfortable attitude. As they were being shown to their table she realized that he was becoming more relaxed with her. They had a delightful dinner from the French menu and shared a bottle of Montrachet wine. She passed on the escargots and started with the salade d'endives au blue. She praised the filet de tilopia sauté, sauce vierge, her entree choice. While saying she should not have dessert she succumbed to the house specialty, Crêpes Suzette.

After dinner, they took a slow, scenic route home. The romantic mood became unhurried, soft, and soothing. Their chemistry was changing, quieter, closer and more comfortable. The unspoken change ushered in the night. Back at the apartment their evening was tame in comparison to their previous encounters, yet the sweetest ever.

On Thursday Eileen awoke to the aroma of coffee. She eased out of bed and found Robert pouring himself a cup. Seeing her he poured a second cup. She walked up to him, looking into his face and said, "This must be Heaven, waking up to coffee prepared by a prince." He replied, "Tis indeed Heaven, my dear, when a man can wake up with an angel in his bed. What would you like for breakfast? I can do cereal, oatmeal, or scrambled eggs and hash browns."

"You can? I'll take whatever you're having. I'm on vacation, no decisions."

"Oh, these are small decisions. Bigger ones await you."

Curious, Eileen wanted to know, "What does that mean?"

"I'll tell you later."

Elusively, Dupree told her he had to go to the office but would like for her to meet him there at three p.m. In the meantime, she was free to do anything she liked. She could use his car. It would be no problem for him to catch the subway. He stated it would be nice to have the car there when they were ready to leave. He told her, "By the way, there is a senatorial reception this evening. You will be my guest and will see Senator Johnson, and several others. I will be the proudest man there, certainly the most envied."

"Smooth talking Prince Charming this morning, huh?"

Handing her his car keys, he departed for the office.

Eileen tried to deduce what the surprise could be. She eventually decided it was an impossible task and gave up the effort. She worked on her business plan for the Moon City project. She felt guilty that she had spent so little time and effort on her important project over the past few weeks. She consoled herself however, that it had not been her intent. It had only been happenstance. Too may problems. She thought of Broadman. He had been so helpful in her crisis. He was such a big investor she could not let him down. She had to do everything in her power to make sure this project was completed.

At five 'til three p.m. Eileen walked into the reception area of Dupree's office. She announced herself. The receptionist stood up, extended her hand and said, "Miss Robbins, I'm Gina. We've talked on the phone. I am happy to meet you, Mr. Dupree is expecting you; won't you have a seat?"

She did not press the intercom so Eileen correctly assumed that he was with someone. Promptly at three the door opened and Dupree came out with another gentleman. As Dupree walked the gentleman to the door, it appeared that purely by chance he noticed Eileen. "Oh, Miss Robbins," he said, "So good to see you. Oh, what a coincidence, let me introduce the two of you. Dr. Ackerman, this is Eileen Robbins. She is also in the space business. Miss Robbins, this is Mr. Don Ackerman. He's from Houston, Texas. He has done some freelance work connected to the Houston Space Center. Dr. Ackerman, Miss Robbins is from Birmingham, Alabama. That's just a few miles from Huntsville. She's been working on an unannounced project that involves space and she has completed a successful fund raising campaign like the one you are just now planning to launch. I'll see that the two of you get each others' phone numbers and addresses. I think you could be fast friends and mutually helpful with an alliance between the two of you. Thank you for letting Senator Johnson be in on this with you, Dr. Ackerman. He has asked me to give him a full report of our meeting. Rest assured, I'll do that promptly and we will be in touch."

Eileen was impressed and pleased. Robert had done something important for her, she reasoned. And with great finesse. What was this big surprise? She couldn't wait to find out.

Dupree invited Eileen into his office and closed the door.

"Listen my dear. Ackerman has just invented and patented something like tough-skin. It withstands heat like nothing ever before invented. It's going to make space vehicle re-entry easy as pie. His problem is that he doesn't have the money to manufacture it, so he has come here to ask the Senator if the government will underwrite the manufacturing. The government is not going to do that but you and your investors may want to team up with him. You're going to need something like this product, as it will take you months, if not years or decades, to get to the fulfillment of your project, but his product can be used now. You've already got enough investment to bankroll his manufacturing business. That way, your investors are going to be impressed and quite happy. It will give you breathing room on your main project."

Eileen was spellbound. She was trying desperately to comprehend the magnitude of what Dupree was saying. She needed to compute the ramifications, 'the potential is enormous.' "You would do this for me, Robert?"

Dupree said, "Someone has to help this man and it's going to help our space program. It'll help everyone. I just happened to be in the right place to facilitate."

"But what do you get out of it?"

"How about another night with you?"

"Don't be silly."

That evening at the reception Dupree introduced her to everyone he knew. She realized later that it was not by chance that when he introduced her to the Chairman of the Appropriations Committee and later the Chairman of the Finance Committee; it was while each of them was talking to Senator Johnson.

The Senator had been in rare form. He had said essentially the same thing to each one of them. One by one, Dupree brought Eileen over to introduce them; Senator Johnson called them each by their first name. "Miss Robbins here represents our fine State of Alabama in many ways. The first is obvious, her exquisite beauty. I've been trying to get her to present herself for the Miss Alabama pageant but she is too busy with other more brainy things. She is working on some real important space travel plans I think your Committee is going to be interested in before too long. I'll give you more of the details when the timing is a little better. Don't forget her pretty face, you'll probably be seeing her again." She knew then that Dupree had not misled her. Johnson really was interested in the project and obviously doing what he could to help set the stage for her.

The rest of the week was more routine with no other high profile power meetings. She and Dupree had an exquisitely fulfilling couple of days, just being together. They drove to Mt. Vernon and Monticello. Friday evening they took a romantic dinner cruise on the Potomac. The experience surpassed her expectations; she was deliriously happy. Dinner was elegantly presented. The historical sights along the riverbanks were rather serendipitous.

On Sunday morning they attended the church of Presidents, St. John Episcopal Church. Eileen was aware that Dupree knew how much spirituality meant to her. They had not talked about it all week so she was surprised when he told her on Saturday night that he wanted to take her to church; she drifted off to sleep with no idea what was in store for her.

They sat through the service as the minister gave a sermon on faithfulness, to God of course, but also to self, to values, to profession, and to mates. She had not thought of faithfulness in so many different ways though it all made perfect sense.

At the end of the service the parishioners began their egress through the front door, but Dupree had Eileen by the hand and they proceeded counter to the others. As they reached the altar, the church was nearly empty. He held her hand and asked her to stay there with him for a few moments. She thought, 'This is weird. What are we doing?' When the church had cleared he reached into his pocket and brought out a gorgeous traditional marquise cut diamond ring. He dropped to one knee and proposed: "Here in this sacred spot with our God witnessing, I ask you to be my wife. To be faithful to me and I will be to you for the rest of our lives. I love you. I want to be with you forever."

Eileen began crying even before he finished his proposal. Tears were streaming down her face. She was ecstatic, but simultaneously frightened. In her mind she wanted to know, 'why has the big question come so soon for me. I'm not ready. He doesn't know everything about me. I haven't told him about my Bipolar Disorder. Will he still want me when he learns everything?'

Robert slipped the ring on her finger. Eileen couldn't resist.

"Oh, Bob, it's so beautiful and that was so sweet. I want so much to say yes."

He interrupted, "Then please do. The sooner the better. The waiting makes me nervous."

"You have a right to know more about me. Everything about me. It's not fair to you."

"I don't care what's fair. I'm in love with you. You don't know all about me." She looked at the ring and loved it. She looked in his eyes and cried. She put her arms around him and kissed him. "Take me to the apartment. I'll cancel my plane reservation. We have to talk. I'll go back tomorrow or the next day. We have to talk this through. I'll wear it now, but you might want it back later."

Driving to the apartment Eileen snuggled up to him with her head on his shoulder. Neither said hardly a word. Both preoccupied, calculating what they would say to each other back at the apartment.

She canceled her flight and advised she would reschedule within a day or two. They prepared sandwiches for lunch. Eileen dreaded revealing her secret to Dupree. She contemplated waiting until later 'but he would think that I don't want to say yes. I have to tell him and take the consequences. Besides I need to know more about Bob.' She spoke first, "Robert, there is a gene that runs in my family that causes me to have mood swings. I have an illness. It is called Bipolar Affective Disorder. In the past it was called Manic Depressive Illness. It is treatable and I am in treatment and doing well. Each of my children will have a 25% chance of inheriting the same illness."

Dupree interrupted, "Darling, if that is what makes you my Eileen, I hope all of our children will have it."

"That's sweet, Bob. You need to know that I will likely need to take medicine my entire life. Lithium is the best medicine for now. There will undoubtedly be other medicines in the future. I'll never be able to drink much alcohol and you would have to help me monitor my moods; if I get too low or too high you would need to point it out to me, gently, I would hope."

Dupree had reached over to hold her hand. At this point he moved around the table, stood her up, hugged and kissed her. He told her that he loved her and walked her to the sofa, sat down with her and held her while she sobbed.

Dupree told her, "one confession deserves another." He said, "My father is the youngest of five children. He has two older brothers. The oldest one has Alzheimer's. The next oldest one may be beginning to have memory problems. Alzheimer's might run in my family."

Eileen asked, "But how old are they?"

Dupree said, "The oldest one is in his eighties and the other one in his seventies."

Eileen said, "Heck, we can live two lifetimes by that age."

Dupree held Eileen close to him. They kissed reassuringly. He looked directly into her eyes and asked, "Won't our vows say for better or for worse? I can live with that if you can. I love you. I want you to be my wife."

Eileen with tears in her eyes said, "Then I will be Mrs. Dupree, yes. I'm going to sleep with the ring tonight. I won't ever take it off. I love you Robert. I do want to be Mrs. Dupree forever. The answer is definitely yes!"

Chapter 30
Faces With Veils

Before leaving Washington, Eileen called her mother. She feigned being homesick for one of her mom's meals and asked to join them for dinner. Her flight would arrive in Birmingham at four-forty-five, and she expected to be home by six.

Even though the call had been unusual, her mother took it at face value, and did not in the least suspect Eileen's motive.

Eileen had traveled comfortably dressed, so she made a quick stop at her apartment to dress more pleasing to her mother. She wanted her news to be happily received. Her mother would be the key.

Arriving at the Robbins' home she pressed the doorbell, but opened the door and walked in as the chimes announced her arrival. Passing through the door she turned the diamond to the underside of her finger. She called out for them, "Hello, Mom, Dad," and walked towards the kitchen where her mother would likely be."

Mrs. Robbins estimated that dinner would be in about 20 minutes and intuitively suggested, "Why don't we take a few minutes to relax, and get filled in on your trip before dinner? Your father is in the den. We'll sit in there."

Entering the den, Eileen announced to her mother and father that she had some good news to share with them.

Mrs. Robbins asked, "Is Senator Johnson going to sponsor your project?"

Eileen, laughing, said, "Well, as a matter of fact, he is helping. He talked to a couple of important people while I was there, and introduced me to some influential people, but my news is even better than that."

Eileen's mother now alerted that something big was up, was staring intently at Eileen. She said, "Oh, well, come on, out with it."

"You do remember me telling you about Bob Dupree, the nice Senior Staff Member for Senator Johnson. The one who came down and helped me a couple of weeks back? He has been so nice and so helpful and we have so much in common and we enjoy each other so much, well, he has asked me to marry him." Eileen repositioned the ring and held it out for them to see. "I said yes. We're engaged, Mom, Daddy. I am so happy. We talked about everything, absolutely everything. We are going to be so happy."

Eileen's mother, ever the protector, and doubter, responded with an emphatic, "But your father and I haven't even met him."

Trying not to be deflated, Eileen responded, "But you will, Mom, you'll like him."

"I'm not sure. Where will you live? He's not going to want to leave Washington for Birmingham. You'll have to give up your position at LRS. We need to think this through."

Eileen's mother had yet again failed to share enthusiasm with Eileen or even offer support. She felt as if her heart were pierced, and reflexively wanted to hurt her mother. Without thinking of consequences, Eileen blurted, "Mom, why must you throw cold water on everything? I'm 26-years-old and I can make my own decisions."

"Well, I'm twice your age so I'm more experienced, and knowledgeable. I'm old enough to know I made mistakes at your age."

Eileen personalized the comment and retorted, "You're saying it wasn't a good decision to have me. You've been taking it out on me ever since. I told you we had talked about everything. He's dying to come meet you and Daddy. He told me to work out a time. He wants to ask properly for my hand but don't you see, I'm too excited to keep it from you."

Her dad had listened once again to his ladies escalate into an emotional war. To intercede he interjected, "Of course, dear and we are happy for you. We'll do everything we can to help insure it's the right thing and that all goes well for you."

"Thanks Dad."

His soothing words defused her anger and restored her to the hopeful aspect of the engagement.

During dinner Mrs. Robbins softened her inquisition somewhat, but continued probing to learn as much as possible about her soon to be son-in-law. She could not, during the entire evening, bring herself to offer congratulatory words or emotions to fill Eileen's cavernous need for her mother's affirmation and approval.

After dinner Eileen decided to opt for more ego stroking from her father, and sat with him in the den where she enjoyed telling him about Robert and their mutual excitement.

Mrs. Robbins took a phone call just in earshot of Eileen and her father. Eileen timed her conversation so as to kibitz as much of the conversation as possible. Not surprisingly, her mother was telling a friend that she was to have a new son-in-law. Eileen thought 'How ironic, she's not even saying that I'm engaged, only that she would have a new son-in-law.' Eileen thought 'she is kidnapping Robert.' She heard her mother brag about Robert's importance; telling that he was the Senior Staff member of Senator Johnson. He was the Senator's right hand. He was indispensable." She even suggested, "Eileen might have to move to Washington." Eileen's anger brewed more intense. 'This is pure vicarious robbery and I'm left empty.'

Eileen thought to herself, 'I will be wearing a soft, transparent pure white veil. I will lift it in full revelation to my husband. Mother wears veils of disguise, designed to be non-transparent, and showing only her own prideful needs.'

In her next session with Dr. Griffiths she relayed this scene, and her emotions. Eileen wasn't formally a paying client of Dr. Griffiths but she had settled into a dependent role where she used him as a counselor. He made an observation that afforded her a never before realized insight about her mother.

"Eileen, you've previously told me similar scenarios about your mother. It is usually the same with her. You are now 26 years old, and continue to expect nurturing from your mother, but she may not be able to provide the particular type you are seeking. She nursed you when you were young. She clothed you, fed you, trained you, and pushed you to excel through the technique of never giving you credit for what you did right, only giving less criticism. In the old days before Enfamil when a mother did not have sufficient milk in their breasts, the babies would continue routing and sucking because they were still hungry, but they were fed by what was called a wet nurse or by goats' milk. My professor used to say of people like your mother, 'Eileen dear, you are still sucking on a dry tit.' The nurturement you are looking for must be obtained elsewhere but you should not ignore the good things you have received from your mother. You can still love and respect all of the goodness that has been there, is there, and will be there. It's incumbent on you to recognize appropriate ways to appreciate your mother. When you develop that technique you will be happier with her. This also is a lesson that you should carry with you for future relationships, your husband, your children, and friends."

Dr. Griffiths and Eileen talked earnestly about her project of flying to the moon and building a city there. He was dedicated to the project, and remained fascinated with the prospect of actually taking a space bus, loaded with people, to the moon. If he could stay involved and insure the continued prominence of spirituality in this project it would be an enormous boost for his theological principles. He dreamed of being able to network with similar believers and to have a spiritual home for the many who were disillusioned with some of the more traditional organized religions. Hopefully, the more rational and open-minded leaders could solve the diversity problems and find a way to establish unity. He would love to be a part of that accomplishment.

Dr. Griffiths' knowledge of Eileen's disorder did not inoculate him from being infected with her enthusiasm and her fantasy.

Chapter 31
Taking Care of Business

Mr. Broadman called Eileen, inquiring whether or not there were any new developments in their space travel project. He related that a couple of the investors were concerned because they had not received any recent updates.

Eileen's thought process was too flighty to stay focused. She meant to answer his question, but in her excitement, she skipped over it to tell Broadman her great news of being engaged to Robert Dupree. She gushed with excitement. She was unconstrained in her descriptions of Dupree's good qualities, and potential, but particularly the deep love and romantic attraction they had for each other. "Oh, Mr. Broadman, I just know we're going to be the happiest couple ever."

Mr. Broadman was glad to be on the phone where he could surreptitiously feel anger at Eileen for dodging his question. Yet he was gentleman enough and savvy enough to understand that women have different priorities. Wise men know this and refuse to let it encumber necessary details, or to interfere with business. He would politely indulge her exuberance, offer congratulations, remember something kind about Dupree and then bring her back to his question and pressing need.

Mr. Broadman said it was time to have a meeting of the investors. A couple of them were antsy. It would help to have a meeting where an encouraging update would be offered.

Mr. Broadman's forthrightness edged Eileen back on track. She could most likely surmise the two who were nervous about their money. She realized that she had not devoted enough time and energy to the project lately and that progress had suffered. She needed to consult with her engineer. New charts would be necessary. The investors needed a pep talk. Eileen considered mentioning Dupree's idea to him, but decided to hold it off for now because he might perceive it as a diversion technique. She would save this as a surprise finale for her meeting with the investors. She would be proactive. "I'm glad that you called. I am working on some new projects that should prove to be interesting. Can we meet with investors this Saturday afternoon?" She was making it more feasible for the investors from Montgomery and Mobile. Also, importantly, she was saving Saturday morning to put the finishing touches to her presentation.

Surprised, delighted and encouraged, Broadman agreed to the time. He offered his company boardroom, and to contact the others. He teased them with the possibility of new ideas and a hint of optimism. He would never give a guarantee that he could not uphold. Backing down was anathema to him. His reputation was always at stake. Even though he had not been the first investor, he now was the pivotal investor and Chairman of the Board.

Eileen had only two days to prepare her presentation. She was back at LRS, reintegrating into the office. Fortunately, senior management had not placed any major or urgent projects on her original to-do list. Mostly it was minimal proofing of forms, and setting a tentative calendar of appointments for the coming week. Even as she contemplated these items, her mind was at home on her drawing board, scheming new ideas for Moon City. She designed new overheads to use for her vision of their space company. Space Travel, Inc. would dominate space travel for years to come. She needed to know cost per delivered pound and ratios of how many pounds that are taken aloft versus how many pounds will be returning to earth. She knew the ratio would be disproportionate. Essentially, the pounds returning home would be the pounds of paying passengers versus the payload of material left on the moon and used fuel.

Her energy was soaring and her thoughts were fast-paced, ideas were rapid fire, and her euphoria snowballing. Eileen recognized it. She even realized that she was not taking her Lithium. She had not taken enough with her to Washington and had run out on Sunday. In her excitement she had forgotten to restart it on her return. She reasoned this was not the time to be slowed down, and, so elected to leave off the Lithium for now. She calculated that if she ever needed to have extra energy and mental sharpness, now was the time. She had only two days to get everything together for the investors. She felt sure that she would be able to keep focused and be productive for the next couple of days. Perhaps, then she would restart the medicine, if she felt the need for it. She was in denial. Her mind raced ahead rendering it ineffective as a race car going too fast for the track. All she could think about for the moment was being productive, and getting the necessary work done, following her destiny. The line between reality and fantasy had disintegrated.

Eileen felt a major obligation to Broadman. He had been there for her each and every time she had needed him. Now he needed her. It would be unthinkable to let him down, and the others for that matter. They believed her. They believed in the project, the business. It was up to her to make it happen, to satisfy them.

She definitely could not let God down. He made it all possible for her. Her delusional fantasy was intensifying, characteristic of the "highs." She needed to update Dr. Griffiths. He should be in on the meeting. She would invite him. She asked Mr. Broadman about this, but he reminded her that Griffiths was not a Board member or an investor, so inviting him would be inappropriate.

After finishing the necessary tasks at the office, Eileen made quick rounds to speak to the staff and was about to leave early, eager to work at home on her project. Mr. Levine spotted her and motioned her into his office.

His office now felt like a trauma room. She would have felt trepidation entering his office had she not been energized. Energy always helped her to accentuate her positive. Chipperly she greeted him, not as Jack now, but "Hi, Mr. Levine, it's good to see you. It is so good to be back. I'm really looking forward to getting back into my work. This is really what makes me tick, being able to help people with their accounting needs. Of course, you know I especially love the tax aspect of it. It is good to know that you are always there to keep me legit. I wonder what firms do that don't have a senior partner who is a tax attorney to guide them. Well, I'm just glad our firm has you." Even Eileen realized she had been more effusive than believable.

Levine was different today. She found herself suddenly quiet and listening. He comforted her, "We're glad you're back. Thank you for your kind words. It has been different with you on sabbatical." He had chosen that term advisedly. "Let's just say it was too quiet around here. Too staid. The staff smiles more when you are here. Eileen, we were too harsh on you and we realize it. Thank you for coming back and staying with us. We are going to make this work. You are going to be happy here. We are happy that you are still here. In business things happen sometimes that shouldn't. What's important is that things work out right and I believe, in fact, I know I speak for the Board and everybody else; it's working out right for you to be here with us. So, personally, welcome back. If there is anything I can do to help you, please don't hesitate in the least to come see me."

Eileen searched his face and his body language. She needed to determine if he was being disingenuous. Was he putting her off guard? She decided she would talk to Dr. Griffiths about it. "Mr. Levine, that is awfully kind of you. I can't tell you how much it means to me. I just know we are all going to be fine. We will be good for each other. If there is anything I can do to help you, you just let me know."

"Thank you."

"I think I have taken care of everything that was needed; so I was headed out, if that is okay with you, sir."

"Of course that's okay. Have a good afternoon. See you tomorrow."

On the way home Eileen scarcely thought of LRS. Mentally she was preparing pie charts. These showed the original investment, the minimal spending thus far, the tremendous progress in terms of actual planning of the various aspects; marketing for more investing, marketing to obtain passengers, time-frames for project development, and for the first planned actual trip to the moon with passengers. Also, they showed the procurement of a space bus, Moon City landscape, and building time frames, and perhaps most importantly, the governmental interface. She could show excellent progress on these fronts. She intended to show this as a phenomenal accomplishment, especially with so few staff, and in such a brief period of time.

At home she worked endless hours on the actual numbers and chart options. She strategized over the best way to present to skeptical investors.

She concluded that the first pie chart would show each development segment as an equal slice of the chart. There would be one empty slice called miscellaneous and unexpected. All projects must plan for the unexpected. She decided to put this one at the top of the pie chart in the eleven to twelve space. Each one of the pie slices would be color coded for a proportionate segment showing that there had been progress in each segment. Theoretically, when the entire chart was filled in, they would be ready to launch their first space voyage to Moon City. The miscellaneous segment would be her finale presentation to them. It would be blank. Nothing unforeseen had happened. They had so far predicted everything prior to it happening. There was no unexpected expense in time or money. Outside of the circle there would be a mirror pie segment above the empty segment and this, indeed, would have a healthy shaded green area because of one unexpected delightfully positive development for them, outside their business plan. She would announce to them, in great detail, how Dupree had brought in Dr. Ackerman, the inventor from Texas.

By the time Eileen arrived at her apartment, she had mentally analyzed each section of her pie chart. She cleared her desk, retrieved her protractor and began working on the outlines of each segment. She intended to present the information in the most favorable light. She needed to devise an appealing approach, yet an accurate representation of where they were. Her investors were some of the brightest people in Alabama. If she tried to exaggerate the accomplishments they would spot the deception immediately.

Before Eileen began microanalyzing the first component, ideas bombarded her. A visual person, her mind projected the chart. She realized that if she shaded in a representative portion it would look skimpy in comparison to the long and protracted work necessary to complete the project. She shifted paradigms to use a bar graph. The same scenario was immediately visible to her. If the bottom starting point was zero and the completion point one hundred at the top, and the time to completion was all the way from the left side of the graph to the right side, the bar would only show an insignificant progression up and across the page. That image was unacceptable. Thankfully, enhancement techniques came to her. She envisioned a more graphically positive manner to present their accomplishments.

Each segment of the chart would be divided into three equal phases and each phase represented by a separate bar graph. The first phase would be organization and recruitment. She sketched the first bar graph on a sheet of paper. Zero percent at the bottom, one hundred percent at the top left and across the bottom she wrote one through twelve months. At zero she wrote the word "begin." Under twelve she wrote, "target date." She thought for a moment and then at the top left she wrote, "Phase One" organization, recruitment, and capitalization." The printed goal was ten million dollars. She plotted on the graph that at the end of the first month, two million dollars were pledged. At the end of the second month six million dollars were pledged, and by the end of the third month twelve million dollars had been pledged. This was exactly what she wanted to show. With a twelve-month goal of ten million dollars she had reached beyond the goal in a ninety-day period. The graph was shaded in very quickly and went out through the roof. This would convert to the twelve to one section of the pie chart.

The first bar graph obviously, was not the entire picture. There would be a second and a third phase of segment one, but these were easily explained. For example, on the same investment scale would be a second bar graph representing the second phase. It would already have two million dollars in it, even though that phase would not begin for several more months. This phase of investment would not be needed until all prerequisites for building and licensing and feasibility studies had been firmly met. The third phase would be the third bar graph, still blank. She would place all three graphs on the same page. The third graph would be at the bottom and would not be scheduled to begin until contracts were in place for all the materials, government cooperation, and target date for construction and launch. This composite page of three logical phases, represented in easily understood bar graphs, would be extremely pleasing to the investors. She doubted the investors' other ventures could boast being so far ahead of schedule in such a brief time.

Furthermore, breaking it up into three phrases would allow her to divide the segments of the pie chart into three corresponding phases. This offered an obvious visual advantage. The space between lines expands as the pie reaches outward, shading from the inner portion of the pie would require a longer radius to encompass the same enclosed area. This would give the visual effect of having completed a great deal of the overall goal, yet it was perfectly legal and ethical to present it this way. In fact, it would be cruel not to project their positive accomplishment in the most encouraging manner.

Eileen proceeded through each segment with the same methodology. With the political for example, the goal was to get senatorial backing. This was also accomplished sooner than expected, and the Senator was already introducing her to the other political figures, again spilling into expectations of the second phase.

On the budget segment Eileen filled in the entire first phase, and during her presentation she would say that they were well within the budget. She would concede it to not be that we were in the second phase because we could not predict total expenditures for the remainder of the year. Nevertheless, we have spent less than budgeted for the time in business.

On staffing she again filled in exactly the full phase of that segment. "We are on schedule with personnel, and they were working diligently on their assigned task," Eileen confidently would tell the group.

On the business plan and design segment, she spilled over into the second phase, stating that the preliminary designs of the space vehicle and the delivery vehicle were complete, as were Moon City accommodations. At this point they were working on refinements and embellishments to both projects.

When Eileen arrived at Mr. Broadman's corporate boardroom, her energized state caused some investors to wonder if she might "be on speed." She scarcely spent any time organizing her notes and overheads, dropping them nonchalantly on the projector. She worked the group as if she were a politician. She spoke to one investor then another, thanking them for their support and enthusiasm, and for coming to this meeting. She delved into their personal lives as much as time allowed. None of the investors could have known, or would have believed, that she had slept for only two hours since Wednesday night.

Mr. Broadman finally boomed out over the cacophony of chatter, thus bringing the group's attention to the purpose of the meeting.

Eileen exuded total confidence. She began her presentation, "I am so fortunate to have the backing and belief of the executive and financial elite of Alabama. Because of this group we have been able to exceed the expectations of the first phase, both in an accelerated time-line, and in qualitative and quantitative measures. I will illustrate this in graph form, and will detail for you each facet of this fascinating project." Attempting to prevent their prerogative to interrupt, she encouraged them to "take notes, but interrupt me only if you urgently need an answer." She explained that, "many of the segments will overlap and answers might well be in another of the upcoming segments." She hoped that she would not be interrupted and possibly distracted or sidetracked.

With confidence and aplomb she placed the pie chart on the overhead projector and turned it on. She had chosen different colors for each segment. She called attention to the twelve to one position being "Investments," acknowledging the investors being the number one importance. At eleven to twelve was the "Miscellaneous and Unexpected" with the inverted pie pointing outside the circle. This was done deliberately for suspense and skillfully ignored by her until last. She decided to name each segment, but then to remove the pie chart and use the bar graphs for her detailed reports. Between each segment she briefly reintroduced the pie chart because it had such a convincing visual effect. It also showed where they were in reference to the progression around the pie chart.

When Eileen finished progressively going around the clock through the ten o'clock position up to eleven but before mentioning "Miscellaneous and Unexpected," she complimented all the investors for a successful completion of the first phase, well ahead of schedule. She cautioned them that the most difficult challenge lay ahead, successfully implementing phases two and three. The infrastructure was in place. She said, "An analogy would be that the foundation has been poured for a skyscraper while the plans are still being drawn. The materials have not been fully designed or purchased. The contractors and the tenants were, as yet, unidentified."

"But we should take heart," Eileen happily told them. "Mr. Dupree who is Senator Johnson's Senior Staff Member, has been able to give us a contact that will be invaluable to us." She then explained the Texas inventor's need for capital. "Fortuitously we have raised more than we currently needed. Dr. Ackerman, the inventor, has guaranteed contracts that will make millions in profit."

"In fact, his material will be needed for use as the outer shield of our own space bus. For that reason we have a unique situation of potential unexpected profit opportunities outside the pie chart with no unexpected expenses. We can more than cover his capital requirements. We have a parallel business opportunity." When she finished the last segment of the presentation she turned to the investors and asked if there were any questions. Mr. Jewel from Mobile surprised her and the other investors by initiating what quickly became an infectious hearty applause.

Eileen had pulled it off. In two days she had done two months of pie charts, bar graphs and speech writing, and they had bought it. She felt invincible. She thanked them for the warm ovation and began talking about filling out the top part of the inverted pie. Eileen expanded out of bounds, declaring that, "as people learn of our project we can license toy replicas of our space bus." She implored further, "shirts and caps with logos and other, perhaps endless, commercial opportunities for spin-off projects could be developed."

Mr. Broadman had heard enough. 'This sounds almost too good to be true. She's going too far with this rubbish about toys and hats. I wonder if she is manic. Yet it did look plausible.' However, it was up to him to stop her, and keep everything on a business footing. "Eileen, you've done a great job. We'll make copies of your presentation and generate some minutes."

"Would anybody care to make a motion that we contact Mr. Dupree and begin arranging a meeting with Dr. Ackerman, and further, to consider an invested position in his company provided the details are favorable?" There was a motion by Mr. Thomason and a second by Mr. Halls. The motion carried unanimously. "Now, is there any other business to come before this meeting? Let's set a time for another meeting. Is one month okay to get back together?" Everyone agreed; the time was set again for Saturday, four weeks hence at two p.m.

Chapter 32
Hedging the Bet

The purpose of the lunch was business, but Eileen unpretentiously enjoyed the side-benefits. She was meeting with her favorite entrepreneur, Mr. Broadman, and at her favorite lunch spot, The Club. It provided an unparalleled view in Birmingham, overlooking the entire city. The view had become one of her favorite joys. The food was not haute cuisine nor would it receive five stars, but it was always fresh, tasty and satisfying. Her choice consisted of fruit salad, entrée and hot tea as usual.

Mr. Broadman had a shrimp salad smothered in remoulade dressing followed by an open roast beef sandwich and unsweetened iced tea, all consumed enthusiastically.

“Let's talk about our Texas deal. I'm sure you've studied these figures and the business plan just as I have and probably more. I'm impressed. I think we're damn lucky to be invited in on this. What’s your read on it?”

Eileen reminded him, “It's not luck, Mr. Broadman, it was our friend Robert Dupree. I believe luck is mostly restricted to genetic heritage and our geographic birthplace. The rest is what we do with it, and I must say, you are a very fine example of that on both counts.”

“Thank you Eileen, flattery is not necessary in this business deal.”

“Mr. Broadman, I haven't memorized enough of the dictionary to adequately flatter you for all you've done for me and this project, let alone what you have done for yourself, your family, and the community.”

“Now stop that, Eileen. Dr. Ackerman has got himself a helluva product and an airtight contract. He had a good patent lawyer but he is cash poor. The timing is perfect for us. He has an immediate timetable and ours is on delay. He has a virtual lock on space travel contracts and can put the skin on everything that flies. It's obvious he hasn't talked to his lawyer about this business plan. He is offering fifty percent of his business to capitalize the first contract. For less than five million we can have half of his business. That means we would have what is tantamount to control of his business. He couldn't move left or right without our permission. He wants ten percent of our company, and he wants to see a convincing balance sheet and business plan. In short, he wants to make sure we're legit. So, we need to get him out here, show him who we are, and convince him that we are a responsible financial resource for his project. Preferably, I think we should request to see his facility and how he makes those chemicals. He needs to see more than our money. He needs to see our curiosity, commitment and enthusiasm. We need to see more detail on how he plans to build his plant. I think if we do our dog and pony show in his arena, it will be more impressive than if we bring him here. We don't have anything to show him that we can't show him from our balance sheet."

"Well, of course you're absolutely right, Mr. Broadman, and it is a perfectly legitimate desire on our part to make the trip and to inspect his product."

"Well, no one can present this moon project like you; you developed it. It would have to be you."

"I would love to do it, and certainly no one can show the confidence and strength behind our company better than you. I hope you would go as well."

"Unless someone knows a reason that I should not go, I see it the same way. Why don't I give him a call and get this thing all arranged?"

Eileen chose to ignore, if not outright deny, the swell of energy building in her body. It had become evident to her that she was stimulated by Broadman. She was less likely to be depressed when around him and more likely to be energized. He was like an approving father. She loved the power he symbolized. She knew he liked her professional prowess. She had done so much for him, but he had also been very helpful to her. They had mutual appeal. She thought, 'Although he pays me for my professional service; he does not owe me any business advice or allegiance. He has no obligation to a business partnership or the mutual flattery we enjoy.' Her thoughts were new and intriguing. 'He is nice looking, especially with his silver gray hair. It makes him look more powerful.' She knew herself well enough to know; 'power is one of the characteristics that attracts me.' This was an innate talent of Broadman's, embellished through the years with numerous and formidable accomplishments. This was in stark contrast to Levine's acquired, but unnatural and unattractive power.

Eileen and Mr. Broadman finished lunch and completed their plans agreeing to look forward to their visit to Texas.

No one can know for sure, even Eileen, whether her forgetting to take her medicine that night was completely unconscious or a semi-conscious decision. She worked into the night later than usual, preparing new overheads to show Dr. Ackerman. She was alert and creative. She retired long after midnight. Awakening early, she rushed into her work routine. She waited until later for breakfast. It dawned on her that she had not included a church in her Moon City plans. She asked God for forgiveness, and promised to rectify this oversight. 'After all, none of this would be possible without His power and permission, so there definitely needed to be a place to glorify Him.'

Though it was quite apparent from Griffiths' voice that she had awakened him with her phone call, Eileen seemed unfazed. She started, "Dr. Griffiths, it has just occurred to me that I have been so remiss in not incorporating a church to glorify God in our Moon City plans. I will pray for forgiveness. I wanted to ask you to intercede and ask forgiveness for me also."

As Griffiths talked, his voice normalized, "Eileen, do you realize it is five-fifteen in the morning?"

"Oh, no. I was just busy with my thoughts and it didn't occur to me. I'm so sorry. I will call you later."

"It's okay, Eileen, I'm awake now. God is not so unaware of our intentions that he would feel slighted. Relax. I'm sure God will give us whatever reminders we need. Besides, you still thought of it in the planning process. You should have no feelings of guilt about this." He decided not to challenge her in favor of being supportive. But the thought did occur to him, 'this is just another example of humans putting God last.'

"Eileen, let's think about this. We're going to have a very small group of people traveling and working on the moon for the foreseeable future. Most are likely to have a scientific background and will be from unselected, diverse, persuasions, denominations, or religions. That's reality and appropriate. We should probably have a small nondenominational chapel, and more accurately, with a multi-spiritual decor so that individuals, or small groups could worship in their own fashion, and in their own manner. If we were at a point where we wanted to hold larger meetings, I am sure we would be able to use the multi-purpose auditorium."

"Oh, that's so practical. Why didn't I think of that?"

"Perhaps you have too many things on your plate. Everything is on schedule, relax."

"I suppose you're right. I do jump the gun at times, don't I?"

"Don't worry about it. By the way, are you taking your medicine?"

"Actually, I'm not sure I need it. I feel better than I've felt in quite a while. I might have forgotten it last night, but in general I have been taking it. Perhaps I have missed a few doses here and there."

"Have you gotten a Lithium level lately?

"Not lately, but they've always been normal."

"Yes, but that's when you were taking your medicine properly. Have you seen Dr. Lavoy lately?"

"Oh, a couple of weeks ago. I was fine."

"Eileen, you may be a bit high and your Lithium may be low. Seriously, you should check with Dr. Lavoy and perhaps get a Lithium level. You might even be rapid cycling."

"I have another appointment in a couple of weeks, I'll do it then. Thank you for your concern. I am working on some new overheads to show to Dr. Ackerman in Texas. Mr. Broadman and I are going out to talk with him. Sorry I woke you up. I hope it doesn't get you off to a bad start today. I'll go now and see you later. Bye."

"Bye, Eileen."

Mr. Broadman called Eileen later in the day to confirm a trip time for the following Tuesday, and also asked if she could have her presentation ready by then.

"Oh, Mr. Broadman, that won't be a problem at all. I worked on it last night and this morning and have made considerable progress. Dr. Ackerman's foremost interest will be to see our financial soundness. I've reconstructed the pie graph that we went over at the board meeting. I have elaborated on the fundraising segment. You will recall that it shows us to be ahead of schedule on the funding but expenses have not been as heavy as projected. Furthermore, we have abundant cash reserves on demand. So, Dr. Ackerman is going to see that we are capable of funding his needs immediately."

"That sounds great."

"That's just the beginning. I'll have the corporate balance sheet up to date through the day prior to our presentation to him. I also have short dossiers on each of our investors and a corporate organizational schematic which shows each person's relevance in the organization. He will also be able to see that he's talking to the decision-making officers. I am completely prepared to be the dog and pony show. I figure you'll be the horseman and do the straight shooting, handshaking, and contract negotiation."

Neither Mr. Broadman nor Eileen caught the symbolism of her comment and did not understand that often there are fine subliminal symbolic expressions long before the actual manic action is unleashed. In fact, close loved ones or therapists will often sense or recognize a brewing storm before the individual will sense or believe it.

Later, in one of her normally balanced euthymic states she would recall this particular scene in a therapy session with Dr. Lavoy. They would process how the danger signs were missed. The obvious question was why would an otherwise bright individual not heed the warning and do whatever it takes to thwart the predicable manic episode, since they nearly always bring disastrous consequences.

Eileen, like many others, initially could not believe that she was incapable of personally controlling her thoughts and actions. Eventually, she comprehended the reality and tried to explain, "This is where we are not understood. Maybe it's too complicated to explain. It is like running or driving and we go faster and faster while excitement builds. During the escalations we are still in control, but eventually the speed pushes us beyond control. It's as if we forget about needing control. The speed keeps building and our control is reduced to steering only, because we have no brakes. Momentum carries us. It's impossible to make an abrupt turn or stop. But we feel too good to be afraid. Besides, if we've been there before, we know that it is going to be an insidiously deceitful euphoria. We embrace it happily, chasing after the thought of the moment. We don't know or understand at what point we crossed over the point of no return; where we yield our judgment to the euphoria, and then have no conscious, personal control of our destiny."

"Well said, Eileen," Dr. Lavoy observed. "Could I add that after you pass the point of no return, it is then up to family, loved ones, friends, society, the law, or the health profession to arrest the mania and perhaps the person in order to reestablish control."

"Of course." Eileen continued, "We are in a sort of meltdown situation. Some will go until we destroy ourselves. Our families think we can just stop. They think we just need to realize what we're doing and stop. Friends are often amused at our energy and generosity, and they take advantage of us. It's an awful situation looking back on it, but when we are manic, it's a wonderful feeling, so the key in treatment is for us to have a continuing awareness, and vigilant maintenance techniques."

"That's right," Dr. Lavoy interjected. "If for any reason the feeling begins to indicate an impending episode, whether manic or depressive, the person should immediately contact their psychiatrist so that the treatment regimen can be adjusted, hopefully quickly enough to avert an outright episode. Points on how to accomplish this are discussed from time to time in the DMDA meetings."

"I know but it's not like we carry around a list and continually refer to it. That's asking too much."

"No, it's not asking one to carry a list; it's living with an awareness. When you first notice the symptoms of mood escalation in either direction, up or down, that's the point to immediately tell your family, especially get to your psychiatrist. Essentially, that is the only time at which you will be able to effectively keep yourself out of trouble with episodes of mania or depression. It is imperative to self-monitor and to force yourself to listen to others when they mention that they think that you are headed for a high or a low. I guess this is a difficult imposition, listening to others, but it often is the only way. It may be the only signal you have before you pass the point of no return."

On that particular occasion with Mr. Broadman, Eileen was not heeding her escalating euphoria. Instead, she had enthusiastically accepted it. She projected herself into multiple avenues of fun; in her work, preparing her presentation, intently enjoying the flirty banter with Broadman and then preparing for her trip to Texas, which she eagerly awaited. She did not make time for a call to Dupree.

Chapter 33
Cozy Flight

Eileen paused temporarily during her pressured, non-stop, one-sided conversation. The brief respite prompted Broadman to think, ‘maybe I should have postponed this trip, she's as high as this plane, thirty thousand feet, and approaching Mach one. She may be too fast, and crash our plans. Oh, well, it's not like she's not making sense. Her highs are part of her charisma.' He remembered the warnings from Dr. Lavoy. “Her judgment could be impaired and her reach overextended. Those around her could become exhausted attempting to keep up, or ultimately frustrated and withdraw from her.” He knew that it was up to him, to subdue her energy, and be a buffer with Dr. Ackerman. They would be in Houston in an hour and a half. 'This trip could be crucial to an immediate return on our investment. We could become wildly profitable, even if the original company purpose never materializes.' He was grateful to Eileen and increasingly captivated by her beauty, charm and energy. Eileen was also a fine person; she invariably includes ways to help others with her creative and imaginative opportunities. For example, he reasoned, 'This trip was not about her but a solidly reasoned opportunity to help Dr. Ackerman, and to negotiate a business arrangement that would be helpful to everyone in our company, her no more than anyone else. The moon shuttle itself, while a big accomplishment for her would be helping the space program. It would help all the investors and all the potential eager travelers. To hear her tell it, it was also going to be a spiritual turning point for everyone.'

Broadman, a religious man himself, harbored doubts about the entire project when conversations focused on the parallel spiritual mission. 'That side of it seems unrealistic, fanatical, and even close,' he thought, 'to those Doomsday prophets.' He was not comfortable with the idea that people were ready for a Messianic awakening. 'It is uncanny. It satisfies Dr. Griffiths' all-inclusive, Spiritual Godliness and, who knows, we could be approaching the end of time. Maybe she is in the grand scheme of things,' he mused, with his guard down, 'and I'm a spoke in life's biggest wheel of fortune. It was all too complicated,' so he resolved, 'to stick to the business aspect of Eileen's life. I'll leave the spiritual philosophies and ministry to Dr. Griffiths.'

Eileen had been silent for just those few moments but was talking again, "And by the way, I don't think I've remembered to tell you that there are many other uses for Dr. Ackerman's product. Our company can help him market this product for new uses because it doesn't matter how hot this material gets, you can still hold it in your hand without getting burned. So, don't you see, all the potential uses? For example, cooking utensils can have the sides and the handles laminated with this so that only the bottom and the interior will be hot to touch. Housewives and kids will be protected from being burned. Radiator caps for cars could be coated with this and steering wheels on cars. My guess is that Ackerman has not yet focused his attention beyond the obvious space implications."

"Eileen, my God. Where do you get all these ideas? Don't you ever stop thinking? But you're right, if the cost isn't prohibitive, those are good uses, and there possibly might be many others."

"I'm excited! I think this is a great opportunity for us. I'm a dreamer. My dream is to build a city on the moon. I dream with my eyes open, that way I remember and collect them, enjoy them, and embellish them. When I can, I do something about them. Too many people dream with their eyes closed and then forget."

"Well, don't stop dreaming, you're a heck of a gal. I'm glad to be a companion on your adventurous trips."

"Oh, how odd that you should say that, Robert nicknamed me 'Trip.'"

"I thought of nicknaming you but decided against it. Miss Robbins is so formal, but of course, it's proper in public."

"Eileen is fine, Mr. Broadman. I also thought of nicknaming you, but it seemed improper and disrespectful."

"Okay" Mr. Broadman summarized, "If you are Eileen, then I'm John, except in the presence of others."

Eileen accepted, "That's fine."

"We should settle ourselves down and plan our approach to Dr. Ackerman, so we don't have any guffaws. I'll try to get him to talk about himself. We need to know the type person we are dealing with. I'll leave the technical jargon to you, but I'll ease back in for the business negotiation. Fair enough?"

"More than fair. You're giving me the easy part."

"Well, what comes natural for me may not come natural for you and vice versa, my dear. Sorry, that just slipped out. Didn't mean anything by it." But realizing her tone had been at least neutral if not a bit warm, he added, "But I did sort of like the ring of it, at least for private conversation."

"Then, we'll definitely have to find time for more private conversation."

"I thought we were settling this conversation down. Things just seem to keep heating up." Broadman observed.

"Well I'm enjoying the warmth, and it certainly isn't too hot yet. It is widely held that there is a time and a place for everything."

They were quiet during the landing. Eileen was completely absorbed in the moment, highly energized and flirting, projecting vivid imagery of romantic dinners and exotic trips abroad. She had her head back and her eyes closed but her hand reached out and took John's and held it tightly.

Broadman became alive with good feelings and happy thoughts, 'Eileen is great fun; I can let my hair down with her, and be open. She makes me remember, and recapture my youth.' When she took his hand it came as a surprise to him. He glanced over but she was merely sitting still with her eyes closed, displaying a contented smile. Holding her hand, he appreciated the softness, warmth, tenderness and smallness of her hand but the quality of the grip brought him abruptly face to face with the dilemma he had postponed. Her hand conveyed a message signaling their bonding. More intimacy was now distinctly possible. It had been years since he had enjoyed such an enviable position. Admittedly, he had fantasized about this moment, but now he was frightened. He knew Eileen was high. Her judgment was impaired. She was fragile. He recalled a previous relationship, his only extramarital foray; the similarity was unsettling. By taking that last intimate step he could destroy their entire relationship, their trust, their business, their friendship. He had thought that he could handle it the last time. He was tempted to believe that 'This is different, we can handle it.' He wanted this possible one last opportunity. Despite her being betrothed, no one would know. It could be her last fling and mine also.'

The jolt of the tires on runway contact brought them both out of their fantasy. They squeezed their hands tighter, but as soon as they were taxiing comfortably they released their hands and awkwardly found another place for them. They avoided eye contact or speaking. Halfway to baggage claim Broadman broke the silence by saying, "What does this Ackerman look like?"

Rather than describe him, Eileen answered with, "Not like a Texan. I'll point him out to you."

Mr. Broadman waited for the right moment to coach Eileen in her talks with Dr. Ackerman, "By the way, Eileen, don't talk faster than he can listen and don't tell him more than he can absorb, or needs to know."

Chapter 34
Houston Day

At baggage claim Dr. Ackerman spotted Eileen waving to him. He spoke first, "Welcome. This is Houston" adapting the space center's famous line. He followed with a gratuitous, "We're Huntsville's counterpart." He assumed their pride with the Huntsville Space Center. Dr. Ackerman proved to be well organized. He had lunch prior to their arrival knowing that Delta had served them lunch.

"I've arranged to take you to the space center to meet Mr. Kurt Rosser. He is in charge of materials procurement. He is our contact for purchasing the product we produce."

The drive to Houston was revealing. Eileen commented on how impressed she was with the city. Dr. Ackerman had very positive things to say about his city and the opportunity it afforded scientists. He moved there more than ten years ago from the University of Iowa where he felt his career was languishing. He contracted for a position with a petroleum company, but had been sage enough to negotiate a contract that allowed him to keep his own inventions, developed entirely on his private time and at his expense. This alerted Broadman to be careful during the negotiations, and not to expect a push-over victory, so he decided to use flattery as a bonding tool.

"That was quite an astute arrangement you negotiated. I'm impressed. You must have already had in mind some ideas for inventions."

"I did indeed, that's why I insisted on it. Even so, I was still able to get a contract making more than I made teaching at the university, but I must say I am quite intrigued with the project you have in Alabama. Mr. Dupree has told me of the progress you have made. You seem to have good resources there in Washington. I have a good support base here in Houston with Mr. Rosser, so it really seems that we might have an opportunity of synergy. I am looking forward to hearing more about your project, and your thoughts on how we might work together."

Broadman was comfortable. It was beginning to sound as if Ackerman had tentatively decided favorably for them.

They had no trouble getting onto the space center property. The guards recognized Ackerman and waved him in without question. He drove them around the complex, impressing them that in true Texas tradition everything was huge. He pointed out the building containing mission control. His excitement to be involved in making space history was evident.

Broadman too, felt grateful to live in this era which made space travel not only possible, but an accomplished fact. Being a taxpaying citizen of the United States of America made him part of this history. To him it was a single and unique opportunity to gaze upon the building that actually guided Apollo XI to the moon and back, and now even as he was in the autumn of his years he continued to posture for even greater space conquests. He vowed not to be envious of Eileen's generation, who were inheriting such an enormous advantage. They have a platform from which they may launch whatever great adventure their destiny affords them.

Mr. Kurt Rosser was a matter-of-fact, no-nonsense busy but pleasant man. As soon as they were introduced he immediately summarized his situation and position.

"Dr. Ackerman has produced a compound which we tested and are satisfied that it will suit our needs. It gives the protection we need, at a weight we can manage, and at a cost we can afford. I am in charge of procurement. If Dr. Ackerman can demonstrate to me a capability of producing the amount of material we need in the time-frame we require, he has my word for an exclusive contract until something better comes along. We know of nothing on the horizon that could be better than his compound. We know of no one attempting to produce a similar compound. I lay this out for you boldly because Dr. Ackerman tells me that your investment group is key in making this happen. Do you have any questions?"

All of Broadman's questions were answered. Mr. Rosser perhaps unwittingly had told him that Dr. Ackerman didn't have a back-up plan for funding that would be serious competition for them. "Mr. Rosser, as one businessman to another, I am impressed. You cut to the chase. You gave us the information we needed in five minutes. I've seen people take half a day to get around to this much specificity. Thank you very much, sir. Any further questions we have would be directly about the compound itself and the manufacture thereof."

Eileen had confined herself to shaking hands, smiling pleasantly, and trying to not appear as a fifth wheel. Mr. Broadman, in fact, had been impressed at her restraint. He wanted to compliment her, but he would wait for the opportune moment.

As Dr. Ackerman drove them from the space center to his laboratory he stated, "I thought you would want to hear it from the horse's mouth that if we can produce the product we have a contract. Now you will see our laboratory. You'll find it much more modest than the space center. I figured we should have an itinerary, and we do, but I didn't print it up. Meet you at the airport, take you to meet Mr. Rosser, check out the laboratory and the product, and then we'll go back to the hotel and get you checked in. I have arranged for us to have a room and an overhead projector for your convenience in your presentation and proposal. I've made reservations at the Auditorium Hotel."

"I figure we'll have a question and answer session that will be reciprocal. We can each, hopefully, get the answers we need. We should be able to finish around five-thirty, and with your permission, we could get together at the hotel dining room around seven-thirty for dinner. They really do a very nice job. My wife would like to join us. I hope you don't mind. She likes to feel comfortable with my business associates."

Mr. Broadman was quick to accept and observed that it was especially thoughtful to have his wife join them. His unspoken thoughts were not even hinted in his quick response to Dr. Ackerman's request. He surmised that Mrs. Ackerman was to do a character assessment of them. Thankfully, he would have time to prepare Eileen. She had been a jewel so far, holding her personal enthusiasm and energy to a minimal level. Mr. Broadman worried; 'as the day gets longer, and she becomes more tired or stressed, or if she has a drink or two, she could begin to lose her composure and judgment, and blow the whole deal.'

Ackerman appeared pleased at Mr. Broadman's acceptance. Broadman surmised, 'These scientists tend to stick together. It wouldn't surprise me if his wife is a psychologist.'

The laboratory was fascinating. Mr. Ackerson had rented warehouse space. The entrance was surprisingly insecure; they walked in with no encumbrances. One person was visible. A balding, tall, six-foot, Caucasian male came toward them. Dr. Ackerman introduced him as Mr. Lonnie Tynes. He comprised the entire staff. Dr. Ackerman introduced them as Mr. Broadman and Miss Robbins from Alabama, who had important connections with the Huntsville Space Program. Dr. Ackerman explained that he and Lonnie were going to demonstrate their product for them, and would answer any questions. "If you'll come with us, we are going to show you the process from beginning to end. On this table, we have four beakers. In the first beaker there is a mixture of solids which has been mixed thoroughly. In the second beaker there is likewise a mixture of different solids, also mixed thoroughly. In the third beaker is a liquid chemical. The fourth beaker contains another liquid chemical. You will notice that we will pour the ingredients from beaker two into beaker three. These will be mixed thoroughly. After sufficient time, which we base on the amount of ingredients mixed and the temperature of the ingredients, generally the ambient temperature, we will then have the ingredients from beaker one poured into beaker three, followed immediately by mixing the contents from beaker four. These fully mixed ingredients will then be ready for baking. You will now observe the processes of curing the product. We pour the contents from the final mixture into this tray of squares. You will note different shapes, sizes and thicknesses. We will pour a slight amount into this separate tray which is simply a thin, aluminum pan. The first tray is a ceramic fired hardened tray. We will then use an ordinary paint brush to paint this material onto this small section of cardboard and we will put several coats on to thicken it. We dry for approximately six hours. We then place it in a kiln and fire it for three hours at fifteen hundred degrees Fahrenheit."

"To expedite our demonstration, Lonnie began this firing process about three hours ago. The material has been in the kiln for three hours. So, we will extract an exact copy of the mixture you just witnessed. Later we will fire those."

With that Lonnie opened the kiln door and with a pair of metal tongs reached inside and pulled out a duplicate tray with all the different design cutouts. He dumped them on the table so that they all fell in a heap.

Noteworthy, none of them cracked or broke. Ackerman asked, "Would either of you be willing to pick one of these up with your bare fingers?"

Mr. Broadman dodged it by laughingly responding, "I'd rather not."

Eileen plainly said, "Not me."

Dr. Ackerman was making his point, 'What? No faith? Let me show you." He picked one up with each hand, and then from finger to finger, from palm to palm and then held them out to Eileen and Mr. Broadman. They each reached out with their bare hands and took the tiles from his hand, and stood there in absolute amazement. Broadman then cautiously picked one up from the pile. He had seen slight of hand and wanted to be to be totally convinced. Ackerman knew what he was doing, but chose not to mention it.

Ackerman said, "This is what will bring our astronauts safely back through the atmosphere."

Eileen added, "And our space bus."

"We certainly hope so," Dr. Ackerman said.

Dr. Ackerman stated they should now see how the remaining experiments had fared. When they reached for the painted cardboard, they found that of course, the cardboard had been burned away, and all that remained were little scattered pebbles and slivers of the material scattered about the tray holding them. "We haven't, as yet, been able to successfully paint our product onto surfaces. We are having to make the small squares and then glue them on to the surface. We had a severe technical problem because the heat could get through the seams between in the tiles. Our solution is old fashioned; we use a 'tongue and groove' technique." He picked up two other tiles from the heap and demonstrated the trough and the protrusion fitting together snugly. "So these will be built onto the spaceship covering every inch. We have a heat resistant adhesive that works well. As to the other tray, not fired in the kiln, you can see that it is still liquid. Do you have any questions?"

"One, how did you know you could touch it?" Eileen was ever curious.

"I didn't. I discovered it accidentally. As I was bringing it out of the kiln, I dropped it. Before I could react, my dog jumped at it and sniffed it. I noticed that his nose touched it and he didn't jump back, so I took a chance and touched it cautiously but felt nothing. I touched it again more confidently. Finally, placing my finger firmly on it, I felt no heat. Accidents account for many discoveries."

Dr. Ackerman drove them to the Auditorium Hotel in the Pioneer section of the city. He pointed out the proximity to the theaters, performance halls, and restaurants. It was, however, the understated luxury, charm, antiques, and gracious staff that most impressed Eileen and Mr. Broadman.

Mr. Broadman had no questions. At the hotel, Dr. Ackerman prepared the meeting room while Broadman and Eileen checked in. Broadman took the opportunity to plead with Eileen to keep her pace consistent with what she hears from Dr. Ackerman, and not to speed through things, not to try to oversell their proposal, not to get expansive about the details of Moon City. He asked that she "Just get the basic concept across: we are building a bus for civilians to travel to and from the moon. Show the interest that we have from our investors, and our potential base of customers. Show him the pie charts and bar graphs which portray our financial stability. Give pertinent history of our company, how we got started. Conclude with our financial strength, the cash on hand, and on-call revenues waiting in the wings. Don't forget our political connections, their desire to partner with Dr. Ackerman as someone who shares enthusiasm for space exploration and travel."

Eileen did all of that flawlessly. Dr. Ackerman was intent throughout the presentation. Mr. Broadman read his interest. He had not counted the head nods but there were many. Broadman was happy that Eileen was following his advice, taking her time, and sticking to the script. Broadman knew that she was about to wrap up, but suddenly she moved off script.

"This has been such an incredible project. I feel that we are a part of destiny; that God is making all of this possible because we will be able to spread God's word to all mankind."

Mr. Broadman's face froze and he gave a cold, fixed stare at Eileen. She caught his stare and realized that she should stop.

"God uses all of us. He puts all of us together as He chooses. I feel blessed to be a part of this project, and I feel He has had a hand in bringing us here to Houston to meet you. We have a great program and you have a great product. We should be a wonderful partnership." Then she stopped.

Finally, Broadman took a breath. A deep one.

Dr. Ackerman had a few questions about the other investors and their commitments, and about their Washington connections, their solidarity and dependability.

As Broadman hesitated one second to formulate his answer, Eileen held her engagement ring to Dr. Ackerman's eyes. As he looked at it, Eileen dispelled any doubts, "Rock solid." All three laughed heartily and no further explanation was requested. This mirthful moment concluded the meeting.

Chapter 35
Houston Evening

Mr. Broadman felt relieved. It occurred to him that he had been tense all day. Actually, quite pensive, fearing that Eileen's high would cause her to inadvertently sabotage their entire negotiation plan. One more big hurdle remained. Broadman doubted they would get through an entire dinner without Dr. Ackerman's wife sensing Eileen's hypomania. He feared this would come across as an undue eagerness. If Mrs. Ackerman felt rushed or uneasy she would advise Ackerman to seek funding in a more conventional manner. This was the Ackermans' first opportunity to reap bountiful rewards for his years of scientific research. She would scrutinize them closely for signs of character flaws, deceitfulness or incompatibility.

As soon as Dr. Ackerman exited the lobby, Broadman put his hand in the small of Eileen's back and escorted her to the lounge, "We have a few extra minutes. Why don't we relax and coordinate our plans for the evening?"

Eileen easily followed the direction of his firm touch just as a dance partner might follow a lead; she relished the moment. "Well, so far it's been a great day. I would say the prospects are looking pretty good for the evening. Let's relax and enjoy the evening."

Mr. Broadman continued, "It has been a great day. You have been wonderful. You have been beautiful in all respects. Vibrant with enthusiasm, smart with restraint, socially charming, and you gave a superb presentation. In fact, the best I have ever heard you present it. You stopped me cold, and Ackerman too, with your 'rock solid' answer. That was priceless."

The barmaid sat a tray of nuts on the table and asked if she could get drinks for them. Broadman quickly raised his hand to hush Eileen before she could answer, and asked for a few more moments to talk it over.

Eileen was puzzled. 'I know what I want, and if he doesn't why did he bring me here?'

"Eileen, my dear, you have been brilliant today. We have passed through several tests, I believe with flying colors. The next one will be more difficult. Please hear me out. The last thing I want to be to you is a father or your shrink."

"Then don't."

"I want a true friendship. Sometimes this means a little of everything, so don't get upset."

"Am I about to get a lecture? If I have done so well, then why?"

"Because tonight is different. We will be in a social setting, we'll be quite relaxed, our guard will be down and his wife will be psyching us out. If we don't pass her test we don't get the contract. She will advise him to seek conventional financing despite it being more controlling and more expensive. She can count on institutional rules and regulations. With us, she has to rely on her instinct, her calculated observations of whether we are fiscally and characterologically right for her husband's, and consequently, her big opportunity. This is their big chance and she knows it. She will be a tough judge tonight. I am asking you to not have any alcohol now, or at dinner."

He had done the best he could. He had tried not to sound too authoritative, yet firm, but kind, and almost pleading.

Eileen heard this with the background of her mental references. It sounded like ownership. What would give him the right? She reacted differently now than she had at any previous time with him.

"Well, for someone who doesn't want to be my father or my shrink, you did a strong impersonation of both."

"I did neither. You are my friend and business partner. I admire and adore you. Our relationship is unique. I admire your beauty, your charm, your intellect, your education, professionalism, elegant social grace, even your expansive thinking and energy, but you have little experience in the business world which is our stage tonight. You have, in fact, very little experience in controlling your chemical imbalance, but what we both know from what you told me, and what the doctor says, is that alcohol causes major problems. You, I, nor our business can afford to have a problem tonight. Ackerman is a Ph.D. I'm betting his wife is a Ph.D., probably a psychologist. At any rate, she will be bright, and she will be psyching us out for everything she can. If she picks up any hint of problems that makes us look unstable, she will insist that he obtain his financing elsewhere, and we will be out in the cold. Our investors are enthusiastic, but now it appears that it is going to take years to get our project accomplished, it would give us needed and comfortable breathing room to seal a deal like this early in our corporate life. After dinner, if you would like to come back here and have a drink I'll have one with you."

"Oh, I hate this illness. I am a prisoner to it."

"Don't hate me or yourself. We all have things about ourselves that we don't like, but if we hate it we hate ourselves. We must accept ourselves and live with who we are, and what we are. It is up to us to make the best of our talents or lack thereof. In your case, we might never have met except for your high level of energy. Your incredible drive propelled you to do things that were like a magnet for me. I love that about you. Let's just make sure that it's always used positively."

The barmaid was approaching, Eileen looked at her and said, "I will have your very strongest tonic water with lime, please."

Broadman laughed. He thought he should follow suit but instead he ordered bourbon, telling Eileen, "I am the opposite, I do better with a drink."

Eileen was mellowing, "Oh, you always do fine. I'm sorry to be so testy."

"Don't give it a second thought, you're entitled."

It's uncanny how people use words that define a meaning far deeper than their conscious awareness. When two people notice one another in a positive way and steer their relationships on an intersecting path, there is a point at which they assume an entitlement. That becomes the Entitlement Intersection. It may be spoken as in marriage, it may be tacit, soulful, eye-to-eye, or it may be symbolic hand clasping such as Eileen's and Broadman's had been earlier that day. Once this happens the relationship is significantly changed with each person assuming an entitlement of partial ownership of the other. There are many complicating ways the relationship proceeds, but in essence each begins to use the opportunity for the task of remodeling or fine-tuning the other.

At dinner that evening, Julie Ackerman was, at least to Broadman, surprisingly attractive, very well groomed, impeccably mannered, and most charming. In fact, the amount of charm was incongruous to her detailed perfectionism in all other areas. He decided to meet her charm with as genuine and equal presentation as possible, but resolved to not let his guard down. He hoped Eileen would be up to the task and follow his lead. He was still doubtful that she could maintain control throughout the evening. After the pleasantries, they gave Mrs. Ackerman the opportunity to lead with her questions. Broadman and Eileen appeared completely unguarded, and spontaneously answered questions with enthusiasm and assuredness. They further displayed their confidence by sharing a couple of small setbacks which they had already overcome. They were sure that the Ackermans had no doubt experienced setbacks. She would be familiar with surprises and glitches and surely be suspicious if they seemed so perfect as to have no warts or scars. They would avoid being categorized by her as the proverbial, "It sounds too good to be true."

Red wine was served and Eileen allowed the wine steward to include her. Broadman watched with concern, but he paid no obvious attention to it. He noticed Eileen picking the glass up several times during dinner but he also noted the volume tended not to diminish. Julie also noticed and surprised them by asking Eileen if the wine was okay.

"Oh, the wine is perfect, in fact delicious. It's me that's the problem. I couldn't pass it up, yet I usually get headaches from red wine, so I try to enjoy the taste, but not enough to get a headache."

"Oh, you poor dear. I don't know what I would do if I couldn't have my red wine." Julie had bought Eileen's explanation apparently with no reservation. She offered white wine, maybe a Chardonnay, but Eileen declined with thanks anyway.

Broadman was so impressed with Eileen's handling of the evening that he felt guilty for having discussed his forebodings with her.

Bonding ensued progressively throughout the evening. In fact, the Ackermans expressed their desire to come to Huntsville, and also to visit them in Birmingham. Mrs. Ackerman even asked them to return for a longer stay in Houston. When the Ackermans departed the hotel, Eileen and Broadman directed themselves to the lounge as if they were on automatic pilot. As soon as the server reached their table, Eileen ordered a gin and tonic. Broadman did not protest and ordered bourbon. They were both pleased with the day, and felt confident the breakfast meeting would bring an agreement between them.

Eileen laughed, "You were so close. How did you know? Though she wasn't a psychologist, she was a doctor of social work. I noticed when she had a couple of glasses of wine she was more open about herself and had fewer questions for us."

"I noticed that also."

Chapter 36
Houston After Hours

Into her third drink, Eileen raced ahead of her partner. She was alive, vibrant, needy; her body transformed and full of hormones. She reached out to Broadman, touching him: holding his hand, stroking his cheek, touching his thigh, looking directly into his eyes, and talking non-stop. She asked question after question about him, his life, his likes, his dislikes, but rarely gave him time to answer.

Broadman, into his fifth drink of the evening, laughed heartily, obviously enjoying himself. He consciously decided to risk making a pass at her. Her eyes and her touch were beguiling. He signed the tab and asked Eileen to invite him to her room. He could bring a bottle of champagne. She admitted that sounded quite fun. It was only ten-forty five.

In Eileen's room Broadman uncorked the champagne with merry fanfare. They each enjoyed half a glass and laughter. Eileen excused herself to go to the powder room and returned shortly wearing nothing but her panties and alcohol breath. Broadman's pupils expanded to accommodate her voluptuous beauty. He stood motionless, drinking in her beauty. His youth was reborn; he embraced and held her perfect and eager body. He could not remember when he had felt skin so soft and warm.

A sharp knock on the door arrested their lustful merriness. They jumped as if the sound had been a gunshot. They stared at each other in frozen fear, but looked toward the door as a second knock demanded attention. A voice pierced the silence, "Room service." It was her room so he urged her to go to the door. Eileen slipped on a robe and looked through the peephole. A gentleman stood there holding a tray that, indeed, appeared to be room service. She asserted through the door, "I didn't order room service."

"Ma'am, we have this order for, oh, oh, I am so sorry, I am on the wrong floor please forgive me. I hope I didn't disturb you."

"No, that's quite all right," she said but her heart was pounding a different answer.

Broadman visibly shaken, sat down on the bed as soon as their safety was apparent. He quickly rebuttoned his shirt.

Eileen came and sat beside him. Reading his nervousness she took his hand and said, "I am so sorry."

"Eileen, my dear, two minutes ago was one of the most exciting moments of my entire life. One minute ago had to be the most frightening moment of my life. How often would a room server go to the wrong room? I think your God has just given us both a wake-up call. Can you ever forgive me? You are high, my dear, you have had alcohol; I even provided it. Your judgment is impaired. I am old, greedy, and horny. My judgment is clouded. I was completely out of bounds. We both need to take our medicine, and say our prayers. I'm married. You're engaged to a fine man. I had a good marriage. You aspire to a good one. Don't spoil it, ever. I will be content to be your business partner, your client; and we will have a secret smile for each other once in a while. That will have to do. I'll just go to my room, and see you in the morning."

"I understand. I bet Griffiths put a spell on us." They both laughed.

The next morning, Eileen decided to skip breakfast and Broadman was grateful. He didn't want to face her until after his meeting with Ackerman.

Ackerman entered with a friendly smile and warm handshake. Unsolicited, he offered up front that his wife had enjoyed meeting them. Broadman assured him that it was mutual and he hoped they had as good a night as his. Broadman and Ackerman enjoyed a hearty breakfast buffet. They ate and talked of their future partnership and worked on the details. Broadman accomplished all he had hoped for. He offered to have his legal team prepare the documents in draft and forward them to Ackerman for his confirmation or critique. When they were comfortable with their agreement then they could have their respective attorneys get the wording exact before executing them.

Broadman was now confident of their partnership. This was a solid deal. A sure-fire investment. If they never even build a space bus or Moon City it really wouldn't matter from an investor standpoint. Their ROI would beat the stock market handsomely. He decided to keep this insight to himself for now.

The flight back to Birmingham was initially awkward. For the first hour they discussed ramifications of their new agreement, and what they would be able to do with it. Eventually the conversation gravitated to themselves and turned gratifying. They skirted around embarrassment and expressed joy for their closeness. They decided to be happy that they'd had an opportunity, but exercised the willpower to forego carnal pleasures, even if with a little help. Had they not resisted, it likely would have reduced them to jealous lovers, rather than effective business partners and friends for life. They sealed the thought with an impassionate, acquiescing, soft kiss of their lips. As they sat in silence, each rubbed their eyes to hide the moisture.

The long flight was tantamount to forced reflection. 'What if I destroyed my marriage before it ever began? No, not me, but this illness, this inner beast. It's so insidious. It feels so good. It's so seductive. I thought I knew what to expect, but I didn't know it was happening. Wow! This is frightening!'

Eileen decided to call Dr. Lavoy. She wanted to ask if he could recommend a book for her. She would also ask him if a medication adjustment was in order.

Eileen was too embarrassed to tell Robert, but she would discuss with him the extent of the danger and ask for his loving observation of her mood level.

Chapter 37
The Wedding

Eileen dreaded discussing the wedding guest list with her mother. The concern wasn't about the numbers. She, being their only daughter, would provide her parents' only occasion to showcase their vaulted status. The more the guests, the bigger the splash, the more important they would appear and feel. She worried about her mother's reaction to inviting members of the support group. She held one ace as she broached the subject.

"Mom, I'm real excited about our guest list. My maid of honor and attendants are perfect. Can you think of anyone we have overlooked? Did I tell you that Mr. Broadman is definitely coming?"

"That's very nice of him, dear."

"Oh, I know, we haven't invited Freddie yet."

"Freddie? Why would we invite Freddie? He's not one of us."

"That's just it mom, Freddie is one of us. Freddie is my friend. In fact, I need to invite Freddie and his wife, Alma, and, of course, if I'm inviting them, I will need to invite at least a few others from the support group; it wouldn't seem right not to."

"Eileen, you can't be serious. Not those people! What would everyone think? We are not like them."

"Mom, don't you see, I am them. We fight the same beast. They, like me, aren't non-persons just because they have this illness."

"Stop it! Just hush! You are not like them! I won't hear it!"

"Then you shouldn't have given me this gene!"

"I didn't. Don't blame me. You got it from your father!"

"Well, you married him, and frankly all things considered, I'm satisfied and you should be too. You have been pretty lucky. Look around you. Listen to me, Mom, these are my friends and my support group. They know what I go through because they also live it; you don't. You can't understand it. You have never felt what I feel when I'm flying on top of the world, or for that matter being consumed by unyielding black quicksand. They know. They have been there. When you tell me everything will be better, it's platitudes and bullshit. When they tell me things will be better, I know they have been there and come back. They are reaching out to pull me back. Freddie has protected me from those who you would say are 'our people'; Freddie is my friend. I can't, and won't dishonor him by not inviting him to my wedding. There are a few others that have been close enough to be invited. It's not carte blanche. I'm not inviting everyone I've met, just some meaningful friends that include Freddie and a few others."

"Oh, I wish you wouldn't. I am afraid they will be disruptive."

"They are civil people, Mom." Then Eileen played her ace, "I suppose you don't want me to invite Senator Johnson either?"

"Did you say Senator Johnson? Do you think he might come; are you sure? Her mother's intrigue was showing.

"No, Mom, I'm not sure but Robert is very close to him and I do think there is a good chance that he will come. I'm sure it won't matter to *him* who else is there. One thing about politicians, the more hands they shake, the more votes they get and it doesn't matter to them what color hand casts the ballot."

Knowing she had been played and lost, her mother yielded without agreeing, "You are going to be the death of me; I just know it."

"Oh, Mom, get over it. These are the 70's. It has been more than a hundred years since the Confederates lost. Let's move on."

The irony had not escaped Eileen that one of the first persons her mother had wanted to invite was Florene, a black domestic helper, who had been with the family throughout the years since Eileen was a small child. It had never occurred to her mother not to consider inviting her to the wedding and the reception, and not as a helper, but rather, as a guest.

The wedding was planned between congressional sessions, more for

Robert's convenience than anything else, but it did allow the opportunity for Senator Johnson to attend. He sent his RSVP of his intent to attend. Eileen's mother made sure that some of her most gossip inclined friends knew of his planned presence.

Eileen and her mother decided to have the wedding at the Episcopal Church of the Advent – a historical and gloriously beautiful church in downtown Birmingham, coincidentally established in 1873, the year Birmingham was incorporated.

When Robert entered the church for the first time, he felt a compelling spiritual presence. The stained glass windows provided both beauty and access to light. The vaulted, open ceiling seemed like an anteroom to Heaven. He felt a warmth and comfort and knew God was present.

Eileen and her mother looked at every wedding gown available including the Bridal Shoppe in Mountain Brook Village and Loveman's in downtown Birmingham. The invitations were custom printed at Dewberry's.

The reception would be at the Birmingham Country Club. But the bride and groom's cakes had to be from Waites. They could not pass up the traditional sugar-spun frosting, always eagerly anticipated, and a work of art.

On the wedding day, when Robert Dupree took his position as the groom in waiting, the congregation was duly impressed with his handsome stature. Eileen's parents had never been more proud.

When the trumpets blared and the bridal march commanded all heads to turn, Eileen's beauty caused an audible gasp. Eileen was queen-like, and radiant in regal beauty. Herschel beamed as the proud parent ushering Eileen slowly down the center aisle. It would be the slowest walk of her life. She felt the warmth and joy of every eye focused on her. The excitement and anticipation kept her from recognizing all of the guests but on her left she caught a glimpse of Freddie who had staked out an aisle seat and wore the biggest smile she had ever seen.

The ceremony proceeded with breathtaking beauty.

The reception was large, loud and festive. Eileen busily introduced Robert to many of the guests.

Senator Johnson took advantage of the occasion and spoke to as many of the guests as possible. It would have been obvious to any observer that he spent more time talking to Freddie than most of the others. He was politically savvy.

Freddie and Alma were appreciative of being included. They were polite and instinctively talked about everything but illness. Freddie talked about having mutual friends and he praised Eileen for once saving their daughter's life.

Eileen praised Freddie as having defended her honor and prevented an unwelcome assault. Freddie was the tallest man at the reception. When he left, it was with pride and happiness, feeling taller than ever before.

Many of the guests offered their congratulations and well wishes as a prelude to their exit. Others milled around excitedly awaiting the bouquet and garter toss. Robert had no interest in who caught the garter. Eileen passionately wanted Missy, her maid of honor, to catch her bouquet. Missy, more than any of her friends, had been a constant and loyal confidant, a safe haven, a hideaway, a ready escape from the maddening pressures of life. It had been with Missy that she first cried about her illness, fearing that it was going to ruin her life. Would it stigmatize her and isolate her from all her friends, even Missy? It had been Missy who had encouraged her during her low points, and especially when she was doubting the saneness of marrying a Yankee working in Washington. Eileen knew how desperately Missy wanted to be married and have children. She could not have been more the quintessential Southern Belle who wanted a good husband, a home, a family, and eventually grandchildren. After high school she had gone to Auburn University, graduated with honors and was now teaching at Mountain Brook Elementary School. She was a human recycle machine.

No one knew, not even Robert, that Eileen practiced throwing the bouquet over her head using a rolled-up newspaper. She wanted to aim as close to Missy as possible. When the photographer gathered all the young hopeful ladies, Eileen stood exactly the distance she had practiced the throw, and turned her back. She became nervous because the photographer would not quickly signal for the toss.

Missy was equally nervous because Eileen had told her, "Once you take your position and I see where you are, don't move for anything. I am going to throw it directly to you." Neither of them needed to worry. Missy was surrounded by all the bridesmaids and a host of others. She thought the bridesmaids were competition, not realizing they were actually forming a buffer of protection for her. They knew her passion for romance and family. Each of them wanted Missy to catch the bouquet as much as she desired to catch it. No one had said a word to each other. It was a spontaneous, intuitive conspiracy. All other hopefuls were on the periphery with no chance of penetrating closer.

The photographer signaled and began to count. Exactly on three, the bouquet was in the air. It was a perfect pitch directly to Missy. A crowd of aspiring maidens from all sides rushed toward it, but were hopelessly stalled by the circle of bridesmaids whose hands were in the air perfunctorily leaving Missy's hands above all others for the perfect catch.

The photographer assembled all the available bachelors behind Dupree who was instructed to toss the garter on the count of three.

Eileen saw Griffiths in the group. Though uncomfortable being there, his presence would prevent unpleasantries that would be consequent to a refusal. Her first thought was 'wouldn't it be neat if he catches the garter,' but her second thought was 'No, I don't want that. If he were married, he might not be as available,' she had grown to appreciate and depend on his availability. The garter was in the air. Eileen willed it to go away from Griffiths which it did, to her and his relief. She did not even know the man who gleefully snatched it from the air.

Eileen and Bob were told it was time to leave. The car was waiting. They began saying their repeated and increasingly abbreviated good-byes. It suddenly and ominously occurred to Eileen that she did not know where they were going. She had planned everything to this point, but from this point forward Robert had made the plans. Griffiths would later postulate that it was Robert's way of asserting dominance immediately upon transforming her to Mrs. Dupree. Griffiths would add the observation that anyone should see that Eileen would not be the submissive, genteel Southern Belle. In the honeymoon surprise she had nevertheless been all too willing. Her hands had been full with the planning of the wedding and coordinating the varied things necessary for it. Anyway, he had asked her for destinations of interests. She felt certain that her choices would include his and she would enjoy being anywhere her new husband decided to take her.

Approaching the car she met with her first surprise. Freddie was chauffeuring. Bob had arranged for him to drive them to the airport. He would have the car cleaned and stored until they returned.

The hail storm of rice continued until they pulled the door to, closing themselves off from their friends and their past and their individual lives. The only remnant was the continued rata tat tat of rice pelting the windows.

The motor was idling. Freddie's foot lifted off the brake and the car began to move. Eileen was on the right, closest to the crowd and in a surreal scene she was moving away while the well wishers were yelling and throwing things at her. Tears began to stream down her cheeks. Her life was changing forever. Her friends were falling away. How would they be to her when she next saw them? What if she could no longer see them?

Eileen turned to Robert, and reached for him, pulled at him as if to reaffirm that she was alive and this was a new beginning and not an end.

Robert saw the tears and thought she regretted marrying him, "What's wrong?" he asked.

"Oh Robert, I am so, so happy. We're married. I am Mrs. Dupree. Where are we going? You didn't tell me we would have a chauffeur."

Robert, though relieved, wondered, 'Is she truly happy?' He could only hope so. "All in good time. You'll know soon enough where we are headed. You could at least speak to the chauffeur."

"Oh, hi, Freddie! I was preoccupied. Where are we headed?"

Freddie teased, "On your honeymoon."

"So, it's a guy thing, huh. You've both teamed up on me. Where am I being taken?"

Freddie defended, "I am quite sure I don't know, ma'am. I'm just drivin' you to the airport, and then I'll take care of the car for you, but I bet it will be nice and ya'll will have a great honeymoon. Life is a wonderful thing, just like families. Ya'll don't wait too long to start a family, you hear? That was the most beautiful wedding I ever saw. I want you to know how much I appreciate being there, Alma too. We had a good time."

Shortly they were at the Delta departure station at the Birmingham International Airport.

The SkyCap was with them momentarily and loaded their luggage onto his cart. Freddie looked at Dupree and offered, "Don't ya'll worry none. I'm going to take good care of the car. I'll leave it back at Ms. Eileen's place. Ya'll need to have fun and I'll be here with the car to pick you up when you get back Sunday two weeks from now."

The two men shook hands. Dupree thanked him and told him how much easier it was on them to have him drive them to the airport. He transferred a folded fifty dollar bill from his palm to Freddie, signaling the sincerity of his comment. Although Freddie felt the bill in his hand he didn't look at it. He kept his eyes on Robert and Eileen as they followed the porter into the building. Just as they were entering the door, they simultaneously stopped, turned and waved to Freddie, as if they had heard his silent mental call to them. Freddie smiled broadly and waved them on to their future.

Chapter 38
The Honeymoon

Inside the terminal, Robert led the way to the ticket counter as Eileen held on adoringly, as new brides are prone to do. At the counter, an attractive, pleasant attendant took the ticket from Robert.

"Where will you be traveling today?" she asked.

"Atlanta," Robert chose a brief reply.

"And on to Hawaii tomorrow I see" prematurely announcing his surprise destination.

Eileen squeezed his arm, "Hawaii? That sounds romantic." Robert looked straight ahead at the attendant and said, "Oh, is that where we will be headed tomorrow?"

The attendant's puzzled appearance was understandable.

"It was a surprise," Robert lamented.

"Oh, I'm so sorry; I didn't know."

"Of course you didn't. It's quite alright."

"It's more than alright, it's fantastic," Eileen chimed with delight. Hawaii had been at the top of her hint list. It was her dream vacation. She had heard about Waikiki Beach, Diamond Head, Pearl Harbor, pineapple fields, Macadamia groves and much more.' Eileen was eager to see it all. She really wanted to go to the garden island and was now hoping desperately that it had been included in his surprise. "Oh, Robert, I'm so happy. Thank you for choosing Hawaii. How did you know it was exactly what I wanted to do?"

"Oh, I couldn't know for sure. I listened to your words and your tone of voice. I prayed that I was right. I didn't know until now. Maybe this is a good omen for reading each other."

"Oh, I hope so. You are so wonderful. I love you."

After the bags were checked, they sat and talked softly. Deliberately Eileen raised her head and looked around and then with bright eyes and excitement turned to Robert and observed, "Do you realize that since becoming Mrs. Dupree, this is the first time we have not been in conversation with someone else? This is the first time just the two of us are talking."

"Yes, my dear. I was formulating a way to thank you for becoming Mrs. Dupree. I shall forever be thankful, grateful and happy. I trust that you will also. I know at this moment I am the happiest man on earth."

"And I am the happiest woman. I eagerly look forward to the rest of my life with you. For the next two weeks I shall think of nothing but you and us."

Robert confided that he had fallen hopelessly in love the moment he first saw her. "Each and every subsequent encounter has deepened my love, admiration and appreciation of you. Until meeting you, no one met my needs so well. You make me feel free to be in love" He confided that it was easy for him to relax and have a good time. His difficult task had been to commit to any relationship until her. He explained that other men have the same problem. "It was not just liking you a hell of a lot, or even being in love with you. It was a need to feel an overall security that I am all that you need and that you are all that I need."

Robert had thought about this. He was about to say more. As his lips parted, her right forefinger sealed them with a deft touch. She was looking into his eyes reading his thoughts. She would take a chance on hearing them later. This timing was good but the setting was wrong. She softly put her head against his shoulder to signal that she understood and that she was content.

The flight to Atlanta was short. In thirty minutes they were taxiing to the terminal gate at Hartsfield International Airport. After deplaning they made their way to baggage claim. Robert spotted the limo chauffeur first, only because he knew to look for him. However, he stayed quiet allowing Eileen to find the welcome sign.

"Robert, look." The chauffeur was holding a sign that read MR. AND

MRS. ROBERT DUPREE. I like it. I'm proud of you. That's impressive. You've thought of everything."

The chauffeur was a courteous and well-spoken gentleman. As they approached him, he said in a questioning way, "Mr. Dupree?" and seeing the nod from Robert turned and stated, "Mrs. Dupree, a pleasure to have you in Atlanta. Your bags should be out shortly. The limo is right outside."

Before long they were comfortably cruising into Atlanta, and shortly checked in at the downtown Hilton. Robert had reserved the honeymoon suite which was decorated more for the pleasure and taste of the bride than the groom. Eileen loved it.

After a few possessive and meaningful hugs and kisses Robert announced, "Let's get ready for dinner, we have reservations."

"Where?" she wanted to know.

Still being mysterious and controlling, Robert said, "You'll know when we get there."

When they were dressed they caught the elevator up. When the door opened they were at Nicolai's Roof.

"I'm speechless," Eileen exuded excitement. "I have heard of this place. Oh, I can't wait." She was like "Alice in Wonderland." Her pupils dilated to take in all of the Russian décor. It was charmingly different from his Washington haunts. The waiter addressed them professionally. He explained the possibilities of drink. Robert astonished her by ordering the vodka straight, and took the first shot Russian style. She selected a martini and sipped slowly. The waiter took their eleven-course order without notes. She was astounded, 'Surely he can't remember everything.' Amazed, she watched and found that all the waiters took all orders without notes, even at tables of eight or more.

Robert selected buffalo, rare, and declared it to be excellent. She selected petite filet mignon, medium-rare, and declared hers to be wonderful. As they went through the courses, each and every one arrived exactly as ordered.

At the end of the evening as they were about to leave, Eileen complimented, but quizzed the waiter, "The meal was awesome and your service outstanding. What a remarkable memory, or do you have a tape recorder?"

The waiter was accustomed to the frequent question. "Thank you, ma'am. No, ma'am. We are trained to remember. For example, I will focus first on one person such as yourself, and you start with a particular salad and then you move on to the next item." He proceeded at that point to recount for her everything that she had ordered in detail and then switched to Robert's and repeated the same for his order.

Eileen looked on in disbelief, and could only muster, "That's marvelous, simply marvelous."

They returned to their bridal suite with a wonderfully full wedding day behind them that was filled with joy, fulfillment, promises, friends, family, well wishes galore, surprises, and delights. Easily the most elaborate and memorable day of their lives. Finally alone they held each other, touched, kissed, caressed, and ultimately translated all of the day's promises into wonderfully passionate consummation of their new union.

Sunday morning's alarm jarred them from a deep sleep, tenacious because of physical and emotional exhaustion. With hardly a word between them they dressed and made their way to the airport. After checking in they found a light breakfast including coffee. Finally, their conversation picked up. They became excited rediscovering they were Mr. and Mrs. Dupree on their way to a fabulous Hawaiian honeymoon.

In the air their conversation continued, mostly about their excitement of being on their way to Hawaii. They talked also about being happy that they were together, and ready to be a couple, with the single life behind them.

By the time they were moving out of Georgia's air space, weariness and sleep enveloped them. Arriving at the Los Angeles stop over they awoke rejuvenated, and they had partially reset their biorhythms to Pacific Time.

From LA to Honolulu they talked about more practical topics. Subject number one was the Moon City project. Robert reiterated his intrigue and enthusiasm for the project. He told her that he was delighted that Senator Johnson was talking up the project to his colleagues but he also mentioned the difficulty of melding private projects such as this with governmental interests and funding. He didn't dwell on it and it did not stick with her. She rather selectively heard that Johnson was talking it up to his colleagues.

They talked about themselves and about how fortunate they both were, having good positions and connections. Though the flight was long, they passed it quickly. They would have many hours of sharing and learning about each other before their conversation would begin to dwindle to routine and mundane topics of marriages gone flat.

This was the first trip to Hawaii for each of them. It would be the experience of a lifetime. It should be, and they both hoped it would be symbolic of an adventurous life full of exciting trips. Each one hopefully satisfying some yearning of the mind, whether for pleasure, spirit, soul, profession, or mere curiosity. They would be world travelers but aspiring, of course, to space adventures.

As soon as they deplaned at Honolulu International Airport they were met with a cadre of beautiful native maidens. Each of them with traditional flowers over their left ear. Each had arms laden with leis made from the Plumeria flower. Before the newlyweds realized it, they had leis over their heads and around their necks. One maiden spotted Eileen's ring and stated knowingly but questioningly, "Honeymoon?"

Eileen gushed, '"Yes." The maiden ceremoniously placed a flower over Eileen's right temple and offered a wish, "May you enjoy the Islands and your honeymoon, and may your marriage be filled with love, happiness, prosperity, and children." Eileen thanked her for the most beautiful welcome she had ever received. As they were walking toward baggage claim, Eileen told Robert, "Freddie was right. Life is wonderful. I hope that one day he and Alma can make this trip."

Robert noted to her that, "The white petals were soft like your skin and fragrant like your body, beautiful like your spirit and yet delicate like you. I'll be here to nurture and protect you."

"Oh, how sweet, Robert. I am going to love being married to you. You're spoiling me. I hope you never stop."

"You must remind me if I'm failing in a husband's first and foremost duty. If your mere presence doesn't bring forth my effusive appreciation of having you, please feed me brain food because you'll know I have lost my wits."

They made their way to the Honolulu Hilton and checked in. Eileen was surprised, but undaunted by the big and crowded feel of Honolulu. She was caught up in the excitement of their honeymoon and being Mrs. Dupree! Besides she could smell the salty air. The beach was close-by and calling. Robert would learn that the beach would be a lifelong competitor for her time. Rather than resisting, he decided to join her. They walked up and down for about a mile while holding hands, kicking the sand, and observing the scenery. Above and distinct on the shoreline beyond the buildings, she could see Diamond Head. The landmark that had guided so many ships of old, both legitimate and pirate to the safety of this harbor. She looked forward to the beach and sunshine. The long day of travel had not been kind to their gastronomic needs. A leisurely dinner afforded them time to satiate their appetites, and discuss the various sightseeing opportunities. The plan was to stay a few days on Oahu. Next, they would fly to Maui where they expected less wall-to-wall hotels, shops and people. Finally they would visit Kauai. Robert had pre-arranged the itinerary. This part of the surprise had remained intact. Robert was expressly happy to satisfy her desires, even beyond her dreams.

Their accommodations were comfortable and suited the occasion well. Despite the length of their day, they laughed and played at being Mr. and Mrs. Dupree until well after midnight.

The following morning Eileen wanted to dress and go to the beach. Dupree wanted to dress and go for breakfast. They compromised, having breakfast by room service, followed by going to the beach together. It had not occurred to Eileen that Robert would not be thrilled to go to the beach. At least he conveyed enthusiasm to be with her even at the beach.

In the afternoon they visited the Arizona Memorial at Pearl Harbor. They stood side by side with Japanese and various other visitors, all contemplating the hundreds of sailors in the watery grave below them. Neither had been prepared for the emotional impact despite the fact that it memorialized an event which happened thirty-three years ago, six years before she had been born. It had been the year of Robert's birth, he was still in diapers. His father enlisted and fought in the war until its conclusion. Their emotions mellowed into the solemnity of the memorial. The silent meditation was for peace and comfort for the souls lost there and their families, for peace and comfort to the dangerous world they were living in and for protection for themselves, their family, friends, and unborn children. The same tacit prayer could be read from the eyes of each visitor, all appearing to have been programmed by the same sad choreographer.

Robert confided, "My dad's best friend from high school is in that tomb. He went Navy. Dad went Army. He liked solid ground under his feet. Dad took a bullet in the thigh at Normandy. He said it kept him out of battle long enough to keep him from getting killed. He received a Purple Heart. Many of his buddies got buried."

They left the memorial vowing to do all they could to improve the world, to promote peace and harmony. For now, they needed livening up, so they went to see the legendary Don Ho. The evening of fun and frivolity worked its magic to pry their memory away from the past and reorient them to the joy of their honeymoon.

The third morning they boarded a small plane and flew Hawaii Airlines to Maui. It contrasted nicely to Honolulu, much less crowded. They drove to the hotel on Kaanapali Beach. Accommodations were spacious, and the beach was inviting. The facilities were grand, with friendly accommodating natives. No matter what the service, it always came with genuine friendliness.

Eileen had been told that there were a couple of things that are "must do" experiences. The hotel concierge conceded that was affirmative. They were not to leave the island without ascending Mount Hiliaauckya. This should be accomplished during the night so as to reach the summit in time to observe the sunrise, which they duteously did. To Eileen the awesome sight was nothing less than if she were watching a sunrise for the first time. For Robert it was just another sunrise, but it was with his new wife, and he was making her happy and thereby himself. What was unique to him was to be with his bride, his love, and to experience this ritual with her. The man in him was proud for having made it happen. For her, it was being part of *the* happening.

As the sun peeped over the eastern horizon it began illuminating the voluminous volcanic crater. Robert read the historical markers and was astounded to learn that the entire city of New York could sit in that crater. This definitely impressed him. Both were glad they'd made the trip.

The drive back to the hotel was anything but anticlimactic. On their descent from Hiliaauckya's peak, a spectacular discovery developed. Looking out over the valley below, Robert spotted a rainbow. They shared the discovery as a symbolic and poignant moment for their honeymoon. Eileen described the beauty almost in spiritual terms. Neither of them had previously viewed a rainbow from above. From that position, they viewed the rainbow as a complete circle. Its appearance was as a floating halo of every imaginable color, suspended between them and earth below. It resembled a giant hologram. They would refer back to this unique moment as a special signal to them for the remainder of their years. Unbroken beauty in a circle of love.

The long day required rest, for much of the night had been spent driving up Hiliaauckya. They also found time to play on the beach, swim in the ocean, and to walk around the upscale shops. Everything was available from the most economical straw market hat to exquisite jewelry and clothing.

Arrangements were made to pack a lunch the following day and boldly attempt the road to Hana.

To experience the road to Hana is like a dare to adventure. Anyone who drives it and returns safely will show off their valor with a t-shirt which states, "I survived the road to Hana." The Hana road is fraught with more potholes per mile possibly than any road on earth. It must be intentionally left unrepaired so as to be uninviting. Naturally this contrarily guarantees high vehicular usage. The drive takes a half day each way. The road is narrow and rarely straight or level. They traveled across a beautiful section of beach, unspoiled by civilization, except for the road. Drastic scenic changes would occur abruptly; ascending a steep incline, into a veritable rain forest. Before they could absorb that new beauty, they were descending back toward a beach. The cycle seemed endless, all the while dodging the potholes.

Hana, they discovered, was home to two rather famous people. The first having finished out his life and now buried there. Each had wanted privacy and solitude for different reasons. The first was Charles Lindbergh. The second was Jim Nabors. The latter had grown up only forty-five miles from Eileen's birthplace.

While at Hana they visited the nine pools. They watched in disbelief as the young native boys dived into the water from the bridge, which was several stories high.

There were no snack shops between Hana and Kanapauli Beach. Robert drove the entire distance. No previous driving had produced such tenseness. He would not risk letting Eileen drive as the road was too treacherous. Neither of them had experience driving on this kind of road.

They decided the drive was not worth the required effort to get to Hana and back. But they, like so many before them, would tell everyone that it is a "must experience." The sights were indeed spectacular, more so for the passenger than the very focused driver.

Back at the hotel, Robert's tight muscles found relief with the liquid Maui tranquilizers, heavy Rum with pineapple juice and coconut milk. He was consuming his third drink before he began to relax. Finally, he commented to Eileen, "How could a place of such beauty be located on the other side of hell?"

Eileen could only say, "Honey, I'm so sorry. I had no idea it would be such a tough drive. Thank you for taking me. At least I won't ask you to move there."

"On the bright side, this should definitely reduce my complaints of the Beltway traffic."

The following day was their flight to Kauai, the garden island. The oldest island. A place so beautiful it should be called "The Garden of Eden."

Eileen knew more of the history than Robert. This was the island where "South Pacific" had been filmed. It was the island where Elvis Presley made his Hawaiian films. It was the island loved by surfers. It was the island of the new and splendid, spectacular resort developments. The island of the Little Grand Canyon, and the rain forest atop the mountains.

On Kauai they relaxed and detached themselves from the world and all of its cares. Peace seemed to envelop this very different island. Every breath was to succor tranquility. They held hands as they walked peacefully along the trails and beach. They took guided tours through the pineapple plantations and the Macadamia groves. Most of their honeymoon days were spent and enjoyed on their veritable little paradise.

They decided to view the canyon by helicopter, despite being ambivalent and skeptical about the safety. It would be an extremely dangerous adventure. They had no way of knowing the quality of the aircraft, its maintenance or the pilot, but decided to risk it.

As soon as they were in the air they knew they had made the right decision. The terrain below was gorgeous: lush green trees and golf courses, expansive pineapple fields, competing farms of Macadamia trees with copious nuts on tired, sagging full boughs.

They flew over beautiful areas and often were surprisingly close to the ground. Abruptly, and without warning, the helicopter moved over a quite unexpected cliff and dipped several feet creating the illusion that they were falling. Eileen pointed at the huge canyon below and around them. The helicopter then leveled and flew around inside the canyon. Robert observed aloud, "Hawaii's own Little Grand Canyon." It was impressive. Its specter magnified superbly by the unsuspecting approach devised by the pilot.

The pilot then flew the craft to an isolated beach, where he landed. They deplaned and walked on an unspoiled virgin beach strewn with seashells. This beach was unaccessed except by the helicopters and by arrangement they came there only one at a time. The pilot gave them ten minutes to stroll their private beach.

At first they strolled hand-in-hand. Eileen stopped and turned toward him. He mirrored her. "Robert, how have we found paradise? Was it by luck? By cunning or planning? Tell me, please."

"It was through love. We are fortunate to get such a unique precious moment. I love you, Eileen."

"And I love you, Robert."

"This trip has surpassed all that I ever imagined. I never dreamed we would have time on a private beach. I never dreamed I would marry a man like you. I never dreamed I would be so happy. Tell me I am not dreaming."

"A kiss should prove to us both that our dream is real. I pledge myself to your happiness. I look forward to waking up every day for the rest of my life because you will be there."

"It will be my privilege and joy."

The helicopter pilot had one more spectacular surprise for them. They were flying toward a mountain. As they approached he explained to them that when the volcano erupted it had torn off one side of the crater top. He would slowly circle around the mountain until he came to the opening. They should not be afraid but relax as he would fly the helicopter into the crater through the opening. This was a slow and tricky process but he did it beautifully. Inside the crater the peaks were high above them. The mountain continuously caught the clouds. There was constant rain and moisture, consequently there were streams of water coming down so that everywhere they looked they saw waterfalls. Over a dozen waterfalls streaming down from the top flowing past the aircraft further down into the crater. As they marveled at the scene, he slowly turned the helicopter one hundred and eighty degrees, and reversed his path, and slowly flew out through the opening. It was breathtaking. Before long they were on the ground again. Eileen told Robert that she had seen so much beauty during these two weeks that she admitted thinking why would anyone want to ever go to the moon or anywhere else for that matter?

"Robert reminded her that "There is beauty in diversity. This corner of heaven exemplifies one type of beauty, but there are many other forms of beauty and I am sure that we will find beauty on the moon."

"You're right. Today we flew to the Little Grand Canyon, the private beach, and the spectacular ring of waterfalls. My space bus will fly us to the moon."

That afternoon they sat on the beach and enjoyed piña coladas. Eileen asked Robert, "Do you think our honeymoon could be symbolic of our marriage?"

"How so?"

"Great honeymoon. Great marriage?"

"I hope so."

"Well, think about it," she said. "A spectacular wedding, divine dinner and honeymoon evening, and then a practical day of travel. At Pearl Harbor we had to deal with tragedy. It was necessary that we include that, but it was difficult, and emotionally draining."

"Then we pushed ourselves onward to get out of the slump. We toiled and exerted ourselves beyond usual endurance in order to get where we wanted to be. We were rewarded with the full circle rainbow and beautiful memories. Then we took a chance on a flight that was risky, but we found our beauty and love entwined and enmeshed through adventure. Will our marriage and our lives be similar?"

"Gosh you're philosophical. I don't know. Most of that sounds okay, but I would prefer to pass on a few of the chapters if we can. I guess I am more the pragmatic politician. Show me what I've got to do and let's get it done. I don't need all that much analysis. I just need you."

"Don't be silly. Griffiths says 'God's hand is in everything.' Most of the time I think I can feel it. It's very comforting, you know."

"Yes, I know."

Arriving back at the hotel, a message to call Rachael Robbins awaited Eileen.

"My word. What could be wrong?" It was already ten p.m. back in Birmingham but she called anyway.

Mrs. Robbins answered, "Hello."

"Mom, what's wrong?"

"Eileen, honey, I thought you'd want to know."

"Is Daddy alright?"

"We're fine, but there is some sad news here in Birmingham. Dr. Griffiths called me."

Chapter 39
Tears

That same morning back in Birmingham, Alma had been the first one up at the Freeman house. She began preparation for their all day outing and picnic. Nevertheless, she appreciatively watched the eastern horizon unfold its daily ritual of painting the sky so completely and richly in ever deepening orange. She continued her glances at it as it melted and faded away into one concentrated orange ball climbing above the horizon. It would be a beautiful day, Alma was sure. She had checked the forecast and there was to be no rain. The temperature would be eighty-five degrees. She was happy that Freddie had agreed to this all day family outing. A trip to the zoo had been a family aspiration for several months.

Freddie missed the sunrise, but she guessed he had seen thousands of them by getting up early for work. He deserved this rare sleep-in. She waited to wake him and the children until half-way through her breakfast preparation. It was a special day, so breakfast would be special.

Freddie awoke instantly and fully despite only having slept three and one-half hours. Eagerness and enthusiasm for the day was evident. He bounced out of bed and helped Alma get the children up and ready for breakfast.

At the table before anyone took a bite, they held hands and asked blessings. Freddie, as always, led the prayer and thanked God for their family, their food, and pledged their service to Him. Despite the eagerness of the children, Alma insisted on fully cleaning the kitchen and making all beds prior to leaving the house.

They packed the car with their picnic supplies, themselves, roughly a ton of laughter and excitement, and then headed off to Birmingham's world class zoo.

As they approached the zoo, Alma commented to Freddie that they had never gone to the botanical gardens directly across the street, and she wanted him to take her there one day. He promised he would, but today was the day for the zoo.

Amazingly, the parking lot was already half full. For some strange reason, this surprised Alma. Just before entering the gate Alma stopped and said to Freddie, "Hold on a minute. Something's not right."

Freddie inquired, "Are you sick? Is something wrong? Are you feeling bad?"

"No, I'm feeling funny. You know how I get these funny feelings. You know zoos can be dangerous. They've got lions, snakes, elephants, tigers, I'm just uneasy that's all."

"Don't be silly. This was your idea. Relax. We'll be careful."

"Don't let the kids out of your sight. Do you hear me? You kids listen to me: Stay with your dad and me. Don't go near the animals. Don't wander off anywhere."

The kids chimed an inpatient chorus, "Oh Mama, come on, let's go!"

Freddie's excitement would not be dampened, "We're going in there and we're going to have fun. I'll watch the kids. You relax and have fun too, you hear?"

Alma was the last one to walk through the door...definitely anxious.

The first thing the kids wanted to see was Monkey Island. Although Alma had not been there in years she remembered the smell and quickly agreed so as to get that behind them long before lunch.

The children laughed and giggled and picked out favorite monkeys and followed them around watching them intently. They commented and had questions about how the monkeys groomed each other and cared for each other. They asked if monkeys were families too. Freddie expounded on the virtues of family even amongst the animals. Alma wondered why he talked so much. For the moment, she chose to ignore the clear signal.

When they got to the giraffes they thought their height was half-way to the sky and teased Freddie, "Look Dad! They're taller than you!"

Although the family walked through the reptile pavilion it was a more perfunctory or mandatory walk. None of them had any interest whatsoever although it was surprisingly large for a city of this size. Alma was more nervous and was constantly looking around to make sure there were no loose snakes stalking them. She was relieved when they passed through the exit door.

The kids spotted the "choo-choo" train and insisted on a ride. This had been a special feature of the zoo for years. The ride gave them a reasonable tour, with commentary, through much of the zoo.

Freddie was constantly talking. Alma noticed that he was overly energized and this disturbed her. She had seen this lead to bad judgment and bad decisions. Her premonition grew worse. He was excited about each animal and though he had not particularly studied any of them he was expounding on their virtues and suggesting that perhaps they should consider having more pets at their house.

Alma thought the goldfish and the dog were all the pets they were going to have.

Freddie was still expounding how an expanded pet world at home would make the children more popular.

Alma reminded him that they were popular enough. They had no difficulty making friends. In fact, with as many friends as they had there was no room for more animals.

Freddie remained undeterred. He chided her for not having vision and ambition.

Alma redirected him to the business of the day, which was to enjoy the zoo and the family.

Freddie always listened to Alma even when he was high. Now she was certain that he was high again.

When the train ride terminated Alma suggested it was time for lunch. Alma had prepared adequate lunch with lots of lemonade, yet Freddie insisted they embellish lunch by buying each person a hotdog.

This frustrated Alma because she had gone to the trouble to prepare a full picnic lunch. Seeing the excitement of the kids getting their hot dogs, however, she relented and after all, it would be something hot to go with the cold sandwiches and chips. All in all, it made a fabulous picnic lunch.

Alma tried to stretch the lunch as long as possible in an effort to draw Freddie into a lengthy conversation. Her intent was to make sure that he realized that he was into a high and needed to be careful. She asked, "Freddie, have you been taking your medicine or have you been forgetting to take it?"

"I've been taking my medicine. I might have forgotten a few days. I've been working so hard I felt like it was dragging me down a little and I needed to work hard."

"Freddie, every time you quit your medicine you have one of those highs. You need to be careful. You know how you think everything is great when you're not on your medicine."

"Well, today everything is great. This is a wonderful day. Let's just have fun. I'll take my medicine tonight."

Freddie, Jr. observantly defended his dad, "Yeah Mama we're having fun, he'll take his medicine tonight, don't be a party pooper."

Alma decided she had made her point. She dropped the subject, not wanting to sound argumentative to the children.

At the tiger cage Freddie held young Mary Jo much too close to the cage for Alma's comfort. She moved closer to him. She understood that his judgment could be unsound. He would not be reading danger into anything, even the animals. She encouraged them to move along.

Alma was unrelieved to find that it seemed the further they went, the more potentially ferocious the animals were, and the more foreboding she felt. The lions were huge and prowling the entire length of their enclosure. They seemed unhappy to be there. Her anxiety escalated.

Freddie picked Mary Jo up again and held her high so she could reach over the top of the fence. Alma practically screamed, "Get away from that fence. Those lions are hungry."

Freddie put Mary Jo on his shoulders, straddling his neck, and they walked on to the next cage. They viewed the bears and the elephants. Alma remained tense. Freddie kept his distance from the fence preventing further nervous instruction from Alma.

Eventually, to Alma's great relief they finished their tour of the zoo and loaded into the car. Her foreboding had been for naught. They were safe and sound and headed home.

Driving home the kids were full of energy and excitement. They remembered aloud some of their observations of various animals and mimicked their sounds. Freddie was very much in the conversation. He was now back to his ideas of expanding the home pet world.

Alma became increasingly frustrated, "When we get home you're taking your medicine," she told him.

Freddie slowed the car just slightly going through "malfunction junction." Shortly, he exited at Fourth Avenue North and then was headed into West End. He stopped at a 24/7 convenience store because they needed milk and bread.

Freddie went inside, still high and happy from his day with the family. After he had taken about three steps inside, he realized that the lady clerk behind the counter had her hands up. It was then that he noticed the young hoodlums at the counter, one with a pistol.

Freddie, undaunted, started walking toward them, obviously believing he could save the situation. "Now wait a minute, fellas." he said. "We don't want to go getting into some kind of trouble this early in life."

The robber closest to him swung directly toward Freddie and pointed the pistol toward him.

Freddie paused. "Now wait a minute, brother. I'm one of God's angels and I'm here to keep you out of trouble. Listen to me. I can help you get a job, a car, a family. You're just setting yourself up for jail time now. I'm special, don't you see? God has put me here to keep you out of trouble." And he began walking purposefully toward the robbers and extended his hand. "Now, just give me the gun. We're going to sit down and talk about how to get you fellas home."

The horrified young robber looked frightened, his eyes getting larger with every step that Freddie took. He was certain that he was about to be grabbed and turned over to the police. Reflexively, with fear, panic, and self-preservation, he pulled the trigger twice.

Freddie fell at his feet, clutching his chest.

The two robbers fled through the door.

Alma had heard the shots and saw the robbers run past her car. She felt sick and knew something terrible was wrong. She ran inside screaming, "Freddie, Freddie!" She ran to Freddie where he lay, face down, still holding his chest. Alma rolled him to his side and saw the blood.

It was obvious that Freddie had been shot. His shirt was bloody over the left side of his chest.

Alma screamed and would not quit screaming. The clerk called the police. New customers and neighbors began offering help and embracing Alma. A lady realized the children were still in the car and stayed with them and comforted them until Alma could be reunited with them.

The scene was totally chaotic, with lay people attempting to administer first aid to Freddie. The police arrived and debriefed the witnesses. Meanwhile the ambulance arrived and whisked Freddie away, not announcing whether he was alive or dead. But Alma knew.

Back at the house, Alma answered the phone and called relatives. Shortly after five p.m. the phone began ringing nonstop. The shooting was the lead story on the five o'clock news. One of the calls around five-ten p.m. had been Dr. Griffiths. " Alma, this is Dr. Griffiths. I'm coming right over. I'll bring some food." Within an hour he was there with two family sized buckets of Kentucky Fried Chicken. Griffiths offered more than food. His presence and his condolences were heart-felt and tearfully received by Alma. It would have meant a lot to Freddie to know of Griffiths' support. He could see her hurting. She knew that he prayed and worked for a more spiritual and harmonious humankind.

Alma asked Griffiths if he had called Eileen.

"No. Actually I don't know how to reach her." He said he would contact her mother, which he did.

"Mrs. Robbins, this is Dr. Griffiths, Eileen's friend. I don't know if you have heard, but something tragic has happened. It was mentioned on the five o'clock news."

"No. What happened?"

"Freddie Freeman was shot and killed this afternoon."

"Oh, my God."

The conversation proceeded through descriptions of the senseless event and ended with Mrs. Robbins promising to help in any way that she could. She said she would reach Eileen. "She is still in Kauai, but will be leaving there early tomorrow morning to fly home. She told Griffiths to tell Mrs. Freeman that she would make sure to have lunch there for them the following day.

When she was off the phone with him she tried to reach Eileen but had to settle for leaving a message asking her to return the call. Next she called Browdy's and ordered a take-out for the following day including a meatloaf, green beans, potato salad, congealed fruit salad, cornbread, rolls, and banana pudding. She then called the country club and changed her lunch reservation from twelve-thirty to one.

Chapter 40
Change of Plans

Hearing the tragic news, Eileen immediately checked with the airline. She was just in time to make a flight back to Honolulu International and catch an eleven p.m. flight to Atlanta. A connecting flight would put them in Birmingham shortly before noon on Sunday. Eileen and Robert hurriedly packed, checked out, and headed for the airport. In the air from Kauai to Honolulu they remembered Freddie and talked of his goodness and friendship. They missed him already. He would not be there to meet them. Eileen said that was going to be unbearably sad. Now, every time she returns from a trip she will remember that Freddie is not there to meet her.

Back in Birmingham, Eileen and Robert took a taxi to the Freeman home. She and Robert missed Herschel and Rachael only by minutes, with neither knowing the other would be there. When Eileen and Alma saw each other, they embraced, and spontaneously cried in mutual grief. Each asked the other, "What are we going to do?" They both felt the loss of support in which they had been so secure. There had been no hint that he might leave or be taken. Alma said she was probably going to be looking for work. Eileen tried faintly to lift their spirits and said she would likely be looking for a new bodyguard.

Eileen made sure that Alma had enough cash to get her through the coming week. She was delighted to learn that Freddie had provided mortgage insurance and life insurance. She was quite surprised to learn that the current timetable for Freddie's funeral was the following Saturday.

She told Robert, "We live in such close proximity but are so ignorant of our cultural differences. I assumed the funeral would be Monday."

During the following week Robert learned and shared with Eileen that the recession was causing several governmental projects to slow down, one of which would be space travel. It would not be closed completely and work would continue on the Apollo plans but on a smaller and slower scale. Future moon trips would be on a slower pace and interplanetary voyages would be on hold. This of course, meant that any possibility of teaming up with her project would be on indefinite hold.

Eileen had been deliberately skipping some of her medicine before the honeymoon and had completely stopped it during the honeymoon. She had felt too good to make herself take medicine. She didn't want any blunted feeling on her honeymoon. Consequently, she had become fairly high by the time the honeymoon ended.

Eileen had lost sleep. She had a major loss with the death of her friend and now she learned of a major setback with her special project. Her high faded and in short order was gone, leaving her enveloped in the familiar black cloud, where no light can penetrate and there is no hope for rescue.

"Life is pointless, Robert."

"Ridiculous," said Robert. "We just got married. Life is just beginning. The whole future is ours."

"Future?" You told me the economy is killing my space project, weirdo dope heads are killing my friends. I feel like a piece of crap. Is that a future? I've just burdened you with me and all of my faults. It is not fair for you."

"Hush, Eileen. Who said anything about fairness? We both knew what we were getting into. You've been off your medicine, haven't you? Call Dr. Lavoy and get your medicine regulated. You'll feel better in no time. We have been through this before. You have to take your medicine."

"I don't want to be dependent on medicine."

"I don't want to be dependent on water. Diabetics don't want to be dependent on insulin and a needle. It's just the way things are, so we all make the best of the hand we are dealt. Make the phone call."

"I'm going to be this way all my life."

"No, you're not. You have the gene but you have the power to stay balanced." You just have to keep your medicine straight."

"You make it sound so easy."

"I don't mean to. I know it's not easy, but the key is, we can do it. The future will bring even better treatment, maybe even a cure."

"How can they cure genetics?"

"Scientists are projecting fantastic things with genes. They're even talking about engineering special people to be incubated on space ships. For example, people without legs because there would be no need for them. Legs would be an unneeded extra weight resulting in unnecessary food consumption."

"That's gross."

"I know, I'm just saying that these scientists are working on everything. We are young. We'll probably have a cure for this in your lifetime. If not, certainly in our children's lifetime."

"You really think so?"

"No doubt about it. I'm convinced."

"Oh, Robert, I hope so. I feel so hopeless, so useless, so worthless, so guilty."

"Call Dr. Lavoy."

"Okay. Okay."

Dr. Lavoy also had been shocked and appalled at the tragic loss of Freddie's life. He listened to Eileen's situation and decided to increase her Lithium to three hundred milligrams four times daily and switch her antidepressant to Pamelor. He started her on twenty-five milligrams twice daily and told her to go up to one tablet three times daily after five days. He wanted to be aggressive and get her out of the depression as quickly as possible. He cautioned that it might take one to three weeks for this to get into her system since she had been skipping some doses of her medicine for two weeks and not taking any at all for the past week.

She acknowledged understanding, but hoped it would work more quickly.

It was Wednesday afternoon. Eileen procured the prescription and took one Pamelor and then took a second one before bed.

By Saturday Robert could tell that Eileen was responding to the medication. She woke up in the morning more alert. She interacted more appropriately. They talked about plans for the funeral. It was time to think of getting back to work.

The funeral was extremely emotional for everyone. Eileen's mind defended against the pain by jumping from one thought to another. In addition to her thoughts involving past interactions with Freddie, she remembered her envisioned future interactions with him on the space mission. She also had other flighty thoughts, which were sporadic "thoughts de jour."

At the gravesite she saw Freddie's family and friends, DMDA members and co-workers; black and white, young and old. Her mind saw the love and goodness of this man whose life brought races together. He continued to do this even in his death where togetherness was still evident. Freddie loved helping those in need. His eulogy lionized him for his devotion to God, family and friends, and his exemplary life of values and courage.

Eileen vowed silently and that night wrote in her diary: "My cause will be to advocate for the less fortunate of the mentally ill. I will work for the elimination of stigmas, and for fair and equal treatment for all the mentally ill, for the elimination of prejudice toward the mentally ill, and between the races. Freddie deserves that. Humanity deserves that. I have been richly blessed, and therefore I must be generous in my service and my giving. Robert will be my stabilizer. He will be proud of me. I will work in conjunction with the organizations for self-help, the Birmingham Alliance for the Mentally Ill, the National Alliance for the Mentally Ill, and the Depressive Manic-Depressive Association, local and national. I will encourage others to tell their story along with me. Together we will be a veritable education brigade. We will write articles and books, and we will speak wherever people will listen."

Freddie was dead, but his life and his death had opened her eyes, unveiling her ultimate calling. She was exhausted and needed sleep, but tomorrow she would begin her new project.

The End

APPENDIX A
TELL THE PEOPLE

As I wrote Eileen's story I sometimes discussed aspects of the story with my patients who have Bipolar Disorder. Consequently, I was provided with two valuable benefits: (1) a constant source of encouragement regarding the book, (2) an endless stream of personal insights and thoughts which they invariably urged me to "Tell the People." Some were woven into the story. A few others I will share in the following vignettes.

The sincerity of my patients' desire to communicate their thoughts and feelings to the general population compels me to pursue that avenue for them and others like them in a collective way. Therefore, the following thought process ensued, and I present to you.

It has now been three decades since Eileen's foregoing story concluded at the beginning of her pilgrimage to advocate for those with mental illness. She has fought the effects of the illness in all aspects of her life: Raising a family, being a professional in the business world, in her marriage, in her spiritual world, and in her advocacy for appropriate recognition, treatment, and parity for those with mental illness. I have no doubt that a significant number of the readers of this story have personally experienced similar kinds of difficulties in your lives. I am convinced that by adding experiences from many of you to the experiences known to or experienced by Eileen, we could, together, construct an informative chronology of the tribulations and triumphs of the past thirty years. Hopefully, these individual insights and efforts could be woven into Eileen's life and acquaintances in updating her story. I believe that this could effectively demonstrate not just where we are on our quest for "appropriate recognition, treatment, and parity" but also provide direction for expediting the remaining journey to our goal.

A significant number of you must have personal experiences that are poignant, compelling, interesting, uplifting, tragic, or shocking. For those of you who would like to participate by sharing your story or insights you are invited to communicate your thoughts or story to the author by snail mail:

Eileen's Project
c/o H.E. Logue, M.D.

Affiliated Mental Health Services, Inc.
100 Century Park South, Suite 206
Birmingham, AL 35226

or e-mail at eileen@amhsinc.net. Of particular interest would be your experience with:

1. obtaining a job
2. insurance companies
3. obtaining disability
4. relationships
5. government applications
6. bias or prejudice due to mental illness

I will dialogue and correspond as my schedule permits. I apologize to not offer quick and immediate response.

I would publish nothing you submit without your permission which you may; if you desire, include in your original communiqué. I would obtain an updated permission if there were significant editing of your submitted material.

Thank you for your interest in this important task.

H.E. Logue, M.D.

APPENDIX B
SOME PERSONAL EXPRESSIONS

(1) Name: Call Me Grateful

"Tell your readers they can't possibly comprehend what depression does to one's perception without personally experiencing it. I shall never forget the dramatic moment when I first realized that treatment was benefiting me. I was sitting in my kitchen and for the very first time realized and experienced that color was all around me. Until then it had been non-existent, as if I were living in a black and white movie. I cried for the joy of discovery and the sorrow of the lost past."

(2) Name: Maurice

"When I was first diagnosed I was considered a family disgrace, not merely mentally ill. I was kept separate and uninformed. I wasn't even told when my mother died. To the public I say, we are educable. Keep us mainstreamed in as much as we are capable."

(3) Name: Gayle

"The picture is without color. The touch that should soothe instead produces pain. The personality is crushed and the soul is dead. Yet, guilt and fear prosper and grow.

Past feelings of comfort and love can evoke no response from me. The unaffected caring desperately tries to revive me. I cannot be reached. There is no need to tell me that the sun is shining, I cannot feel it; that life is good, because I am in pain; that I should, 'Get up and do something,' because I cannot, I have no energy, interest or motivation; there is no need to tell me that God is in His Heaven because I am surely in hell. My soul is vacant except for guilt and pain.

Life is unbearable. I pray to God, My Creator, to restore and release me from the torture. I cannot reach Him. Trying is endless and futile. He must not hear me or love me anymore. My last thought is of love of family, and God and I offer a final prayer for their ultimate understanding and forgiveness.

What's this? I have awakened. Has God intervened? Did He prod my ever vigilant parents? Must he punish me more? After nearly three days in hell the light is so bright and my skin is tingling. I hear their voices of jubilation. I *feel* caring and love. I have bounced off the floor of hell and I'm on my journey back.

I remember and accept Romans 8:28, 'All things, though not from God, can work to make us more Christ-like if we allow him to work through us.'

I daily thank and ask blessings for those who have been kind to me, God, family, friends and doctor. I gave up. They did not. Now when I meet someone downtrodden I avoid platitudes. Instead I give of myself. I impart true empathy gleaned from having been there. I assert an earned authority to lead them back to health. There is immense joy in knowing that I have helped someone return from their loss of self.

I pray that my words and this book will help others find balance and joy in their life."

Author's note: Many thanks to Gayle for her poignant, painful revelations. I apologize for condensing your noble effort and encourage you to write your own book.

(4) Name: Martha

"Get help. Don't listen to the voice of doom and destruction. So many have died because they pulled the trigger, yet I was spared after pulling the trigger six, maybe seven times. When I pointed it away from my head, and toward the floor and pulled the trigger once more; it fired. Why? But to give you this message. Treatment works and life is wonderful."

(5) Name: Jolene – a mother

"If you have a child that is moody and irritable and ADD or ADHD is being considered as a diagnosis, consider the possibility of Bipolar Affective Disorder. Do this especially if there is depression or Bipolar or a history of heavy drinking by any family member."

(6) Name: Rachel

"This illness destroyed my marriage and many others. I would not wish it on anyone but everyone with it needs to respect it. It deserves daily attention just as any other destructive illness."

(7) Name: Donald

"If a family member has an illness that is detrimental to the family and that member refuses to get help, one should seek advice from a mental health professional. A family intervention should ensue with as many significant family members as possible and hopefully with a mental health professional in attendance."

(8) Name: Charlie

"I identified with Eileen in considering marriage. Somehow it is okay if I'm single and I make myself miserable but it is unconscionable to burden a spouse with my miseries. I am glad to see this handled well in Fly Me to the Moon.

Please hear my advice. Don't put off getting help so long, as I did. We and our families need to understand the sufferer has no more control over Bipolar illness than one has over a physical illness; though it might seem so, it is not. It is sad that such illness can affect one's mind, judgment and life."

(9) Name: Sylvia

"No high can match my mania. Drug highs are fleeting and unreal. My highs *feel* wonderfully coherent with grand and euphoric dreams, schemes, plans, and ideas. My lows are so indescribably bottomless. The darkest, most hopeless, helpless place. Each extreme devastates me."

(10) Name: Ellen

"Spouses should be made to study the illness. They don't understand. They are overbearing, forcing us to take the pills, but naively expecting that we should be instantly normal."

(11) Name: Joey

"To put depression in perspective the average person would need to consider the difficulty we face where everything is magnified unbelievably. For example, picking up a cup is tantamount picking up an anvil."

(12) Name: Bill

"It's not a debilitating illness. We are productive citizens. My father and, I am sure, others, have lived their hypomanic life and accomplished much." Unfortunately for some, especially the poorly compliant, it can be very debilitating.

APPENDIX C
THE COMPANY WE KEEP

A popular myth of the lay public is that most mentally ill persons accomplish little and are more disruptive than constructive to society. Many defy this categorization, particularly those individuals with Bipolar Disorder or Mood Disorders. With continued publicizing of accurate information, and notable persons publicly acknowledging their illness, in time, we will fully dispel these propagated false beliefs.

Study of articles, books, newspaper stories, and other resources indicates to me, during the practice of my profession, that those persons listed below likely have (if living) or had (if deceased) the Bipolar Affective Disorder gene or at least a Mood Disorder. The history of their life, actions, behaviors, or known illnesses indicates the strong likelihood of the illness, though, obviously, one hundred percent proof is not available in all cases. Should the reader wish to study this particular subject further I refer you to what I believe to be a great and definitive published book on the subject, Touched With Fire - Manic Depressive Illness and the Artistic Temperament, by Kay Redfield Jamison, Free Press paperbacks, a division of Simon and Schuster, Inc., copyright 1993. First free press, 1994. You may also find a more inclusive list of famous people at http:/www.mooddisorderscanada.ca/depression/print/p_famous.htm.

My observations parallel others in our profession that persons in a manic state are often in their most creative state. Until they reach the point of poor judgment, their creations often excel over peers. Similarly those in the depths of depression sometimes will more poignantly express despair and futility than anyone would dare believe.

When you hear of a family member or a friend with Bipolar Disorder, Depression, or Mood Disorder, remember and consider the following names:

Victor Hugo
Edgar Allen Poe
Leo Tolstoy
Michelangelo
Lord Tennyson

Vincent van Gogh
Peter Tchaikovsky
F. Scott Fitzgerald
Charles Dickens
Robert Louis Stevenson
Sylvia Plath
Walt Whitman
Irving Berlin
Steven Foster
Lord Byron (George Gordon)
Noel Coward
Alexander the Great
Edwin "Buzz" Aldrin
Hans Christian Anderson
Roseanne Barr
Ludwig Von Beethoven
William Blake
Napoleon Bonaparte
Marlon Brando
Art Buckwald
John Bunyan
Mozart
Larry King
Jessica Lange
Robert E. Lee
Vivian Leigh
John Lennon
Abraham Lincoln
Joshua Logan
Jack London
Greg Louganis
Martin Luther
Imelda Marcos
Ann Margaret
Herman Melville
Burgess Meredith

Drew Carey
Dick Cavett
Ray Charles
Frederick Chopin
Winston Churchill
Dick Clark
Rosemary Clooney
Kurt Cobain
Natalie Cole
Samuel Coleridge
Sheryl Crow
Rodney Dangerfield
Charles Darwin
King David
John Denver
Princess Diana of Wales
Charles Dickens
Emily Dickenson
Theodore Dostoevski
Jack Dreyfus
Richard Dreyfuss
Kitty Dukakis
Liza Minnelli
Carman Miranda
Marilyn Monroe
J.P. Morgan
Ralph Nader
Sir Isaac Newton
Florence Nightingale
Ozzy Osbourne
Dolly Parton
Boris Pasternak
George Patton
Jane Pauley
Pablo Picasso
Cole Porter

Ezra Pound
Charlie Pride
Sergey Rachmaninoff
Patty Duke
Thomas Eagleton
Thomas Edison
T.S. Eliot
Ralph Waldo Emerson
William Faulkner
Eddie Fisher
F. Scott Fitzgerald
Betty Ford
Harrison Ford
Stephen Foster
Sigmund Freud
King George III
Tipper Gore
Alexander Hamilton
Joan Rivers
Norman Rockwell
Charles Schultz
King Saul
William Tecumseh Sherman
Neil Simon
Rod Steiger
William Styron
Alfred, Lord Tennyson
King Herod
Nathaniel Hawthorne
Ernest Hemingway
Aurdrey Hepburn
Howard Hughes
Thomas Jefferson
Joan of Arc
Lyndon Baines Johnson
Danny Kaye

Ted Turner
Mark Twain
Mike Tyson
Jean Claude Van Damme
Queen Victoria
Vivian Vance
Kurt Vonnegut
Mike Wallace
George Washington
Robin Williams
Tennessee Williams
Thomas Wolfe
Virginia Woolf

It is sad to even contemplate our world absent their contributions.

If you would like to help dispel the stigma by adding your name or if you believe a name should be removed, please contact H.E. Logue, M.D. at eileen@amhsinc.net.

APPENDIX D
RECOGNIZING BIPOLAR SYMPTOMS

Persons with Bipolar Disorder may not be readily distinguishable from non-Bipolar individuals because they function normally most of the time. Kreplin was one of our early and most respected psychiatrists. He was the first to recognize that persons who have recurring episodes of depression (or mania) have the same illness known now as Bipolar Affective Disorder. This, he contended, was irrespective of whether or not they had bi-polarity of the disorder, i.e., mania and depression. As the profession evolved we veered away from Kreplin's advice and adhered to insisting on the illness being expressed both in mania and in depression in order to diagnose it as Bipolar Disorder (formerly Manic Depressive Illness). We have now come full circle and recognize that Kreplin was correct. Despite this knowledge some in the healthcare profession including a few psychiatrists, ignore this and fail to accurately diagnose Bipolar Affective Disorder particularly in recurring depression without manic episodes.

Some persons with Bipolar Disorder may have quite mild symptomatology. They may simply have mildly exaggerated moods and may more appropriately correlate with the diagnostic and statistical manual (DSM) criteria for Cyclothymic Disorder. These are personality variations of alternating moods. Others have periods of depressive symptoms and periods of hypomanic symptoms, i.e., energy levels higher than normal in thought and action but not to the degree of classic mania. These symptoms can be seen in children, adolescents, and adults. In fact, there is an estimate that fifteen percent of children with the diagnosis of ADD actually have Bipolar Disorder instead. The following is a quick and condensed treatment of the subject. The reader is referred to the bibliography for more detailed information.

According to the Diagnostic and Statistical Manual of Mental Disorders – Fourth Edition Text Revision (DSM-IV-TR) when a person has reached a manic state you are likely to see three or more of the following symptoms.

(1) Inflated self-esteem or grandiosity.
(2) Decreased need for sleep (e.g., feels rested after only three hours of sleep).

(3) More talkative than usual or pressure to keep talking.
(4) Flight of ideas or subjective experience that thoughts are racing.
(5) Distractibility (i.e., attention too easily drawn by unimportant or irrelevant external stimuli).
(6) Increase in goal-directed activity (either socially, at work or school, or sexually) or psychomotor agitation.
(7) Excessive involvement in pleasurable activities that have a high potential for painful consequences (e.g., engaging in unrestrained buying sprees, sexual indiscretions, or foolish business investments).

A person may also have symptoms similar to the above lasting a shorter period of time and perhaps not as intense so they are classified as hypomanic episodes.

A Bipolar person experiencing a Major Depressive Episode will likely exhibit five or more of the following symptoms for a two week or longer period:

(1) Depressed mood most of the day, nearly every day, as indicated by either subjective report (e.g., feels sad or empty) or observation made by others (e.g., appears tearful). **NOTE**: In children and adolescents, can be irritable mood.
(2) Markedly diminished interest or pleasure in all, or almost all, activities most of the day, nearly every day (as indicated by either subjective account or observation made by others)
(3) Significant weight loss when not dieting or weight gain (e.g., a change of more than 5% of body weight in a month), or decrease or increase in appetite nearly every day. **NOTE**: In children, consider failure to make expected weight gains.
(4) Insomnia or hypersomnia nearly every day
(5) Psychomotor agitation or retardation nearly every day (observable by others, not merely subjective feelings of restlessness or being slowed down)
(6) Fatigue or loss of energy nearly every day
(7) Feelings of worthlessness or excessive or

inappropriate guilt (which may be delusional) nearly every day (not merely self-reproach or guilt about being sick)

(8) Diminished ability to think or concentrate, or indecisiveness, nearly every day (either by subjective account or as observed by others)

(9) Recurrent thoughts of death (not just fear of dying), recurrent suicidal ideation without a specific plan, or a suicide attempt or a specific plan for committing suicide.

It should not be forgotten by the affected person, family of the person, or treating physician of the person that general medical conditions may cause or exacerbate symptoms of depression or of mania. Likewise, drugs and medications (notably amphetamines and steroids) may also exacerbate, cause or precipitate manic depressive symptoms.

To make the diagnosis of Bipolar Disorder consider the author's acronym "SHOT." Take a shot at the diagnosis.

S: What is the symptomatology or phenominology of the patient? Do the symptoms appear to be manic or depressed or repeated episodes of depression or mania or continuing mood swings?

H: History. What is the history of the person? The history of the family? Is there a family history of mood swings, mood disorders, substance abuse in persons with mood disorders or Bipolar diagnosis?

O: Ongoing illness. What is the progression of the illness? What is the course of the disease? Does it continue to go on in a progression appearing as a Bipolar disease course?

T: Treatment response. If one looks at the response of the treatment one should get a good deduction as to the nature of the illness. For example, an unresponsive treatment of a recurring depression may be because its base is Bipolar rather than simple clinical depression.

For further information, see Diagnostic and Statistical Manual of Mental Disorders - Fourth Edition Text Revision (DSM-IV-TR), American Psychiatric Association. Pages three hundred and seventeen to three hundred and seventy-five.

Support Groups

Depression and Bipolar Support Alliance (DBSA)
730 N. Franklin Street, Suite 501
Chicago, Illinois 60610-7224
Toll free: (800) 826-3632
www.dbsalliance.org

National Alliance on Mental Illness (NAMI)
Colonial Place Three
2107 Wilson Blvd., Suite 300
Arlington, VA 22201-3042
Information Helpline: 1-800-950-NAMI (6264)
Main: (703) 524-7600
www.nami.org

APPENDIX E
GENETICS UPDATE

Inheritability is not as simple as one out of four, but remains a relatively safe, rough, guideline.

Many factors obscure the ability to always know a person's exact biological lineage. One confounding aspect is the hypersexuality associated with those who have Bipolar Disorder.

Despite the foregoing, scientists have studied families of solid lineage, consequently giving us reliable statistics.

Worldwide prevalence of Bipolar Affective Disorder, Type I, is reasonably stable at about one percent, i.e., those with both manic and depressive episodes. When one adds Bipolar II where the highs are not clearly manic but rather hypomanic, and has episodes of depression, another zero point five percent should be added to the prevalence. If Cyclothymic Personality or Dysthymic Personalities are added, the percentage is even higher. This has not yet been clearly defined and established. However, researchers such as John R. Kesloe, M.D., Associate Professor of Psychiatry, University of California, San Diego School of Medicine and other psychiatric geneticists are bringing us closer to understanding the complicated genetic spectrum of Bipolar Disorder and for that matter, mental illness in general.

As the research results unfold we understand that many of the studies point to Chromosome Twenty-Two where some irregularities associated with Bipolar Disorder reside. Surprisingly, this is the same chromosome implicated for genetic disorders in Schizophrenia. Possibly, the two disorders are closer than we had imagined. This offers clues to greater understanding of the persons diagnosed with Schizoaffective Disorder, Bipolar Type. At any given time their symptoms might appear more typical of Schizophrenia, but at other times more typical of mania. Many scientists are now talking of a Bipolar spectrum, anxiety spectrum, or indeed a mental illness spectrum. Additionally, chromosomes twenty-one and eighteen have been implicated in aspects of Bipolar Affective Disorder.

Recent studies show strong evidence for susceptibility on chromosome 18p, 18q, and 21q. Obviously, more research detective work remains to be accomplished.

It appears that a predisposition is genetically determined, but the absolute illness awaits environmental impact and initiation. We know this or scientifically postulate this because in identical (monozygotic) twins where one has the diagnosis of Bipolar Disorder only sixty-five percent of the other twins will exhibit symptoms of the disorder. In nonidentical (dizygotic/fraternal) twins we find the same percentage as any other sibling, i.e., fifteen percent. Another interesting phenomenon that we see is in identical twins, four out of five that has the illness diagnosed will have it expressed in the same manner as the referenced twin, but one out of five would have the illness, but expressed differently such as Unipolar Depression rather than Unipolar Manic or Bipolar type.

If we had a simple Mendelian model with one gene trait the above varieties would likely not be seen. What we most likely have is, in effect, different segments of the gene that are affected. For example, one segment may be affected in one person, two segments in another person, three segments in another, or four segments or more in another person. The more of the segments affected, the more likely we see penetration and expression of the symptomatology and the severity of the symptoms. Furthermore, depending on which segments are affected, the type and manner of symptom expressivity will be altered. The foregoing relates to the Polygenic model, many genes, each relating to the expressed symptomatology.

The myth that a person is either manic or depressed and therefore, manic depressive, has been discredited by continual clinical observations and diligent epidemiologic studies. This is being corroborated with genetic discoveries. In the model mentioned above we have what is called an Epistatic model wherein consequences of the damaged genes would have greater expressivity of symptomatology than would a simple sum of each genes expected expression.

APPENDIX F
TREATMENT BEYOND LITHIUM

The following is not a treatment guideline. No specific treatment is endorsed.

WARNING: All medications have side-effects. It is incumbent upon the patient and the patient's prescribing physician to carefully evaluate the condition needing treatment and the particular person's nuances regarding their illness. In that context, one should carefully weigh the potential treatment benefits against the risk factors for any given person with any particular medication. One must also consider the potential harm from non-treatment.

Although the following focuses on pharmacologic treatment, the reader should know that other treatments are available and important including, but not limited to relevant education of the patient and the family, psychotherapy (individual and group), ECT (electroconvulsive treatment), treatment of comorbid conditions which would exacerbate Bipolar illness such as substance abuse, Obsessive-Compulsive Disorder, Panic Disorder, phobias, Post-Traumatic Stress Disorder, and certain medical/physical illnesses.

The American Journal of Psychiatry (The Green Journal) published a practice guideline for the treatment of patients with Bipolar Disorder (Revision) in Volume 159, No. 4, in April of 2002. At nearly fifty pages in length it is an excellent compendium to understand the treatment needs and gives rationalization for treatment modalities. In its statement of intent it states among other things, "These parameters of practice should be considered guidelines only. Adherence to them will not insure a successful outcome in every case, nor should they be construed as including all proper methods of care or excluding other acceptable methods of care aimed at the same results."

As the reader reads the following, the foregoing statement should be borne in mind. The reader should remember that each person's fingerprints are different from anyone else. Likewise, their chemical print, their DNA print, is individual and consequently different from anyone else. Therefore, each person's pharmacologic treatment need, while generally similar to another person, will nevertheless, need to be individualized for that person. The reason for this was made clear in the section on genetics. The reader should be aware that the following statements and comments from the author regarding various treatments are general and **cannot** be assumed as a treatment need for any particular individual. Treatment of Bipolar patients should be by a psychiatrist. Other modalities such as psychotherapy by clinical psychologists and others are desirable adjunctively. However, the main treatment must remain somatic, i.e., from an organic basis such as pharmacotherapy or ECT in the same manner that Diabetes Mellitus needs medication, dieting and counseling.

Mauricio Tohen, Ph.D., M.D., notes that Bipolar Disorder is the most lethal mental illness. Twenty-five percent attempt suicide with ten to fifteen percent completing suicide. Less than ten percent of bipolar patients will get through life with only one episode. Patients with two or more depressive symptoms during a manic episode will relapse at a higher rate and earlier than will those patients without depressive symptoms. Patients who have psychotic symptoms during their initial break are more apt to relapse sooner and more frequently than those without psychotic symptoms.

Fifty years ago (1953) Chlorpromazine (Thorazine) was introduced. Historically this was the first medication introduced to treat mental illness. It was used to treat the psychotic symptoms of Schizophrenia but it was noted to be effective and was used in the treatment of mania. While it could be used for maintenance with Schizophrenia, it could not be used for maintenance with bipolar patients. Other medications followed: one was Haloperidol (Haldol), another antipsychotic more powerful than Thorazine. Amitriptyline (Elavil) and others were developed as antidepressants. Diazepam (Valium) and others were developed for anxiety. The pharmacotherapeutic age was ushered in very rapidly in the 1950's and 1960's.

In the early 1970's, Lithium gained respect and wide acceptance for its ability to effectively stabilize the mood in two-thirds of the bipolar patients. It quickly became the standard treatment for Bipolar Disorder and even today vies for first-line treatment. Lithium remains the only scientifically proven effective medicine to reduce the incidence of suicide. Since Lithium's introduction it has been re-introduced in various forms both proprietary and generic. Two notable introductions were Lithobid, a three hundred milligram tablet to be taken twice daily and Eskalith, four hundred and fifty milligrams to be taken twice daily. Both of the former were controlled release Lithium providing a smoother or more level blood concentration of Lithium. Lithium is an important treatment option in the pharmacological treatment of Bipolar Disorder.

Prior to Lithium one other treatment was significant for Bipolar Disorder and other mental illnesses, particularly depression: That treatment was electroconvulsive treatment (ECT). ECT was often necessary to treat the manic states and the severe depressive states prior to the widespread use of Lithium and other medicines. It seldom was used as a maintenance therapy. Even today, ECT is used in cases resistant to pharmacologic treatment. It is also the treatment of choice in severe episodes during pregnancy. Thereby avoiding long-term exposure of the fetus to medications. ECT can also be used judiciously and highly selectively in a maintenance treatment mode.

The foregoing symbolically skips an important discovery by a non-scientist businessman. Jack Dreyfus in 1958 discovered that Phenytoin (Dilantin) successfully treated depression. The medical/scientific community discarded the discovery, just as in many cases where the message is discounted because the messenger is ignored. Mr. Dreyfus, a successful Wall Street businessman suffered from severe depression. He reasoned that the symptoms of depression were due to electrical changes in his body. He therefore asked his physician to prescribe Dilantin as a trial. In Mr. Dreyfus the results were miraculous. He became enamored with his success eventually leaving his successful business to establish a charitable medical foundation. He zealously, but unsuccessfully promoted Phenytoin as an antidepressant. The medical community did not give adequate attention to this remarkable find. His case was anecdotal rather than scientific. Though Mr. Dreyfus continued to collect many anecdotal successes, this treatment never caught on. Chronic use often caused side-effects including gum hyperplasia, possibly one of the reasons it did not gain wide favor. The underlying message to explore anti-convulsants as potential treatment of mood disorders was most likely overlooked because the messenger was ignored.

It would be decades before the discovery by Dreyfus would resurface with other anticonvulsants. The physician community began experimenting with Depakote, Tegretol and other anticonvulsants, finding that indeed there was efficacy in the use of anticonvulsants in mood disorders. Abbott Laboratories is to be commended for hearing from practicing physicians that Depakote was useful in treating Bipolar Disorder. They should further be commended for sponsoring the research and clinical trials to prove the efficacy of Depakote in the treatment of Bipolar Disorder. In so doing, Abbott Laboratories gained FDA approval in 1995 to use their anticonvulsant, Depakote, to treat Bipolar Disorder. Consequently, the standards of treatment for Bipolar Disorder changed dramatically and forever. Other pharmaceutical companies with anticonvulsants soon followed in their path. It had been nearly four decades after Dreyfus had made the anticonvulsant discovery.

In 2003 Lamictal was approved by the FDA as another anticonvulsant efficacious in the treatment of Bipolar Disorder. It appears that it is more efficacious in the treatment of the bipolar depression rather than the Bipolar mania. More recently, other anticonvulsants have also been approved for treatment of Bipolar Disorder. Tegretol (Carbomazepine), Topamax (Topiramate), and Trileptal (Oxcarbazepine) are examples.

A new generation of antipsychotics, known as Atypicals, has come into being during the last decade. These have fewer severe side-effects than the older, conventional antipsychotics. The pharmaceutical companies have been testing these medications for efficacy in the management of bipolar symptoms. One, Zyprexa (Olanzipine) gained FDA-approval (in 2002) for treating Bipolar Disorder. More recently others, notably Risperidal (Risperidone), Geodon (Zyprazidone), Seroquel (Quintiapine), and Abilify (Aripiprazole) have gained FDA-approval for treatment in Bipolar illness.

In 2001 the National Institute of Mental Health launched a five year, twenty-two million dollar study. Already more than half of the anticipated five thousand volunteers are enrolled in this study, The Systematic Enhancement Program for Bipolar Disorder (STEP-BD). The study is to find better bipolar therapies.

One treatment plan that is counter-intuitive is sometimes difficult to get the patient to accept. Even treating physicians are slow to accept this new twist in the treatment of bipolar patients. Patients who have Bipolar Type I, which is with manic episodes as well as depressive episodes, have in the past been treated with antidepressants and a mood stabilizer. Data collection over the years has convinced some leaders that often the antidepressants in this particular class of patients causes further destabilization rather than supporting continued antidepressant treatment. Treatment by a mood stabilizer or a combination of mood stabilizers often will more efficaciously stabilize the mood, protecting from the high as well as the low of depression. Other leaders continue to doubt this approach.

Various pharmaceutical companies continue to spend millions of dollars looking for better pharmacologic treatment of Bipolar Affective Disorder. They research better models for current treatment medication classes. They also research basic biophysiological and genetic structure looking for new insights and avenues to treatment. Eventually genetic splicing may play a role in treatment.

Continuing Medical Education

Credits are issued only as CME. Your professional discipline must honor CME units for these to be of value to you. To obtain continuing medical education credit, please visit www.loguemd.com for instructions.

Information may also be obtained via postal mail:

Eileen's CME
c/o H.E. Logue, M.D.
100 Century Park South, Suite 206
Birmingham, AL 35226

References

Adams, A. (1993). *Almost perfect*. New York: Knopf.

American Psychiatric Association (2000). Diagnostic and Statistical Manual of Mental Disorders, Fourth Edition Text Revision (DSM-IV-TR™). 317-375.

Andreason, N.C. (1987). Creativity and mental illness: Prevalence rates in writers and their first-degree relatives. *American Journal of Psychiatry, 144*, 1288-1292.

Barrett, T. B., Hauger, R. L., Kennedy, J. L., Sadovnick, A. D., Remick, R. A., Keck, P.E., McElroy, S. L., Alexander, M., Shaw, S. H., & Kelsoe, J. R. (2003). Evidence that a single nucleotide polymorphism in the promoter of the G protein receptor kinase 3 is associated with bipolar disorder. *Molecular Psychiatry,8*, 546-557.

Bartlein, B. (2003). Depression, anxiety are health matters that need attention in today's workplace. Business First. Retrieved from http://louisville.bizjournals.com/ louisville/stories/2003/01/27/editorial2.html

Bipolar disorder and genetics. (2004). Retrieved January 1, 2004 from http://www.concernedcounseling.com/communities/bipolar/nimh/genetics.htm

Brown, L. (2002). Detour. New York: Simon & Schuster.

Calabrese, C. L. B., Sachs, J. A., Ascher, E., & Monagham, G.D. (1999).

Placebo controlled study of lomogtrigine monotherapy in outpatients with bipolar I depression. *Journal of Clinical Psychiatry, 60(2)*, 79-88.

Castle, L. R. (2003). *Bipolar disorder demystified: Mastering the tightrope of manic depression*. New York: Marlowe & Company.

Ghaemi, S. N., Rosenquist, K. J., Ko, J. Y., Baldassano, C. F., Kontos, N. J., & Baldessarini, R.J. (2004). Antidepressant treatment in bipolar versus unipolar depression. *American Journal of Psychiatry, 161 (1)*, 163-165.

Greenberg, J. (1964). *I never promised you a rose garden*. New York: New American Library.

Kahn, D. A., Carpenter, D., Docherty, J. P., & Frances, A. (1997). The expert consensus guideline services: Treatment of bipolar disorder. Retrieved from http://www.psychguides.com/bpgl.html

Kelsoe, J.R. (2000). The genetics of mood disorders. In H. K. Kaplan and B. J. Sadock (Eds.), *Comprehensive textbook of psychiatry* (pp. 1308-1317). Baltimore: Williams and Wilkins.

Kelsoe, J. R. (2001). Genetic and familial basis of the bipolar spectrum. In Bipolar Spectrum Part 1. *Audio-Digest: Psychiatry, 30(4).*

Liang, S. G., Sadovnick, A. D., Remick, R. A., Keck, P. E., McElroy, S. L., & Kelsoe, J.R. (2002). A linage disequilibrium study of bipolar disorder and microsatellite markers on 22q13. *Psychiatric Genetics, 12*, 231-235.

Niculescu, A. B. & Kelsoe, J. R. (2001). Convergent functional genomics: Application to bipolar disorder. *Annals of Medicine, 33*, 263-271.

Niculescu, A. B. & Kelsoe, J.R. (2002). Finding genes for bipolar disorder in the functional genomics era: From convergent functional genomics to phenomics and back. *CNS Spectrums, 7(3)*, 215-226.

Phelps, J. (2004). APA bipolar guidelines, 2002: A "guided tour." (2004). Retrieved from http://www.psycheducation.org/depression/APAguide.htm

Stewart, W. F., Ricci, J. A., Chee, E., Hahn, A. R., & Morganstein, D. (2003). Cost of lost productive work time among US workers with depression. *Journal of the American Medical Association, 289*, 3135-3144.

Styron, W. (1990). *Darkness visible: A memoir of madness*. New York: Random House.

Sullivan, F. (1996). *Empress of one*. Minneapolis: Milkweed Editions.

Swann, A.C. (2001). Mixed states and the structure of bipolar disorder. In Bipolar Spectrum Part 2. *Audio-Digest: Psychiatry, 30(5)*.

Tohen, M. (2001). Course of mania and schizobipolar variants. In Bipolar Spectrum Parts 1 and 2. *Audio-Digest: Psychiatry, 30(4-5)*.

Zajecka, J. M., Weisler, R., Sachs, G., Swann, A. C., Wozniak, P., & Summerville, K. W. (2002). A comparison of the efficacy, safety, and tolerability of valproex sodium in olanzepine in the treatment of bipolar disorder. *Journal of Psychiatry, 63*, 1148-1155.

Printed in the United States
102742LV00003B/218/A

9 781598 006964